ure &
ture DUNDEE

THE
BREAK-UP
EXPERT

SONYA SINGH

**SIMON &
SCHUSTER**

London · New York · Sydney · Toronto · New Delhi

First published in Canada by Simon & Schuster Canada.

First published in Great Britain by Simon & Schuster UK Ltd, 2022

Copyright © Sonya Singh, 2022

1 3 5 7 9 10 8 6 4 2

Simon & Schuster UK Ltd
1st Floor
222 Gray's Inn Road
London WC1X 8HB

Simon & Schuster Australia, Sydney
Simon & Schuster India, New Delhi

www.simonandschuster.co.uk
www.simonandschuster.com.au
www.simonandschuster.co.in

A CIP catalogue record for this book
is available from the British Library

Paperback ISBN: 978-1-39851-052-4
eBook ISBN: 978-1-39851-053-1
Audio ISBN: 978-1-39851-684-7

Printed and bound in Great Britain by CPI Group (UK) Ltd, Croydon, CR0 4YY

Dear Mom and Dad,

*thank you for teaching me not to
take life so seriously and the art
of telling a funny story.*

❖

To my sisters

*who stand next to me in
everything I choose to
accomplish.*

Thank you, Tina and Rupa.

THE
BREAK-UP
EXPERT

Chapter 1

Dear Breakup,

Curious . . . are ALL emails confidential?

Asking for a friend.

Charlotte

"If we just have you lean a little more to the left and have your lips lightly touch the mug and . . . BIG SMILE!" I shifted my weight on the kitchen island, doing my best to follow the photographer's direction. At least the interview was taking place in my own home.

"And . . ." He clicked the camera one more time. "That's the one. Beauty. Okay, Maggie, she's all yours now."

The photographer gestured to the attractive woman walking across my living room in impossibly high heels. She hopped onto a stool, stretching her long legs to the side, and looked straight ahead with a veteran TV host concentration I was not about to interrupt.

"5, 4, 3 . . ." announced the voice in my ear. "We're live!"

"Recognized as one of California's Top Forty Under Forty CEOs," Maggie Johnson read from her cue cards in her anchor-woman news voice. It was deeper than her real voice, the one she used for meetings and dressing down her assistant. "She was just on *Cosmo*'s list of Top Ten Self-Made Women, and *Forbes* magazine recently celebrated her company as a multimillion-dollar business. Please welcome back to the show CEO of Breakup, Manny Dogra." Maggie smiled, revealing a set of pearly whites that looked almost too bright against the sedimentary layers of TV makeup.

Good Day with Alex and Maggie was the most-watched morn-ing show on the West Coast. Maggie's name appeared alongside Lilly Singh, Kelly Clarkson, and Robin Roberts as one of the most successful hosts on TV. But rankings are fluid. Maggie was fighting for more than the top spot on that list—she was also fighting what the blogs referred to as "the first signs of aging." It was only a matter of time before the show would be retooled as *Good Day with Alex and Someone Else*.

"Manny, it is *soooo* good to see you again," she said, propping the cue cards on her exposed knee.

"Thank you, Maggie, good to see you again, too," I said, using my soft TV voice, the one I had honed over several hours of media training.

Breaking news: Maggie was not only a wildly popular TV host; she was also a client. She had split from her husband using one of my handcrafted breakup letters. A few weeks of coaching followed by the letter was all it took. My one-on-one sessions with Maggie were just the push she needed to break things off without, as she put it, "hurting Frank's feelings and invading his privacy."

Breakup was all about privacy and integrity. I had built an entire company—some might say empire—facilitating client breakups. Then there was the follow-up work, such as the no-regrets sessions and the self-confidence boot camps that encouraged people to put themselves back out there.

"Girl, you are on fire," Maggie said, trying hard to sound like the twentysomething she was dating now.

"Thank you so much," I said, beaming with the TV smile I had perfected.

"Right before we sat down, the assistant producer informed me that Breakup has successfully managed more than 150,000 clients," Maggie stated proudly, as if she had shares in the company.

"We just hit that number as the company went public yesterday. It's all thanks to my hardworking team," I replied enthusiastically, knowing they were more than likely glued to their TV screens at this very moment and would appreciate the shout-out.

"That is impressive, gurrrl."

I felt sympathy for Maggie, trying to stay up on the latest slang.

"A team that is celebrating another anniversary this month, am I right?"

"Three years!" I beamed back at her.

"And it all started with just a simple email?"

"If the emails were so simple to write, Maggie, Breakup would be out of business." I chuckled.

"So true, gurrrl, so true." She leaned in as close to me as she could without risking a fall. "So, what is the secret to your breakup sauce? You've been on our show many times before as our resident relationship expert, but let's dive into the business of Breakup. Tell us how it all started."

"Well, I spent my late twenties coaching friends through crumbling relationships. I guess you could say I had a knack for crafting the perfect email—not only to the men I had dated but also to my friends' partners, who just weren't getting the hint that it was time to move on."

I thought back to those emails. The guys weren't the only ones to blame; some of my friends couldn't be bothered with proper closure. "We'll always be friends," they liked to say in an attempt to soften the blow. "I think we should slow things down," they'd suggest as a way to make the other person feel better. What they didn't understand was that sometimes the soft touch simply didn't work. Not that the opposite approach was any better. A swift "We're through!" or an intense "It's over, I just can't do this anymore" doesn't do anybody any good.

"But what is that essential ingredient we all seem to be missing in perfecting the art of an amicable breakup?" Maggie asked, as if she were considering writing her own breakup emails one day.

"You know, it takes the right balance of firmness and compassion to let someone know it's officially over. My team has figured out that secret recipe. And for now, it's staying in our kitchen." I smiled. "But I will share this. We know that nine times out of ten, you can just forget that nonsense of breaking up in person. It rarely works. Too many tears. Too much sex. Too much opportunity for drama. And texts are bad. Too casual and uncaring.

Emails are best—especially when you have an assist. We follow a thoughtful strategy that involves crafting the perfect email and figuring out the best time to send it—"

"Which is . . . Monday?" she asked, as if emphasizing she had never used our services, so she certainly wouldn't have read the standard client onboarding email titled "Your Essential Guide to What Day of the Week to Send Your Breakup Email."

"Monday mornings—no. Holidays or celebrations—double no. Thursday evenings—yes! Our data tells us that breaking up on a Thursday is best—when it's followed by a sick day on Friday, it gives the client (and the newly designated ex) a three-day weekend to heal and get ready for whatever Monday might bring."

"That does sound so compassionate, and I think we all could use some of that in our relationships, too." Maggie paused as if reflecting on her many failed attempts at being a partner. "And recent relationship polls suggest that people are breaking up in record numbers?"

"That's right, and those people are calling *us* in record numbers. Our services have expanded to include an à la carte menu for all your relationship management needs. No one needs the external anxieties often associated with a breakup: 'Are you sure about this?' 'Maybe you should consider settling?' 'You're over forty, it's going to be impossible for you to start over!' Not when Breakup can handle all of that for you." I smiled widely, feeling good about our recent addition of new services, which had taken over a year to come to fruition. "I like to remind people that Breakup focuses on the real you, not the one who has been filtered to fit the frame of the most popular app."

I thought back to our numerous breakups, realizing that the "real you" aspect of things was tough for many people. In particular, understanding who they *were* rather than who they *thought* they should be, especially when their identities were reduced to a hashtag: #singlegirl #singlepringle #hunkymess #instahot #beautiful #girlswithink.

"We encourage our clients to be proud of who they really are, not who they pretend to be. And we certainly don't want anyone to feel they have to settle."

"I love that. The real you." Maggie emphasized *real* as she tried to move her over-Botoxed forehead. "So, let me tell you, I know many people who use Breakup." Here she cleared her throat. "They always say great things about you. But there are those who find your services to be . . . how should I put this . . . *inappropriate?*" Maggie narrowed her eyes as if she had just broken some White House scandal.

"Well, Maggie," I said, prepared for this, "we're living in an age when we just don't have the time—or even words anymore. We use emojis to describe our feelings, and 'likes' to slide into DMs. Dating apps can create entire relationships based on a few simple swipes. Unfortunately, far too many people try to break up the same way. How many times have you found out your relationship ended by waking up to a 'single' status on social media, being blocked by your ex on WhatsApp, or being dumped through a TikTok video?"

Maggie looked directly into the camera and raised her eyebrows as if to say, *No way!*

"I'm not making this up," I continued. "These days breakups are like proposals on the internet. Everyone's trying to find unique ways to do them." I thought about the bride-to-be who had discovered that her fiancé had hooked up with their wedding planner. Three weeks before the big day he posted a picture of the two of them on his social with the caption, "Some things you just can't plan for."

"Closure doesn't come easy these days, but what does come easy is contacting us." I took a well-timed pause, giving the camera a knowing look to acknowledge that I was going into my spiel.

"Breakup brings back the honor, kindness, and closure necessary to let go of someone and give them the end they deserve. We also help you get back up on that horse after you've been knocked off a few times." Women always laughed at the horse analogy, and Maggie did too, right on cue.

"Because sometimes you just don't want your own friends to help you get back up," she added.

And she was right. People who kept going back to a relationship eventually felt embarrassed and even judged when talking about it with their best friends. And on the flip side, best friends were often exhausted hearing about it. At Breakup, we never got tired of hearing about *any* relationship.

"Consider us a new friend who offers you advice without any judgment, the friend you know will still be there after you break up." *Press release words*, I thought, making a mental note of my ad-lib and patting myself on the back. Figuratively, of course.

"That's a new service you provide, am I right, Manns?"

I grinned at *Manns*; it was better than *gurrrl*.

"That's right! Now Breakup is also offering the Tidy Up package. Think of us as Marie Kondo for your love life. We'll help you clean up with our one-on-one consulting services. New place.

New wardrobe. New start to your dating life," I said proudly. "A whole new beginning."

"Breakups are just so darn hard," Maggie said. "I remember back in the day wondering if I had done the right thing ghosting"—she winked at me, a not-so-subtle way of acknowledging the hip word she had just used—"some of the men I had dated. Now, if only your services had been around ten years ago." She shrugged her shoulders as if in reference to the multitudes of men who had been after her back in the day.

I heard a thirty-second countdown in my ear, and my thoughts quickly went to my publicist's words: "Call to action!"

"Breakup is here now, Maggie," I said, as if to remind her of our repeat client discount. "We understand that regardless of how you decide to move forward, the person you break up with will be thankful that at the moment, we . . . *you*"—I gave her a sneaky smile—"took the time to break up with them tactfully."

She nodded. I could have sworn I saw her wink at me.

"Up next, we return to the studio, where Mark and Katie will be talking to one couple who is celebrating fifty years of marriage!"

Chapter 2

Dear Breakup,

I never get to see my boyfriend anymore. He's always "working." Our relationship didn't start this way, and I totally get that he is building a future for the both of us with all this money that he's making, but I need more than just money.

Also, we are common-law, so don't I get half his net worth when I leave?

Ralph

I walked to the office, soaking in the warm morning sun, the high of the early TV segment slowly wearing off. I'd been up since four a.m. and was now heading into my regular workday. I needed caffeine. Lots of it.

I was almost at the coffee truck when my phone rang.

"B . . . abbb . . . ebb . . ."

"Adam, I can hardly hear you. Adam, are you there?"

"Man . . . eee . . . Ma . . . ee . . . to . . . see you . . ." his muffled voice continued.

"Adam, what are you trying to say?" I said, certain I sounded more frustrated than anything else.

"Mag . . . morning . . . fantas," the muffling continued.

Click.

Call Ended.

Adam always called me after one of my TV interviews, regardless of what time zone he was in. He was a proud fiancé who cared about Breakup and who had helped the company expand.

One of my favorite memories with him was a dinner we shared at Baskin's newest local steak restaurant on a hot summer's night a few weeks into our relationship.

"You know what it is . . ." I asked as I had just taken a bite of my succulent eight-ounce rib eye.

". . . lack of confidence. I wish I could just sit some of these amazing clients down and tell them they don't need to settle."

"Then do it. What the hell's holding ya back?" He swirled the whiskey, neat, in his glass. "Give 'em what they want. Confidence. You need to cater to your clients with more than letters. It's time to create services for clients' needs. It's time to expand and make some more money."

"Maybe it is . . ."

"It's why I love you, Manny . . ."

It was the first time Adam had said he was in love with me.

And it was the first time in a really long time I felt like I belonged to something outside of work. I loved that.

"We make a good team together. A couple of hardworking babes." He saluted me with his glass.

Teamwork. It was one of the words I emphasized with Breakup clients. Relationships required work from both parties.

Adam did see more than I could when it came to the bigger picture of Breakup, especially in those early days when life felt so dark without the two people I would normally have leaned on for advice. It didn't feel so empty now, with Adam filling my cup or glass with love, even if it sometimes felt like we were celebrating more of a business deal.

That night after dinner we'd headed home and planned the Breakup menu, with a serving for every client's appetite. It was what I adored about Adam, how he could get me buried so deep in work that I often lost track of what was going on around me. Including the anniversary of my mother's passing that day.

I was shaken out of my thoughts by a cheery shout.

"Good morning, Ms. Dogra!" Rajiv, owner of one of Baskin's most popular food trucks, greeted me with a burst of enthusiasm and a huge smile. "You were superstar of show! I turned up very high, so everyone on the street could see my dear boss friend Ms. Manny Dogra on the TV this morning."

Rajiv's truck, Aja Raja, was famous for its Indian decor. His family's business in Rajasthan had served as inspiration. He had shown me a picture of their converted moving van: mismatched string lights flickered orange and red over an array of plastic flowers, a psychedelic paint job, and bold striped awnings.

Rajiv knew that gaudy decorations would lure just as many

customers as his world-class chicken tikka masala dosa, which is why he set out to make his truck and food one of a kind. A unique wrap design adorned his truck inside and out, featuring old Bollywood actors from the '80s, like Amitabh Bachchan, Jackie Shroff, and Rajiv's not-so-secret crush, Madhuri Dixit. Sure, the Bollywood-mobile (as it was affectionately known) attracted foodies who wanted to try something more exotic than Outback Steakhouse, but they really came for the photos. Rajiv loved it when his customers posted Instagram pictures of their food. He even liked the corny captions exclaiming "Don't worry, eat curry" or "Paneer death experience!" or about having to sign a "naan disclosure agreement" just to take a picture with him.

Rajiv was proud of his business and happy in his work. When he wasn't tending to customers, he was cooking, singing, and watching Desi movies in the back of the truck. And when the movies weren't playing, loud Indian music was, songs like "Om Shanti Om," "I Am a Disco Dancer," and "Ek Do Teen Char." He smiled every time his favorite track came on, which seemed to be every single one. "Ooh, this is my favorite," he would tell me as he poured me a hot cup of Indian coffee. He was always shaking his skinny hips with the music.

"Just listen, Ms. Dogra," Rajiv would say, pointing a dancing finger to the air like in a scene from one of his beloved movies. "Listen to love in this song. This is true love, because it makes your heart sing," he would say and sing along while he popped the collar of the striped cotton shirt that never quite seemed to match his pants.

He was doing that right now. His voice became louder, his

accent thicker, as he touched his chest and shook his head side to side to the beat of the music.

"What did you think, Mr. Indian Sir? Oy, you, green jacket. Look over here. What do you think about love?" Rajiv hollered to a passerby. "Where you going? Come have cup of Baskin's best chai with me and my beautiful also Indian TV boss friend Ms. Manny Dogra, CEO of . . ."

I widened my eyes in a vain attempt to get him to stop. Why did he persist in embarrassing me like this?

"No thanks, man. Love is overrated," the man shouted back. "Don't bother falling in love, you hear me, 'Indian boss friend,' whoever you are. Forget about it. If you're Indian, you have no chance of it. Especially when it comes to telling your Indian family. Ain't happening . . ." The man continued scoffing at the idea of love as he walked away, and his words trailed off into the wind.

"*You* ain't happening. *You* overrated dumbo businessman," Rajiv murmured under his breath.

Rajiv was all the things my mother and father hadn't been: Bollywood movies and music, saris and kurtas, and Indian celebrations of all kinds. He was also my morning cup of cheer, and I felt lucky that his food truck was always a few steps away from my office when I needed a jolly refill in between breakups. In fact, if it wasn't for Rajiv's loud—more like shouting—introduction on the day of our big move-in, I don't know if I would ever have made my way over to Aja Raja, since I was more of a Starbucks girl. But Rajiv made it difficult to ignore his loud introduction. "Oy, Indian businesswoman. You come here for best coffee from your brother. Come over now," he said, and I quickly converted to the coffee he was serving up. Rajiv also showed me that he was in touch with his American side as much as he was with his Indian side. He was a proud US citizen and always reminded me that he wanted his three Indian daughters to be raised Indian first, *then* American.

"I am a hardworking man. I am on the Chamber of Commerce. I do the vote and wear the sticker to show the world. Sometimes I even listen to country music of sexiest man alive Blake Shelton. But my girls must know that being Indian is just as great as being American. It is same," he would say sharply in an accent infused with English and Hindi.

It was his way of reminding me that I should have been told this growing up.

"Everyone has a story, Ms. Dogra. Each single one of us. One day you will have even bigger story than what you have now."

I had no idea what that meant, but I liked to hear it nonetheless.

"Here you go." Rajiv reached down to pour a spoonful of Splenda into my coffee.

I didn't care much for the Indian coffee/chai he made, so he always had a pot of regular coffee brewing in the back for me. He claimed it was Indian coffee, too, but it tasted suspiciously like Dunkin' Donuts.

"And one more thing before I don't forget." Rajiv grabbed a small red box, hand-painted with gold swirls and tied with a red string. "Happy Diwali, Ms. Dogra. Make sure you eat and put some good weight on, and give some to your weighter." He meant trainer.

I smiled back and said, "Oh, shoot," as if pretending to know what day Diwali fell on or what it even meant.

There was a hint of disappointment in Rajiv's laugh. "Every year it is the same month, and every year you say to me this 'Oh, shoot.' You have to find yourself a good Indian man in your life, Ms. Dogra, and he will make you see all of the Indian celebrations."

"I am sorry, Rajiv. I just don't *see* Indian celebrations like you do, and I don't . . ." I didn't complete the sentence. I was going to say I didn't really understand, but even I didn't understand what that meant.

"Happy Diwali, my friend," I said in the end.

Chapter 3

Dear Breakup,

What about putting the brakes on my relationship with my current girlfriend? I was dabbling in online apps, strictly out of boredom and curiosity, and I met this new girl—and I am intrigued.

Why can't I just hit pause with my girlfriend of two years?

Daniel

I stepped off the elevator into the frenzy that always followed a media segment. The office floor buzzed with bright young men and women attending to their tasks, while the beautiful sound of ringing phones and clacking keyboards filled the air.

"Yes, that's right, we were featured on *Good Day with Alex and Maggie* this morning." The team's excitement was palpable as they answered phones while, no doubt, calculating their next bonus. To a first-timer, the call center would have looked like complete mayhem, but the truth was that my staff was organized and effective, attending to our clients with near-military precision. I liked to see my staff working. That's how I preferred to start each morning. It was one of the qualities that I found appealing about Adam. The way he talked about his team with pride and fondness. He loved being not only their leader but also their biggest cheerleader. Now I had that connection with my team, too.

I pushed through the private client entrance, moving far away from the noise of my team. The matte black glass doors etched with the Breakup logo closed behind me as I entered a serene, soundproof lounge. My shoes echoed across the gray-and-white hardwood, which added a soft glow to the room, providing a temporary distraction to clients who had come to split with someone they had once cared for. Soft music and the soothing sounds from a waterfall filled the air, triggering a relaxed feeling for the person who was about to go into panic mode at the thought of hiring us. Strategically placed reading material offered tips on being "Single and Ready to Mingle" or "Alone and Ready to Bone," whichever the client wanted. The walls, a subtle purple, were complemented by flattering lighting that created the effect of a perpetual golden hour. After all, if you happened to catch a glimpse of yourself in the mirrors, it helped to have the perfect light to enhance your soon-to-be-single features. Clients who lacked confidence also lacked the resolve to carry through with their breakups. The better you thought you looked, the more comfortable you were with being single. It was that simple.

"Morning, Manny," Anjali, our office manager, said as she

popped up from behind the reception desk. The executive of-
fices were behind the client lounge, away from the hustle and
bustle of the busy call center. "You were such a boss on the segment this morning. You totally slayed it. And was it just me or did
Maggie look a little . . ." Anjali waved her hand around her face
and lingered around her forehead.

"Yup, a little too much, huh? But she's also one of our clients,
so we respect all the bad decisions Maggie makes," I jokingly
reminded Anjali.

I placed my coffee and the red box with the Aja Raja logo on
the glass desk.

"Is Rajiv actually selling Diwali boxes this year?" Anjali asked.
"I was on him all last year to do this! I mean, sure, West Baskin
isn't exactly the nucleus of all things down with brown, but with
the Indian families we do have, we can still celebrate and share
our food with other Baskin residents." She started to clean up
the grease ring the box was slowly leaking. "Oh, by the way,
Adam called a few minutes ago. He said he tried to reach you on
your cell as well. Is he back from Europe yet?" she added, all in
one quick breath.

"Not yet, but soon," I said, reassuring myself more than her.

"It must not be easy to be in a long-distance relationship. I
mean, these days I can hardly manage one in the *same* time zone.
Which reminds me of a new Breakup package I was thinking
about. You've Got Mail . . . kinda like the movie but focusing on
how emails are just as important a love language as . . ." Anjali's
words trailed off as I thought about dating Adam long distance
and our love language as of late.

It wasn't easy. In fact, Adam and I had been trying to connect over the last few days. Trying, but not succeeding. Fall was one of our busiest seasons at Breakup. Most clients felt it was the season of reason, as in a reason to break up. It was the same every year: The summer, with its mixture of barely dressed beach bodies, barbecues, parties, and alcohol—a lot of alcohol, usually—all came together in a cocktail of euphoria and brain fog that inspired men and women alike to jump into new romantic relationships. Some people found true love at a beachside house share, which meant cutting ties with their previous true love from the Upper East Side. Others felt an inexplicable connection to the local bartender, who listened attentively as they drowned their relationship sorrows in way too many margaritas—and eventually in each other's beds.

Whatever the reason, September to November were our busiest months, which meant that it would have been difficult to connect with Adam even if he weren't spending so much time in Europe, with a time difference and lousy cell reception.

"You've got mail." I said it out loud. "I like it. Nice work, Anjali. Book in a one-on-one with me later this week."

"Thanks, Manny." She pushed her red-framed glasses back up the bridge of her nose, smiling at her morning assertiveness. I knew she was also mentally checking another task off her list. She was more than organized, she was Netflix's popular TV series "The Home Edit" for our office. She had mastered a solution to digitally organizing Breakup, and she made it fun—at least she made it look fun.

"Manny, we have clients waiting for you. In fact, one is insisting on seeing you ASAP." Anjali scrolled through her tablet. "His name is Sammy . . ." She pushed up her glasses again as she read. "Patel. Yes. Sammy Patel. He's looking for a temporary Breakup, but I told Mr. Patel that Breakup is not in the business of pausing relationships. But he is adamant about seeing you."

Anjali was right. There was no such thing as a pause with us. This wasn't an episode of *Friends*. I mean, with all due respect to Ross and Rachel, there was no "break" in Breakup.

"Patel?" There weren't many Indians in West Baskin as far as I knew. "Tall, green jacket, and a little too much attitude?" I asked.

"Yes! How did you know?"

"Let's just say I've already had the 'pleasure' of meeting him."

"He's waiting in Pod 3, and he really wants to see you now."

"Why don't you tell Mr. Patel that you spoke to me, and we unfortunately will not be taking on his case."

"Sure. Just like always, I promise to be gentle in my breakup with the client." Anjali snapped her fingers just like she always did when we were about to pass on a client.

"Good luck with Mr. Pessimistic Patel." I grabbed my coffee and headed to my office.

My office was big—too big, some would say—but as I walked through the doors, it took me back to my mother and father's work ethic, and how they would have approved.

Damn. It always hit me like this. A moment of thought about my parents and how much I loved them, then—*bam*, the dull ache when I felt their absence. I walked over to the floor-to-ceiling windows, taking a deep breath in as I stared at the clouds slowly floating along, reassuring me that my parents would always be nearby.

It had been three years since the car accident, and Breakup was a one-woman show at the time. A year after that I had met Adam, and now Breakup was a publicly traded company. I had buried my heartache after their loss by building up my company. It wasn't about money; it was his drive to "be the change" that inspired me to mirror his success and work even harder on the business. Adam could set aside friends, family, and the world around him for his company, and ultimately, I trained myself to do the same with my grief.

"Be the change," I said to myself as I walked over to my desk, pushing away my pain as I had so many times before.

A few minutes after I had settled in, there was a knock on my door.

"Ready to get started?" Anjali popped her head in.

"Ready as I always am!" And I was. It was just like every morning, ready to get back into the business of Breakup.

Anjali was now carrying three tablets, each with its own colored case, as she always did for our morning meetings. She liked to color-code everything. Pear green was for new clients, indigo blue was for new packages, and fire red was for a crisis.

"Mr. Patel had a pretty interesting temporary breakup request, but I still asked him to leave. He wasn't too happy about it."

"They never are. I don't think he's a happy person, period."

"He wants you to reconsider. He's willing to do 'whatever it takes,'" Anjali said, using air quotes to make her point.

"Mr. Patel should know we don't need 'whatever it takes,'" I said, already over the client and his request.

She looked down at a tablet and bit her lower lip.

"It's fine, Anjali. This guy is insistent and pushy. That could make for a troubled client later. Mr. Patel can find someone else to help him with his breakup," I assured her. "By the way, how was your date with that new Hinge guy? Vik?" I asked, tired of talking about the grumpy client.

Anjali was on all the millennial dating apps. She hadn't been in a steady relationship for as long as I could remember. In fact, most of the guys she dated—impossible to call them men—had no ambition, living at home with their parents and saving up for a beer pong table. She needed a man with goals, a steady income, and his own place to live. Someone who was heading down the same adult path as she was, not veering off to get in line for the newest video game, like the last guy she had briefly dated. He apparently used up all his vacation time for VIP video gaming conferences. He had six vacation weeks a year.

"Oh my gosh, Manny." Anjali plopped down on the seat in front of my desk. "He actually showed up drunk for our date!"

"How drunk?" I asked, as if that even mattered.

"As in slurring-his-words drunk. He downed a couple of drinks at home alone."

"Maybe he was just nervous to meet you?" I tried to reassure her with what I knew was a horrible excuse.

"Manny, our first date was breakfast."

"Oh, geez. Mr. Vik sounds like he needs one of our emails—"

"Yup. I pressed send on that one."

"Speaking of emails, what's on the agenda today?"

"I have one client who's supposed to get married in two days but wants to call off the wedding. Cold feet."

"Two days?" I said, startled. "That may be a new record. Could you schedule a call for that today?"

"On it. And I have another one who's packed up her bags and is heading for Canada."

"Why Canada?"

"She met this guy online—a ski instructor. She's moving up there to be with him but needs help telling her family and friends because the guy turned out to be her father's best friend."

"So she needs an exit strategy. Gotcha. Okay, this is going to be a call to the family from her. Can you get her on the phone for a one-on-one session? I'm thinking the Family Feud package."

"That's what I was thinking, too, Manny. We may want to consider branching that package out. We seem to be getting a lot more requests from daughters falling for their dad's friend."

"Hmmm . . ." I sat back in my chair.

"It's this whole silver fox thing that's going on right now."

"Silver fox?" I leaned forward.

"Yeah, like the George Clooneys of the world are suddenly hot to thirtysomething women."

"And just happen to be close friends with your dad," I added. "All right, good idea. Split the package up. One for fathers and one for mothers. Who knows where this silver fox trend could take us?"

"On it." Anjali swiftly typed something. "The last one is Scotch PR. They want us to help with Jennifer's breakup—which makes it breakup number four for us. Timing's an issue because she has a premiere next week."

"Didn't we just do the third?"

"Yes, um . . . exactly sixty-four days ago."

"Well, then, we already have a template of emails. Can you gather them up and have them sent to me? I need to review them so we aren't using the exact same copies, in case the exes go to the tabloids."

"Gotcha." She finished up her notes.

Breaking people up was our business. It didn't matter if you were a celebrity on your fourth breakup with us or Client 54689 getting cold feet before your wedding, we weren't in the business of judging.

It had seemed like a simple business idea, and it sort of was, now that I looked back on it. I was having a dinner party for my twenty-eighth birthday—a small celebration at my house—where a friend was consumed with emailing her boyfriend after several botched attempts to split with him. She spent almost the entire evening trying to figure out how to dump Chad. Finally I grabbed her phone and typed out a message, and at the end of the night, she hugged me on her way out.

"He just replied to your email. He was so happy we could remain friends. It worked! Your words worked!"

A few more rescues like that, and word got out that I was the Breakup Queen—#BQ. Just like that, I turned an obsessed girl's birthday takeover into a multimillion-dollar business.

I met Anjali at another celebration. She was a young caterer who had recently moved to Baskin from a small town in the Midwest to get away from her bad breakup. As I watched her managing the logistics of food and catering, supervising the staff, and chatting with guests, I saw a spark and knew I had to have her on my team. A handful of phone calls and a little twist of her arm got her to abandon the world of food and beverage to help me out in the office, which at the time was my tiny condo. Our team of two quickly grew to a group of fifteen in an actual office, and, eventually, to a team of fifty in this penthouse suite.

The Breakup team cared about our clients. Breaking up was awful, but what was the alternative—having no closure or finding out through social media that the person you loved was busy loving someone else? Our crew made each breakup clean and kind. Respectful. Our clients may have checked out a long time ago, but we did everything we could to give their relationships proper closure. Losing someone you loved was difficult enough; not knowing why you lost them was devastating. Our track record was clean, too. Nobody ever suspected the breakup came from us. That's how we knew we were doing a good—scratch that—*great* job.

"Ooh, I almost forgot," Anjali said. "This just came for you!" She placed a plain brown envelope on my desk. "Can't wait to see it," she added as she headed back out the door.

"The cover!"

I was about to peel back the tape on the envelope when Anjali turned around. She was staring at her green tablet. "Mr. Patel is on line one."

"All right, I'll take it."

"You will?" her voice cracked.

"Just the call, not the case." Mr. Patel was getting annoying. Time to set him straight.

"Manny Dogra speaking," I answered the phone when the call came through. I used my *don't mess with me* voice.

"Ms. Dogra, I really need your help, and I'll do whatever it takes at this point. I am pressed for time, and the clock is ticking."

"Mr. Patel, I'm sorry to disappoint you, but, as I'm sure Anjali explained to you, we just don't do temporary breakups. It could get us in a lot of trouble with our stakeholders if we start going against our company policies and—"

"Ms. Dogra, you haven't even heard my story. I just need you to make an exception. My request . . . it's unique, and if you could just hear me out—"

"Mr. Patel, you have to hear *me* out. I get this all the time from clients, but—"

"This is different."

Oh, here we go. It was always different. Just like the client who shared a dog with her boyfriend and needed help dognapping him before their breakup, or the client who was guided by voices to the new love of her life even though she was married at the time, or the client who was having an affair with her neighbor's twentysomething son—we had heard it all.

"And *you* should understand," he continued.

This was going to be good.

"You're Indian, after all," he said, stating the obvious.

"What does that have to do with anything?"

"The girl I'm dating . . . she's not . . . you know . . . Indian. I can't possibly take her to my brother's wedding—"

"Because she's not Indian?" I cut him off.

"It's just never been done before. The oldest son bringing a non-Indian girl to his younger brother's wedding. Hasn't been done with any of the Patels. Never. So I need a week off from my girl, from us."

I cocked an eyebrow. "Let me get this right. You want to temporarily split with your girlfriend while you attend your brother's wedding, and you'll return to her after the wedding, as if nothing happened?"

"Yes. At least by then, one Patel son will be properly married."

My nostrils flared. "I'm sorry, Mr. Patel. I just can't make an exception. And to be honest, I don't understand. It sounds . . . it sounds silly to me."

"Silly? You think Indian tradition is silly?"

"That's not what I meant—"

Click.

I stared at the phone, and then put it down. I had learned early in my business life not to take these things personally. I hated to turn down clients, but it was the right thing to do. What was that saying, when one door closes . . .

And with that, there was another knock on my door.

"Manny, how did things go with Mr. Patel?" Anjali asked.

"Come in for a second!" I signaled her to take a seat. "It was a strange call, no doubt about it. Mr. Patel wants a temporary breakup because—did he also tell you this—he's dating a non-Indian woman and can't tell his family. He said something about tradition."

Anjali looked at me with big eyes. "I wouldn't be able to tell my family, either."

"Really? How could you *not* tell your family if you loved someone? Surely, they want what's best for you?"

"It's just every Indian parent's dream that his or her child will grow up and marry into another Indian family. My parents want me to have my happily ever after with an Indian doctor, lawyer, or engineer. They want to keep all the traditions in the family. Mr. Patel probably feels he would be bringing a kind of disgrace to the Patel family name if he married outside the culture." Anjali obviously had some experience in the matter.

"Well, then, why bother dating a Smith or Jones . . ." I pressed her.

"Because not all the Viks are a dream and instead end up being your worst nightmare," she said, obviously thinking back to her brunch bust.

"So, you're telling me this client would rather lie to his own family and his girlfriend . . . ?"

"At least until his brother gets married. Then it will be less pressure on him because at least one Patel son has married Indian."

So he wasn't making that up. I had never been exposed to this side of being Indian before. But, really, I hadn't been exposed to much Indian culture at all. It just wasn't the way in our family.

"He was still kind of a jerk to Rajiv this morning. And as you know, we don't do—"

"Temporary breakups." Anjali completed my sentence. "I know that Mr. Patel seems like a hothead, but after I spoke with him, I got the impression he's just in a huge Patel . . ." She searched the room. "Retell. Patel retell."

"Patel retell?"

"He's about to make history here, Manny. He wants to change the course of who Patels *can* marry. This is a total Indian narrative. Most of us can relate to this in one way or another," she said in a way that made me feel excluded from her new club with Mr. Patel. "Not that you can't relate to it because you aren't Indian, it's just . . ."

I watched Anjali as she struggled for the right thing to say.

"Don't get me wrong, I love being Indian. But it comes with

a lot of responsibilities, and families are rooted in tradition. That includes mine and, from the sound of it, Mr. Patel's. I know it seems dated, but it's like rice and dal. Culture and convention go hand in hand. From the arranged marriages to the oldest son not wanting to dishonor his family because he's choosing to marry a non-Indian." She got up and headed to the door. "Manny, I thought . . ." She hesitated. "I thought most Indians grew up just knowing that's the way it must be. It's like the plot to almost every Bollywood movie."

I tried to recall the few movies that Rajiv had pressed me to watch, but the truth was I always fast-forwarded to the beautiful wedding scenes full of gorgeous dresses, so I missed out on most of the plot.

"Thanks, Anjali. Maybe I just need to watch a few more of those movies. I'll see you in a few minutes with the rest of the team."

When she left, I thought about my parents. They had never suggested I date anyone. I went out with guys I felt a connection with, and, growing up, I didn't feel connected to anyone Indian. And in our house, dal and rice didn't come together. It was pasta and red wine.

I sat back up in my chair and typed "I am Indian and want to marry a non-Indian" into Google.

Wow.

Forum after forum with men and women wondering how to break it to their parents that the person they were dating or even considering marrying was a non-Indian.

I shook my head. It didn't matter if this was a real problem or not. It wasn't my problem. I had said no.

Chapter 4

Dear Breakup,

My boyfriend has two phones. He claims the one I don't know the password to is for work. But just the other day, I found out from a close friend of his that he hasn't worked in over a year! Could the other phone be for another guy? Either way, he needs to know it's over between us and that this isn't a prank call!

Jonathan

It seemed strange, sometimes, running Breakup while planning my own wedding. Well, trying to at least lock down a date. I'd met my hunky fiancé two years ago when I'd been invited to attend the West Coast CEO Awards at the Baskin's convention center. The function was in honor of the state's most successful young CEOs, and I'd taken Anjali as my date. She was more than a kick-ass masterfully organized assistant—and soon manager; she was an ally, what my father would have called a "good soul." Strong and ethical, she made the best decisions for the company and for me. In days gone by, she likely would have been referred to as the woman behind the man. Luckily for me she was content to be the woman behind the woman.

That awards ceremony was my first big night out after my parents had passed away the year before. It was hard to muster the energy for anything but work, especially attending such a fancy bash—it would be the first time I shaved my legs in months—but as Anjali reminded me, my parents would have been livid if I'd stayed home and passed up the recognition for another night with Doritos and *Schitt's Creek*. "Fine," I had said like a petulant teenager. "I'll go."

Anjali had insisted we use her stylist cousin free of charge for the night, but he couldn't make it, so instead he had sent the hottest celebrity designer dresses to my house. In between reaching for the remote and vodka sodas, and scrutinizing quarterly Breakup files, I mustered up the confidence to go through the color-coded rolling rack. I was immediately drawn to a pink fishtail dress with a long side slit and layered beadwork.

The dresses were also accompanied by an encouraging note from Anjali—something about being a successful woman leader. Under normal circumstances, she also would have come armed with a hair and makeup team. Smart woman, she knew that I needed to be eased back into my full social calendar. I brushed a dusting of powder on my face and added a few strokes of red to my upper cheeks and temples. I looked in the hallway mirror as I slid my feet into my Louboutin heels. My almond-shaped eyes and full lips made me a faint approximation of my mother. I stepped in closer, wishing I could see more of her in me.

I was a little nervous as my car pulled up to the convention center. It was all very LA, with the requisite red carpet and photographers. Anjali was right to have had a stylist dress me for this posh event, as reporters were there, too. I was mid-interview when I saw Anjali arrive. A few minutes later I glanced over to see her talking to an exceptionally handsome man. Not the usual dad bod she found attractive—which, according to Breakup stats, was something most women found themselves attracted to. I turned back to the interview.

"This dress, Ms. Dogra, it hints at the beautiful beadwork you see in Indian dresses," the journalist said as she pointed the microphone at me. "Is it an ode to your Indian ancestry?"

I hesitated. No way could I say, "It's just a beautiful dress that a stylist picked out for me." I thought the designer was KYNAH, but I wasn't sure. Thank goodness for Anjali, who always managed to avert a crisis in the making for me. Stealth—one of the many things I loved about her.

"It's an ode to the hard work Ms. Dogra has done over the past year. The bright colors represent an even brighter future ahead for Breakup," Anjali said. Confidence looked good on her.

She grabbed my arm and yanked me inside, leading me toward the bar. "I want you to meet someone," she said, fluttering her eyelashes.

We were zigzagging toward the only pocket of the room that wasn't packed when the same man Anjali had been speaking to earlier—the same exceptionally handsome man—headed our way, stopping in front of us as the overhead lights lowered. He had his own glow to him.

"I understand your office is something I need to see in person . . . as an architect, of course." He leaned in. "Hi, I'm Adam Jamieson. Lovely to meet you, Ms. Dogra." He reached out his freckled hand to mine.

I glanced over at Anjali and gave her a look, but she only stared back at me with a huge grin that made her seem like a cartoon figure. Trying to play it cool, I shifted my gold clutch and offered my right hand to Mr. Handsome Architect.

"Nice to meet you, Adam. You can call me Manny and—"

Before I could even finish my sentence, he kissed my cheek and untucked my hair from behind my ear.

A little "ooh" escaped my lips. I tried to recover. "How very European of you." I took a minute to breathe in his sharp cologne.

Adam gracefully loosened one of his blazer buttons. He was wearing a royal blue slim-fit jacket with a blue-and-gray vest underneath. Under that, a blue shirt that matched the color of his eyes. I got the feeling he worked out as my eyes landed on his broad chest. I looked up at his tanned face, wondering if he'd just come back from the beach.

Anjali took her cue to leave. "I'll just be over there. I see some clutter that's making me squirm, next to the margarita table," she said, and with that she headed toward the lounge area.

I pushed my hair back behind my ear and smiled nervously.

"My office, yes, umm, it has a really stunning backdrop of the Baskin skyline. It's actually going through some much-needed renovations right now," I managed to say in one nervous breath.

"I'd love to hear more about it and even see it. I grew up here. Manny . . ." Adam moved in closer, and I felt the heat from our bodies escaping what seemed like too many layers of clothes. I was spellbound as every part of me lusted for this Adam. Hell, I was practically posing for the cover of one of those Danielle Steel novels.

"I would love to see you again," he said, interrupting my embarrassing thoughts. "You're so beautiful. You should leave your hair like this," he whispered as if we were the only two people in the packed hall. His hand lingered as he slid my hair to the front of my face, then cupped my jawline, his thumb softly grazing my lips.

And in that moment, I no longer felt so lonely. Adam's presence made me feel *something* at first sight. Something I hadn't felt in a long time. A few weeks later, we were living in Adam's home by the private marina in Baskin. A few months after that, we were engaged.

As if on cue, a call from Adam came in, his face popping up on my computer screen.

"How's my beautiful TV star? You were fantastic!" he said, gleaming.

"Thanks, babe. Thanks for making that time in Europe for me."

"I'm actually back, Manny. I was with Mom and Dad. Got in early this morning for their anniversary. Didn't want to interrupt you at the house on set. You remembered the party, right?" Adam moved closer to the screen, scrutinizing my face to see if I had forgotten.

"Oh, shoot," I replied. It was the same "Oh, shoot" I had used on Rajiv earlier.

"It's in my calendar!" I looked at the side of the large desktop screen, pretending a calendar reminder had popped up—which it hadn't.

"I already have a dress picked out," I said, continuing the lie.

He backed up from the screen. "Manny, it starts at four. Please don't be late. Oh, and I was brainstorming on the flight here and I got a new Breakup business plan I wanna run by you . . ."

"I just want to see you, Adam, and talk business later."

"Yeah, babe, but you gotta hear me out here—"

"Guess what just came in the mail today?" I interrupted him as I reached for the envelope on my desk and proudly placed it in front of me so he could see it.

Adam was already distracted by his work phone beeping in the background.

"Oh, babe, one of the designs is being delayed in Berlin, and you know I am here."

Yeah, I just found out.

"I have to jump on this call. Show me later, okay? Love you."

Before I could even tell him I loved him back, the connection had ended.

What was it with men hanging up on me today?

Chapter 5

Dear Breakup,

It's been six agonizing months since my work crush found a girlfriend. I know we never really dated, but we would take coffee breaks together almost every day, and I would spend my Sundays baking his favorite cookies for the both of us to share on Mondays. Then he found HER, and now he spends OUR coffee breaks with her, and now SHE bakes for him! I am crushed. Can you help me get over someone I never really dated?

Minnie

Our conference room was a huddle space for fifty, with every kind of tech imaginable to gather, store, and analyze data during a meeting. We had interactive whiteboards, a wireless presentation system, the right mix of microphones and speakers, and an

LED video wall that splashed our logo across the screen. Yet as sleek as the room was, it wasn't cold. Floor-to-ceiling windows let in the sun, and the walls, covered in a soothing shade of sky blue, were the perfect background to showcase the work of local artists. Fresh flowers delivered every Monday completed the look—a stunning combination of traditional meets tech, as Adam put it. In fact, the timing of our relationship seemed perfect for many reasons, including Adam's influence on the final renovations to the Breakup office.

Design was important to me, too, something I had picked up from my mother, who loved to stage houses. My parents were also a good team, but mainly when it came to selling real estate. It was the only time I really saw them happy together. Other than that, they seemed to spend a lot of time alone, in different rooms of our large family home. I always assumed it was because they were so busy with their business, but as I got older I realized they were just as content avoiding each other.

"Hey, Manny."

"Hi, Rob," I greeted Breakup's CFO. "And good morning, everyone." I looked around the room at the tired but excited faces that usually followed the success of a PR hit.

"Happy Di-wal-ee," Rob said, gesturing to the array of delicious-smelling food on the conference room table. "Anjali brought us treats."

Rob said *Diwali* in the most American way possible. But who was I to judge, since my Hindi only went as far as a few badly pronounced swear words. On occasion I had heard my father utter some filthy swear words under his breath. I had just recently found out their meanings, thanks to Rajiv, who felt it was his duty to educate me on both Indian street food and street language.

I had to admit, though, I was shocked when he told me that *haramzada* meant "bastard." I learned that one when he put his hand on a too-hot coffee urn. *Harami saala*—literally "son of a bitch"—came out when some guy in an Indochino suit tried to shortchange him. And on those occasional days when it rained in Baskin, well, that's when Rajiv really let it rip. "*Salla Badmash!*" he'd sputter. I never did learn the English translation for that. "There are some things you don't tell a lady," Rajiv informed me.

Usually, the Breakup meeting room smelled of coffee and bamboo—the latter thanks to the Nest diffusers that Rob had insisted we get for ambiance. "The more zen I am at work, the better it is for all of us," he'd reminded me as they were being installed.

Today, it was alive with the aroma of cumin, cinnamon, and cardamom.

I turned to Anjali and mouthed, "Rajiv?"

Yup, she mouthed back, smiling. "Happy Diwali, everyone," she said with the correct pronunciation, "duh-vaa-lee."

Rob took notice and made a few attempts under his breath, but it came out sounding more like Darth Vader, so he gave up and shoved a savory tidbit into his mouth.

Rob was not only Breakup's CFO but my former college boyfriend turned best friend. We had dated for less than a year before I realized he was more interested in watching the men's swim team than spending time with me. I never told him why I broke up with him, and after graduation he wrote a heartfelt email (which later became one of our many Breakup templates) apologizing for not being upfront with me. "It's hard to be honest with someone else when you're not honest with yourself," he wrote.

We emailed back and forth about life, loves, and work after that. When Breakup took off, he was managing the finances at a small tech start-up, and I offered him the executive role. He was quick to accept. Rob may have made a lousy boyfriend, but he had become an incredible best friend, and he was a great CFO. He jumped headfirst into work after a bad breakup left him devastated. After a few months of heartbreak, he met a local bartender at our favorite after-work hangout, and Jay and Rob had been living happily ever after since then. I was pleased for Rob, and even more pleased that our company was reaping all the rewards of his adoring relationship with Jay.

"All right, let's get started. Happy Di . . . Happy . . . Happy Day, everyone," Rob said. "Nice work on the early morning sugar rush, Anjali." He picked up another treat and set it on his plate. "The way to a raise is through food—at least with me." He laughed at his own joke.

"Speaking of money, we made a heck of a lot of it this past quarter." Rob opened the portfolio in front of him. "According to the stats I pulled up, people are breaking up in record numbers along the Eastern Seaboard and all the way through the South. Take a look at the monitor behind me." Rob had put together a map of the country highlighting those states with the highest breakup stats. New York, California, and—Nebraska.

"Hold on a minute," I said. "Why is Nebraska in the top three?"

"FarmersOnly.com," Rob said.

"So?"

"Maybe these farmers are quick to moooove on," he said, making his best impression of a dairy cow.

Everyone rolled their eyes except Jill from accounting, who actually giggled.

"Don't laugh," I said. "It will only encourage him."

"I'm not really sure why Nebraska is up there in the top three," Rob said, resuming his CFO demeanor. "But with all these new apps, people think the grass is greener on the other side, so they're looking for ways to get out of the weeds of their current relationships. We're still getting the greatest number of requests from this age group," Rob said, motioning to the next graphic, which showed what we already knew—people between the ages of thirty-five and forty-five were our best customers.

"All app users!" Anjali added.

"Old and new users. Everyone keeps bouncing around thinking that someone better is out there. Thank god I am finally outta that game!"

"There never seems to be a winner in the app user game," Adele from sales added as she abruptly turned her phone over on the table.

Our database grew year after year, just like the number of dating apps did. Two decades ago, the online dating world was a small market of Plenty of Fish and Lavalife users. Then came the smartphone, and people got smarter with their dating behaviors. Now everyone knew someone who was using Bumble, Tinder, or the newest baby on the dating block, Bender, an app that matched people with similar drinking habits. As the number of users grew, the definition of dating also expanded. A recent addition to the market—*almost* relationships.

"We also have a new kind of clientele. Clients who are looking for closure on a relationship that never got off the ground. A crush who crushed you."

"Like trying to process an ending for something that never really happened, which is what one of our new clients was just inquiring about last week. Actually, make that two," Anjali added as she scrolled through the inbox on her phone.

"Sad for some, more business for us," Rob reinforced.

"People invest so much, and they're not even in a real relationship."

"You just put the last nail in the dating coffin, Anjali. Why are people doing this over a crush? The new Fatal Attraction package—"

"Rob, that's not the name we decided on," I said, giving him a stern look.

"Kidding! We won't be boiling any bunnies here." He put his hands up in mock surrender. "Crushed It is our newest package offering. A weekend boot camp designed to help you move on from someone you never dated. We give you that closure."

"Rob and I are fleshing this out now. We'll send a copy to everyone by the end of the week," I said.

"We've also talked about how the market is getting bigger across the US, and now is expanding internationally. Soon Breakup will be ready to move to the world's stage. Anjali, that's your new account, managing the international market," Rob announced.

"Thank you," Anjali said, turning to me.

"Don't thank me, thank the man with the big wallet. He's

going to have to pay you more if you're doing more work," I said. "But seriously, Anjali—thank you for all your hard work and dedication. And a big thank-you to everyone."

"So, there we have it," Rob jumped in. "The Queen of Clutter—"

"Declutter," Anjali interrupted.

"Yes, the Queen of Declutter is now leading the international stage, which sounds like a new category at the Oscars," Rob added proudly. "Anyway, great stuff all around. We can celebrate midweek at the usual after-work spot! Okay, now back to Anjali for our morning recap of pending clients."

"Thanks, Rob. We have a lot of emails to get through, thanks to Manny's awesome TV segment! We also have the usual odd requests."

"Let me hear a few," Rob said.

"We have a woman who is asking for a breakup with her boyfriend so that she can date the boyfriend's father."

"Easy. Dump City population: one son," Rob declared.

"Rob, be nice." I looked over at him and smiled.

"We also have a woman who is tired of her husband's friends. She's complaining there's more bromance than romance and wants out with their two kids."

"Can't a guy have friends anymore?" Rob shook his head.

"And we have, I mean had . . . Mr. Patel . . ."

"Who is looking for a temporary breakup," I jumped in. "He won't be calling anymore. I took care of him."

"All right, so usual Monday here at Breakup," Rob said.

"I was also mulling over the additions to our à la carte services. If I am leading the international markets, perhaps we tie in a cultural component."

"Keep talking, Anjali. I like where this is heading," Rob said.

I tilted my seat forward.

"My conversation this morning with Mr. Patel had me thinking that we could support things like cultural differences, traditions, values, beliefs—"

"If the traditions are within reasonable limits," I added.

"Yes, of course. There is a whole world out there, and maybe with some coaching packages that involve conversations around understanding . . ."

Was this package made for me? I thought, cautiously listening to what Anjali was saying.

"I smell rupees, yen, and euros making us a lot of American money, honey."

"Rob, no honey, just money," I warned him, putting on my HR hat. "We love it, Anjali. I'll take a look at your first draft. Why don't you work with . . . Erica, Jenson, and . . ." I looked around the table. "Abby."

"Sure."

"On it."

"Awesome."

They all replied at once.

"Thanks, Manny," Anjali finished up.

Anjali cared about Breakup, and you could see that in the way she was devoted to her work. And her new idea had everything to do with her drive and nothing to do with how I had handled Mr. Patel this morning. *This isn't about me,* I reminded myself. As Adam always said, "Don't take anything personally when it comes to work. Invest your ideas in your company, not your emotions." But as much as I admired Adam's influence, we had different opinions on our styles of leadership, including just how close we got to our teams. He always said, "Employees aren't like family, they can always be replaced." But when I looked around the room, I thought there wasn't anyone on the Breakup team who could be replaced.

"Now, can we dim the lights?" Rob called out. "We have something special to share."

As our eyes adjusted to the darkened room, Rob turned in his seat and pointed to the screen, where a large picture popped up.

"How did you get a copy?" I asked Rob.

"It's on every newsstand, Manny."

I didn't know that. I thought I was going to be the first one to see the cover of the November issue of *Beyond More*, which is what the editor, Marie, had promised. She must have forgotten and gone to print.

The boardroom chairs shuffled as everyone shifted to get a good look. The image of the holiday issue was filled with cover lines—"Holiday Hair and Makeup," "Gift Guide for 50 Items Under $25," "Don't Pack On the Holiday Pounds," and "Manny Dogra: The Beauty Behind Your Breakup"—and lit up the room in red and green.

It takes getting used to seeing your face on a magazine cover, not to mention in high-res. I had just mustered the courage to turn to look up at the screen again when Rob swung his seat around to face me. I could tell something was wrong from the expression on his face, even in the dim lights.

"Is it just me or is something off about this picture?" he asked.

"What do you mean?" I gave the picture my full focus.

"I don't know . . ." He looked around the room for help. "You just . . ." He was struggling to find words. The Rob I knew had no trouble with words. They were like numbers to him; the more he used, the better the outcome.

"It's just that you seem a bit . . . how do I say this? Your face . . . it seems a little bit *brighter*."

"Brighter," I asked him. "Or lighter?"

"Hmmm, not brighter. No, not that. It's your skin, the pigmentation. It's just . . . you look whiter than you normally do," he finally spat out.

"Oh, it's just these new screens we put in," I said. "I've got the magazine right here. Look."

I opened the envelope I had brought into the meeting. The team leaned in anxiously.

No difference.

"Manny . . ." I heard a muffled voice say. "I have to say, what I see on the cover versus what I see in real life, it's two different people."

"I think she looks . . . angelic," Alison from graphics added.

"And these days the colors tend to *bleed*, so depending on what magazine you pick up, each cover will look vaguely different. Possibly. Maybe," someone else continued, unconvincingly.

Rob stood up and started to clap. "Manny, you know what, this is the most-read magazine in the country, and you just made the cover. Can we get a round of applause for our CEO?" The room filled with apprehensive applause.

I stood up abruptly.

The clapping stopped.

"I need to see more copies!" I pushed the cover back down on the table. "Anjali . . . can you—"

"Already on it." She jumped out of her seat and rushed out of the room.

"We've got a busy day ahead of us. I'm going to head back to my desk. Rob, can you finish the meeting?" I knew I wouldn't be able to say anything else, so I headed out the door before he could reply.

Plopping down on the sofa in my office, I took a deep breath and reached for the necklace around my neck. The necklace! I had worn it the day of the photo shoot, just as I had every single day since my mother had given it to me. I never took it off. How had my mother's necklace just disappeared from the cover?

Twenty minutes later and Anjali returned to my office with beads of sweat dripping down her face. She looked like a hot mess, but, of course, the stack of magazines in her arms was perfectly organized.

"Here!" She placed a hand on her chest. "I bought up every copy they had and—" she managed to say between breaths.

"Let me take a look." I grabbed the magazines. I studied each one, and then dropped it on the floor. They looked just like the issue that had been mailed to me, just like the one Rob had shown in the meeting. Of course they did. I hadn't really expected anything different, despite Alison's attempt at making me feel better. I looked lighter. My skin was lighter, and my necklace was missing. I looked down at the last magazine in my hand as Anjali anxiously waited for my reaction.

"My skin . . ." I said to her as if she had an answer. "It's light. It's really, *really* light."

"It's true. You don't look exactly like you," she said as she lowered her gaze to her empty arms. "I mean, it's you, but it's not you. Manny, you look like a . . . please don't take this the wrong way, but like a girl who is not Indian?" Her eyes still didn't meet mine as she struggled to find the words, just as Rob had earlier. "Do you want me to call Marie? I'll get her on the phone right now and make her remove that magazine from every outlet in the country."

"No, no," I said. "I'll send her a note. Once I calm down. Once I figure out what to say. I just don't understand how this happened. She promised me final approval."

"Are you sure you don't want me to call Marie?" Anjali could read me. She knew how upset I was.

"I'm sure," I reassured her. "It's okay." But it wasn't.

I took one last look at the cover. Not quite CEO Barbie, but not Manny Dogra, either.

Chapter 6

Dear Breakup,

I have had it! My boyfriend, in all of his forty-seven years, has no manners! Last night was the last straw. We went out for Taco Tuesday and some of the guacamole from his plate fell onto his arm and—are you ready for this?—he licked it off. In the middle of a public place, he sticks his tongue out and licks his arm! Are all men like this, or should I just settle for this barbaric animal, since I'm about to turn forty-nine in a month?

Rosy

I eased my way out of the seat, trying not to catch the short tail of my red cocktail dress in the car. I made my way through the lobby full of guests lingering outside the ballroom toward a server with a tray of drinks. Just a quick sip before making my entrance.

"One second," I said to the server, grabbing a glass of champagne and downing it as if it were a cheap cocktail. "Thank you!" I handed the empty glass back. He nodded as if the events of the day were written on my face.

"You may need one more. It's a Jamieson party, after all."

I turned at the sound of the familiar voice. "Derek, you made it!"

"Of course I did. Wouldn't miss the party—or seeing my future sister-in-law. Not for anything in the world."

"But I thought you were shooting your next film with Zac . . ."

"Efron can wait," Derek said as he embraced me. "How are you doing, Manny?"

"Great, now that you're here." I really was. "Overall, I'm good. I can't wait to see your brother. I haven't seen much of Adam lately. I was hoping to spend some time alone with him tonight."

"You and me both." Derek was always begging us to come to this city or that country while he filmed his latest project. "Let me tell ya, you look hot. Hopefully my brother doesn't forget to tell you that."

"So do you!" I gushed as I squeezed his bulging bicep, part of the Jamieson genes. "How long are you here for?"

"I have to head back tomorrow to finish up the movie, then I'm in Canada for the rest of the fall working on a new series. But first, I'm on this American Bollywood thing."

Derek was the only Jamieson who even acknowledged I was Indian. Last year, he had invited Rajiv and me on set when he filmed a commercial near Aja Raja. Now Derek's beautiful face beams alongside Bollywood royalty on Rajiv's truck.

"Is my brother actually coming tonight or is he busy on another project? I did text him earlier today but must have been a weak signal." Derek raised his phone pretending to look for a Wi-Fi signal, knowing full well that Adam had more than likely just ignored the text.

"He is. We finally talked this morning. Our schedules have been so off. He's been in Europe, and I'm—"

"On every TV show. I caught you this morning with that Maggie. Man, she's got great legs, from what I could see." Derek whistled.

"I actually think those are insured." I wasn't joking.

He grinned. "I should get in there before Dad hits the bourbon too hard. Oh, can you do me a favor?"

"Sure, anything for you!"

Derek reached in his pocket and grabbed a business card. "Can you email Jennifer before next Monday and let her know it's over?"

"Another one? Derek, that's five breakups in less than four months."

"So, I'm averaging one every month. I am trying, Manny. It's hard to make these relationships work when you are on the road so often."

I thought about Adam and me, and all the traveling Adam was doing, but we made it work, didn't we?

"Can you do me a solid and make sure this breakup happens before Monday? Kinda need it done before the next big movie premiere," Derek insisted, then planted a kiss on my cheek.

I couldn't break client confidentiality, even for my soon-to-be brother-in-law—who was already about to get a Breakup from Jennifer.

Watching Derek as he pressed through the reception doors made me realize how much I'd missed him. I cared deeply about my future brother-in-law, and he cared about me. In fact, he once told me I was the best thing to happen to the Jamieson family. He also said I was the *only* thing to happen to Adam—besides work as of late, that is. When I moaned to Derek that he was mean, he backtracked a bit, saying his brother should be putting more effort into all his relationships. Derek had made several attempts to get closer to his brother, but more often than not he was the casualty of missed phone calls, unanswered vacation suggestions, or just lost opportunities to hang out at a local bar when Derek was shooting in Europe.

To Adam's credit he was busy building a successful company, and he just didn't have the luxury of "memorizing lines while getting my hair and makeup done," he would joke to me.

But sometimes I wondered if he truly felt that way about Derek. I had, after all, caught him declining a call or two from his brother that he could easily have picked up. Regardless of him having to cut our conversations short lately, though, Adam never declined any of my calls and always made time to catch up with "CEO Dogra," as he affectionately called me. He especially loved talking work conflicts with stakeholders, and unreasonable clients and financial advice for Breakup. *The more CEO talk, the less time for grief talk*, I imagined Adam would say. In fact, after he had lost his grandmother he sent a text with her funeral details, which was followed by another text:

> She lived a good life, and she would have wanted me to do the same with my focus on work. Back to the grind, Manny.

I never got a chance to meet Grandma Jamieson, but I did know that Adam had been closer to her than his real parents.

"Hello, gorgeous." Adam snuck up behind me and kissed me behind my ears. His lips felt strange after so much time apart. He leaned back out and just like the first time we met, pulled my hair over my ear. "And there's my girl."

"You know, if my boyfriend found out I was kissing a complete stranger at his family celebration he would find it very naughty," I said and grinned. Adam reached in for another kiss, and this time his familiar scent gave me some comfort. He held my hand as we walked over to the other end of the ballroom.

The Jamiesons had chosen a Gatsby theme for the party, with opulent ostrich feathers dangling from a glittery balloon ceiling. Male servers wore cuffed trousers and striped shirts with club collars and collar bars. Women servers were dressed as flappers in sequined fringe with matching headbands, offering cigars out of boxes secured with bands draped around their necks. Black-and-white vintage table linens were set off by elegant taper candles, highlighting the art deco place cards. The whole effect was mesmerizing.

"It takes two to make an accident," he said softly in my ear.

"Oh, are we quoting the impulsive F. Scott Fitzgerald tonight?"

"I only cite the best," he replied, ever his charming self.

We settled by the bar, where a woman had just ordered a Beautiful Fool, and Adam ordered a Bee's Knees for me and a Twelve-Mile Limit for himself. He knew I preferred gin over whiskey.

"Adam, I didn't know you were coming in for the anniversary party. You hadn't mentioned it all week in any of your texts."

"Are you sure? I could have sworn I had texted you this morning on my way to the airport . . . and last week." He scrolled through his phone. "You know, Berlin just has my mind running blanks half the time. There's so much riding on this project. Anyway, enough about me, let's talk about that magazine cover. It was a beautiful shot of you, Manny. And the article was written like—"

I felt my body tense up as I thought back to the magazine. Part of me was still in a state of shock that an editor would go to print without my final approval, another part seeking comfort in the fact that there must be some explanation for the way it looked. The way it didn't look anything like me.

"The Breakup emails *I* write for a living?" I often joked with Adam that if he ever decided to break up with me, I would write his email for him.

Dear Manny,

This transaction has now come to a point where it serves neither of us. With that in mind, I have filed a motion to not continue with our relationship any further, as I feel the next quarter would only draw a loss for both parties . . .

"I don't sound like that, do I?" he would tease back. "And if I do, it's because I know a good investment when I see one. Personal and business, CEO Dogra."

Business was one of his sexiest qualities.

"Yes, exactly like those emails," he responded. "Gracious, effective, attention-getting."

I had to smile. Adam had a knack for making me forget

what was bothering me. We moved away from the bar to a quiet spot off by ourselves, watching the club members celebrate the Jamiesons.

"I really missed you." The blue in Adam's eyes lit up as he looked at me.

"I missed you, too," I said, but absently. I had to admit I was still thinking about that damn cover.

"I have exciting news about work, but I'll save that for later."

Adam must have seen the frustration on my face. "Just hang in there, Manny. I promise the traveling will all come to an end soon. I know it's been a hectic few months for us, but it will all be worth it."

I nodded, and we made our way to Mr. and Mrs. Jamieson, who were gathered in a circle with close friends off to the side of where the band was playing. *Close enough to the music to drown out any real conversations*, I thought. Any time I had attended a Jamieson party, the exchanges between couples were usually limited to how they planned to spend their summers in over-priced European homes, the size of yet another newly acquired yacht, the schedules of entertaining so-and-so, and money-related banter. It was probably the only thing the Jamiesons had in common with my late parents: no real friendships. Although my parents preferred it that way. "Head down and work, Manny. Talk is cheap," my dad would remind me as we sat in his home office separated by a large plate of homemade nachos he had prepped for our study sessions. As "head down" as he was, he was also a man with a large appetite. "Food keeps our minds fueled for great ideas. Just don't tell your mom we snacked after dinner," he would say, followed by his mischievous grin.

"Well, if it isn't our very own foreign model!" Mr. Jamieson called out when he saw me.

That's a new one, I thought. Making me sound more like a car than a human.

"Breaking hearts not only for business—but now she stuns on the cover of the most-read magazine in the country," he boasted to the group gathered around him, raising his glass as high as his voice to make sure everyone noticed.

Although I didn't care much for Mr. Jamieson's small talk, he certainly was business savvy, which Adam had picked up from him. And just like my father, he believed in keeping your head down to focus on work.

"Oh, please," I said to him. "This party is about you two." I kissed him on the cheek and hugged Mrs. Jamieson.

"Be right back, babe," Adam said to me as he slipped away from the circle to take a call.

"That's a beautiful cover, Manny," Mr. Jamieson continued.

"It sure is," Mrs. Jamieson agreed. That was usually as far as she got in a conversation—agreeing with her husband.

"Happy anniversary to you both." I smiled back at her, trying to pivot the conversation away from the disastrous picture of the whitewashed me.

Mr. and Mrs. Jamieson were a friendly couple despite their sometimes odd and outdated look on things. They were dedicated business folks like Adam, and like my parents had been, and although they could *never* replace my parents, I felt a sense of comfort belonging to a family. Less lonely. I could deal with being alone, but the feeling of loneliness was tough, and I had had enough of that after my parents' passing. Brunches, dinners, and the Jamieson parties, as dry as they were, gave me a sense of belonging to people other than my staff, something I longed for.

"Sorry about that. Europe calling," Adam whispered when he came back.

"Maybe Europe can call after our party?" Mrs. Jamieson gave him a stern look.

"Mom, don't start. Please."

"I'm just saying, thank goodness your father doesn't believe in carrying around a cell phone."

"That's right. If anyone wants to get a hold of me, they know where to . . ."

Find me . . . I finished Mr. Jamieson's sentence in my head. A self-promotional line he often repeated at social gatherings. Even Derek once told me he found these "family reunions" tiresome. For the most part I agreed with him, but I also enjoyed seeing Adam with his parents. There was a sense of pride he carried, knowing that he had ventured out on his own.

"Unlike Derek," Adam often said. "Derek flashes his name around Hollywood, and everyone thinks of Dad. But in architecture, no one cares about Jake Jamieson."

I also found comfort in being with family, even if that family wasn't quite mine yet. As I watched the Jamiesons, I couldn't help but think of my parents again.

"It's in their genes," Mrs. Jamieson leaned in and interrupted my thoughts. "Work. They're working men. We keep busy with other things." She waved her hand around, clearly indicating she had spent a great deal of time arranging this party through her confidential Rolodex of contacts who could provide the best in decor, drinks, and dancing.

"It looks beautiful," I said as the shimmer from the diamond chandelier above us bounced off Mrs. Jamieson's pearl Chanel necklace. "All of it," I continued as I watched Adam slip away for another call.

". . . And their parents. What a loss."

I turned my gaze back to the social circle.

"It just happened so suddenly. A car accident in NYC is what I heard," said the woman next to Mr. Jamieson.

My stomach started to turn. Parents. Loss. Car accident. All words I hated to hear.

Adam came back again and whispered in my ear. "You know what, let's get out of here!"

"What? We just got here. How are we going to do that?"

"Like this." He raised his empty glass as he held my hand. "Excuse us, just going to grab another drink," he said, and started pulling me toward the bar.

"Adam!" I smiled, thrilled at the idea of leaving the party and the current conversation.

"You'll see them for breakfast tomorrow anyway." His hand slipped to my lower back.

Even though Adam was often absent due to his work, when he was present he knew I didn't need to hear conversations about death. It was his way of helping me through the grieving process—not talking about what had happened. Seeing Adam and having his arm around me felt more inviting than the dull Jamieson anniversary party and helped me push away the events of today. We slipped through the doors that led to the kitchen, and I saw Mrs. Jamieson winking at us, as if giving us consent to leave the extravagant party she had worked so tirelessly on.

By the time Adam and I arrived home, I was happy to take off my heels.

I wandered into the kitchen and slid open the large rustic barn door that was located in the back of the room.

"How about a vintage Barolo?" Adam snuck up behind me and kissed the back of my neck, as I studied the bottles in the section branded "Italian Reds."

"I don't think we have one. It's on our list of future purchases."

Future purchases. I was starting to make everything sound like business, even at home.

We had almost every vintage red and white wine from the West Coast, mostly because they were often delivered to the Jamieson winery first as gifts from neighboring wineries.

"We do." Adam turned me around and held up a bottle of 2016 Barolo. "Happy Breakup anniversary, CEO Dogra."

"Hey, that sounds like you and I are celebrating *our* breakup anniversary."

"Never." He grazed my cheek with his lips as he handed me the bottle of wine. "And one more thing . . ." Adam reached into his shirt pocket and gave me a box, which I opened.

"Headphones?"

"Personalized AirPods. I was watching your interview on the Jay Shetty show the other day and you had on these big bulky things that pushed back your hair. Now you can . . ." Adam slid one into my ear. ". . . wear these. See? Don't we make a great team?" He kissed my cheek and closed the white charger case that had *CEO Dogra* engraved on it.

I put the earbud back into the case and quickly kissed him back.

Adam's gifts always had a functional purpose. The Montblanc pen for signing new client contracts, the iPad Mini I could carry around to jot down new Breakup packages if I was ever feeling inspired at one of our romantic dinners, the Bluetooth pocket mirror that also functioned as a PDF presenter in case I bumped into a potential investor. We never acknowledged personal celebrations with each other, and somehow over time I had turned my personal celebrations into inconveniences of the day, unlike the festivities my parents used to create around my birthday, graduation, and other significant moments. The less I reminisced about those days now, the less painful the loss.

"Grab the glasses, babe. I just need to check my phone for a second."

Adam slid into the dining area as I reached for the crystal wineglasses. I was just opening the bottle when he returned.

"You know, this place keeps looking better and better by the day," he said.

"It is coming along nicely, but it would be even nicer if we could spend more time in it together." I looked down and whisked my index finger around the mouth of my glass. I was really missing him, now that he was here.

Adam put down his phone. "I know, babe. Soon. Work is peaking right now. Everything is just where I want it. We are finally getting the respect of some of the industry's best. Just the other day Mark Dial called. *The* Mark Dial . . ."

His words became faint as I drowned them out with the sound of pouring wine. As much as I loved Adam and his work principles, I had my limits on how much work talk I could take at the end of what was an overly exhausting and disappointing day for me.

Where were those AirPods again?

"And, of course, when he called . . ." Adam was scrolling back through his phone as he continued with his story. He hadn't even noticed I had briefly tuned out. ". . . Fuck, this Barolo is good. You know, I've been trying to convince Dad to step up the winery game. I think there is so much we can do with that place, but of course, Derek thinks the simpler, the better."

"Derek was at the party tonight."

"Yeah, I forgot to fire back a text to him," Adam muttered. I could tell by the way he moved his gaze from me back to the wine that he hadn't forgotten, he just couldn't be bothered to make it a priority.

He swiftly changed the topic from Derek back to the winery. "I just think if Mom and Dad spent a little more time in Europe, they'd really understand the mechanics of wine, and how it's actually the main course of a meal."

I stared blankly at Adam and continued to drink, and he continued talking about work—his work, or his parents' work. I moved on to my second glass. *Had our relationship always been like this?* I wondered. I didn't think so. I thought back. Adam and I had spent a great deal of time in each other's arms when we were first getting to know each other, making love, planning our future together, but after a year or so of that love language, Adam had been offered the dream gig of a lifetime with the European hotels, and suddenly our dreams took a step back. But I knew that was temporary.

"How about you? How was your workday?" He had poured himself another glass and swirled it, letting the wine breathe.

"Well, it was interesting, to say the least," I moaned. "Adam, did you notice something odd about me on the cover of that magazine?"

"Nope. You looked beautiful. Like always. You know your face lights up when you do this kind of stuff," he said, taking a gulp of his wine.

It did? Most days I just wanted to get media over and done with, but I understood how powerful a tool it was for Breakup. The more eyes on our brand, the more fingers speed-dialing us for help.

"But, it . . . it doesn't really look like me, does it?"

"They Photoshop these things all the time." He shrugged. "You know how it is. You've done half a dozen of these."

He took another big gulp and so did I. The wine was slipping past our lips faster than usual.

"No," I said. "Sure, they Photoshop everything these days, but my skin looked a lot lighter than usual."

"I thought you looked sexy, babe."

"But I didn't look like *me*. I'm going to email Marie. She gave me her word that I'd receive final approval if she made any changes before it went to print. She backed out of that." Recounting the situation to Adam made me realize how upset I was.

Adam glanced down at his phone again. "Are you sure you want to do that?"

I couldn't help but feel annoyed at him for not really being interested in what I was saying. "It's not right. In fact, it feels a little disrespectful."

"You're focusing too much on the picture. People are going to read the article and use the cover as a . . . a coaster."

I bristled.

"You know what I mean. Manny, I didn't sneak out from the party tonight to talk about some magazine cover. I came back to see you and spend time with you tonight," he said, reaching out for my hand.

"Actually," I corrected him, "you came back because it's your parents' anniversary."

"True, but there's nothing like a little multitasking," he said with a grin.

I pulled my hand away. "Dammit, Adam. Don't treat me like an item on your to-do list."

"Where did that come from?"

"We've been together for about two years; we have a house you hardly spend any time in. Every time you do set foot in it, your eyes bug out with all the work *I've* done to it. In fact, I have had to take on all the responsibility of the contractors, design, decorating, everything you promised we would do together. You're the architect, not me. We haven't even settled on a firm wedding date."

"Manny, it's not like I don't spend time with you when I can." *When I can.*

"You spend most of your time on the phone when you do manage to come home."

"I've got a lot on my plate."

"Oh yeah? How about you clear some of that plate off, like

I always manage to do for you. For us. You know, I thought the whole point of being in a relationship was not to feel so lonely."

Adam kissed me. "Let me make you feel less lonely." Adam's preoccupied kisses continued down my neck as he tried to move his phone into his other hand. "I think you're just upset about that stupid cover."

"It may be stupid to you, but that's me on the cover of a national magazine, looking like . . . looking like . . . *not me*. And it's about the fact that I didn't approve it!"

Adam looked at me.

"Manny, I approved it," he admitted.

"What?"

"I approved the damn thing."

"You did what?" My words came out a lot louder than I had meant, silencing the house with my shock. "You saw that whitewash? And you approved it?"

"It was on your laptop on our last Cabo vacation and the sun must have been in my eyes."

"It's not *me*."

"Well, it looked like you in Cabo from the angle I was looking at it." Adam reached for me, but I pulled back. "I thought I was helping you out."

"Helping me out?" I reached for a copy of the magazine that was lying on the island with the rest of the afternoon mail and shoved it in his face. "By making me look like a totally different person?"

"Manny. Relax." He took the magazine and put it back on the island, refusing to even look at it. "It is you. That's what you look like to me."

My fists clenched. I moved the wine bottle away from me.

"What do you mean—*to me*?" I was upset before, but I was angry now. I could feel my cheeks burning.

"You know what I'm trying to say." Adam lifted my arms and wrapped them around his shoulders.

"I really hope I don't!" I snapped back.

"Don't get mad." Adam pulled my hair toward my face. "I just don't see color, especially when it comes to you."

"You have got to be kidding me." I stepped out of his sloppy embrace. "I've put up with a version of that well-intentioned bullshit all my life. I didn't expect to hear it from my fiancé."

"Sorry, that came out wrong. You know I've got my architecture hat on all the time. Even with you. You're like a blank building I can paint whatever color I want. We want."

I felt like I'd been slapped. "What the fuck, Adam?"

"Well, come on, you don't actually think you're . . ." Adam searched for words in the wineglass he had emptied, "Indian or whatever?"

"Yes! I do?" Why did that sound more like a question?

"Manny, you're blowing this whole thing out of proportion. It's not like you know anything about the beliefs, the people, the food—that's for sure. You're not *really* Ind—" he stopped before doing more damage.

I was furious. Pulse rising, fist-clenchingly furious.

"Maannnny," he soothed. "You're beautiful. All anyone will see when they look at that cover is your beauty."

Adam said *beautiful* as if it were my nationality. Which I suppose, to him, it was. He didn't get it, and to be honest, neither did I. But something in me ached, and anger turned into sadness.

"I am getting the fuck out of here." That was all I could manage.

"Manny, stop. Come back here and let's talk this out," Adam said, but his phone started to ring. He looked at me, and his eyes begged me to let him answer the damn thing.

"Just get the phone," I said. "I know you want to."

"This is so ridiculous. It's just another PR push—that cover. Who cares? You'll do another one . . . gimme a second." He answered his phone.

"I care," I said, touching my mother's necklace and feeling the warmth of the gold. She would have cared.

I snatched the magazine off the counter.

"Here." I tossed it at Adam before walking away. "Use it as your coaster; it's fucking Calacatta marble your drink is resting on."

Chapter 7

Dear Breakup,

My boyfriend walks around the house naked all day. At first it was sexy—that air of confidence was hot—but now it's just disgusting. The other day, he was eating crackers, and a few fell into all the wrong cracks on his body, and guess what, he picked them out and ate them. Help HIM. He needs a session with you, or I am out.

Rasheeda

My drunken finger couldn't seem to get Rob's apartment buzzer to work. Damn, that Barolo had made me tipsy. I was about to attempt a text when the door swung open.

"Who are you here for?" two girls asked as I loitered outside their building.

"Oh, Rob, unit 211."

"Rob and Jay. Yeah, go on in. Have fun."

I hurried up the stairs and started banging on Rob's door.

"What the hell is going on out there?" came the voice from the other side of the door. "Jay, if you've forgotten your key again—"

"It's not Jay, it's—"

"Manny?"

I looked up at my friend as the door opened. "Rob, make me Indian." The words had simply slipped out, and I wasn't even sure what they meant.

"Awww, honey . . . come here." He embraced me.

"I just want to be Indian, Rob."

"Let me think. I could look up a Deepica YouTube makeup tutorial. Jay is obsessed with her Live Tinted brand. Or that Diipa Khosla has been all over my 'gram with her hottest makeup tips and hottie hubby."

I tried to smile.

"Manny, come on in. I'll make you some tea."

"I need something stronger."

Rob looked me up and down, no doubt aware that I had already been drinking. "One Rob Bomb coming up."

No one actually knew what went into a Rob Bomb. No one much cared. It was strong and sweet and packed a punch. That was enough.

Rob and Jay's apartment was a mash-up of their personalities made physical—a purple armchair, lavender-scented candles, and intense splashes of Prince. You could see the way they—their love—had come together, creeping into every nook of the apartment. I thought about my place with Adam: blue and brown, which my architect fiancé had insisted was the right balance of minimalism and personality—ironic for someone who said they didn't see color. Our house sat beside the water, and the only sound that filtered through the windows was of lapping waves. No pictures of our favorite musicians adorned the walls; in fact, I had to fight for a picture of Adam and me to go up. He felt images drowned out the presence of the architecture of the house. I was so eager to move in that I agreed.

"By the way, that is one hell of a dress," Rob said. He handed me a glass of what smelled mainly of gin but also other things I didn't care to make out, then took a drink from his own glass.

"Cheers!" I raised my glass like a Jamieson would. I took a sip and winced.

"You said strong," he reminded me.

"Cheers and tears . . ." I let out an exaggerated drunk cry that was more sulk than anything else.

"What happened tonight? I thought you were going to see Adam." Rob rolled his eyes at Adam's name. He wasn't a fan. Rob, just like Derek, had offered up multiple suggestions for double dates, game nights, and vacations together for the four of us, but Adam was always too busy. When I tried to tell him just how off-putting this was to my friends, he would remind me, "Work now, play later." I uncomfortably agreed. After all, Breakup was experiencing an all-time record of success.

I sighed and winced again at how strong the drink was. "Can I?" I reached for the leftover Chinese food on Rob's coffee table as my stomach reminded me that I had had more to drink than eat today.

"Here, let me get you a proper plate." Rob went back to the kitchen as I crushed a spring roll.

"I did see Adam, and Derek, too."

"Derek was there?" Rob handed me a plate of chili chicken with noodles.

"Yup and . . . hold this one second." I reached into my purse. "He needs another breakup."

We swapped back the plate for the business card I had retrieved.

"Sheesh—Derek's breakups are like his Botox. We all know it's coming; we just don't know when. You know, this could actually be a new Breakup package. Guys Who Breakup and Botox Together." Rob was suddenly inspired.

"Hey, that's my future brother-in-law," I teased.

"Sorry. I shouldn't have said that out loud. Go on. What's got you so hot and bothered about tonight—and not in the kinda way I was hoping for when someone hasn't seen their fiancé in some time." Rob shimmied his shoulders in an attempt at some sort of dirty dancing.

"I had every intention of getting hot and bothered earlier. Anyway, it's just that Adam and I didn't seem to connect so great later in the evening." I stared at Rob. Did his eyes just sparkle at the thought of Adam and me not connecting? "Maybe he was jet-lagged and just saying things. He's been working really hard on the—"

"Berlin project," Rob said before I could get out the words. He took my already empty glass and handed me another Rob Bomb.

"There's more. I'm also feeling so disconnected since . . ." I looked down at my drink.

"I know, honey. I know," Rob said. "It's been hard for you with your parents gone."

"I can't seem to find myself. I don't know who I am as of late. I keep thinking my parents spent so much time trying to show me life as an American in Baskin. That's all I seem to really know." I put down the empty plate and sank farther into the couch.

"What else do you want to know?"

"I want to know about life as an *Indian* American in Baskin." Memories of Rajiv's truck, the dinners at his place, Anjali's words about Indian traditions, and that damn cover played back through my mind.

Why hadn't I said *I do* with more conviction when Adam had asked me about being Indian?

"I don't know much about that, Manny, but what I do know is that I remember talking to your dad the few times I came over when I was your boyfriend."

We smiled at the memory of Rob being my boyfriend.

"We'd had a few too many glasses of Canadian Club and he mumbled things in Hindi that I couldn't understand. He did mention that he didn't have much of a childhood and that his life was simple. Manny, he wanted you to have more than simple. He wanted you to have everything that you do have now. And you have a lot to thank your parents for."

"Why haven't you ever told me any of this?"

"I'm sorry, but I was so busy hiding my own secret, and you know what? Once I came out to my parents—nothing changed. They were still the kind, loving people they'd always been. We really lucked out with our parents, Manny."

"I know, Rob. But I also know it was hard for my dad to be married to someone who loved someone else."

Rob furrowed his brows.

"It was a marriage of convenience. Didn't I ever tell you that?"

"Um, no," he said, shifting his brows to a raise. "You left out that little detail."

"I found out that my mom was actually in love with a man from the local village in India but was forbidden from marrying him because of an old family disagreement. So her father set up a meeting with a neighboring family, and she was introduced to my dad."

"Well, that's one hell of a meet-cute." Rob gulped his drink.

"She wasn't forced to marry him, but she was so heartbroken at being forbidden from marrying the man she really wanted to, she went along with the idea of marrying my father."

"What disagreement could have caused such a rift?"

"It was over land. Farmland. Both families claimed that more belonged to them."

"Manny, don't take this the wrong way, but this sounds incredibly unbelievable. Are you sure you haven't had too much to drink, and this isn't a movie-of-the-week suggestion from Rajiv?"

"I wish it was, but it happened. Over time my father could see that my mother's heart belonged to someone else." I swirled a cube of ice around in what was left of my drink.

"It sounds like maybe they set out to forget her unpleasant past and decided to make an entirely clean break and start a new life here in California," Rob suggested. "Do you think your father was actually trying to help your mother by not dredging up any memories at all from her past, so he pulled back on everything Indian for you?"

I thought about that for a minute. "I guess that is one way to look at it. But I missed out on so much of being Indian."

"I guess the question now is, how do we get some of this Indian back *into* you, if that's what you really want? Maybe start with an Indian toddy?" Rob snagged his phone, searching for recipes.

I sat back and searched for an answer. An honest answer.

"It's going to take more than that. But, you know, I wish I could wear an Indian outfit, like a sari, to a Jamieson party and not this!" I gestured down at my dress. "Just walk in there and be proud of knowing how to wrap it. And, maybe, accidently fling it in Mr. Jamieson's face when he refers to me as a 'foreign model.'"

"Ouch, he didn't? Well, if you are ever going to do that, you better make sure there's no drink in that old man's hand."

"I also wish I could understand when Rajiv references holidays and celebrations. I had to be reminded that today was Diwali by him and Anjali. How pathetic is that? I wish I knew more about Bollywood plots. I wish Adam wasn't so color-blind."

"What do you mean, color-blind?"

I didn't feel like telling Rob what exactly had transpired earlier. I would later.

"He just mentioned he didn't really think I was Indian when he looked at me."

"There's no such thing as looking *like* something. People don't look at me and think I am gay or not gay enough—or at least I hope they don't. Forget about what Adam said tonight. Think about all the great things your parents did do for you. You went to private school, traveled the world, and can speak four languages. You're the freakin' CEO of a million-dollar company because of what they instilled in you. Those are your family traditions."

We both worked our way to the bottom of what was left of our drinks.

"*Multi*million-dollar company," I finally said. "You should know, as my CFO." I leaned in and hugged him as we both laughed. "Strong drink! I'm going to head out."

"Drinks," Rob corrected, and then said, "Yes, go home. Sleep on it, and in the morning this will all blow over. And the next time a magazine comes calling to put you on the cover, we'll make sure you're wearing a sari!"

I hugged Rob again and headed out into the building hallway. "Apologies for dumping all this on you at this time of night. Please don't feel sorry for me!"

"You mean . . . *sarry* for your sari?" Rob said loud enough that I could still hear him as he cracked up at his own pun and closed the door behind me.

Chapter 8

Dear Breakup,

I just found out that my partner has a secret "get the hell out of Dodge" fund. I think that is me. I am the Dodge. Should I be worried? Should I have my own fund?

Jacob

The city seemed extra bright as the stars twinkled across the Baskin skyline. Tiny bungalows lined the streets below, and backyard pools caught the reflection of the large moon. I looked around my office and headed to the minibar. When the penthouse was being renovated as Breakup headquarters, I had decided to design my own space so it was equipped more like a hotel room. Spa shower; a large hotel-like armoire full of clothes for every meeting, after-work schmooze event, and last-minute PR stint;

and, of course, the minibar hidden just below the oak bookcase. I grabbed the bottle of champagne and sat back on the corner of my desk, still in my dress, watching the world outside since everything in here felt small compared to everything out there.

Adam's parents had sent me the bottle to congratulate me on making the cover of that dreadful magazine, and I chugged back a glassful, just as I had on the many nights I had spent alone after my parents' passing. Alone, but in the company of work.

I looked at the card that had been stuck to the bottle with a purple bow. At least Adam's parents remembered my favorite color. At least their assistant did.

Congratulations to our beautiful light-skinned daughter.

Love, Jake and Laura Jamieson

Okay, so maybe I added the bit about light skin.

Jake and Laura Jamieson knew nothing about me. Up until a few months ago, they had thought I was Spanish.

They had joined Adam and me for dinner one night at our favorite sushi restaurant. I had spent the night before going through old boxes I had found in my mother's closet. That's where I'd located the gold bracelet that I slipped on my arm before dinner.

As the waitress took our order, she stopped and took a closer look at my wrist. "Do you mind?" she asked as she leaned in to examine it. "What a beautiful piece of jewelry, and the spiral is so unique," she said.

"Thank you," I responded, pleased that someone appreciated the exquisite artistry.

"What part of India are you from?" she asked.

"India?" Mr. Jamieson jumped in, as if offended. "For god's sake, she's Spanish."

Mrs. Jamieson asked him to lower his voice; she was always afraid of making a scene in the presence of other "socialites."

"Laura, I got this covered," he said, his words a little sloppy. "Sí, señorita. She is Spanish," he added, in his best Speedy Gonzales accent.

"I'm so . . . sorry," the waitress stammered. "I just thought . . . because of your bracelet. I saw a few on my last trip to India."

"This belonged to my mother," I said, turning the bracelet over on my wrist. "She was from a small village outside New Delhi."

"I'll be damned," Mr. Jamieson said, smacking his hand on the dinner table.

I could tell Adam was mortified, but he said nothing. Once we got home later that night, Adam apologized for his father's drinking, and the next morning had a diamond bracelet delivered to my office.

"Now you'll have one for the other wrist" were the words on the card that accompanied the piece of jewelry. I preferred to wear just my mother's bracelet, but I always appreciated Adam for trying.

My phone beeped with a text message.

> Please come back home. I love you.

> Let's both finish up the Barolo and talk this out. We can plan something special to do together soon. I promise.

Plan to Adam meant a business plan on how to find a solution for the night. That was also Adam trying. I wanted to tell him all his promises seemed to be broken lately.

I started to type a response when I saw reply dots show up on my phone. I stopped. A few seconds later, Adam stopped, too. There was nothing more to say. How did I have nothing more to say?

My imagination began running as freely as the drinks I had had earlier. I could picture the scene now.

"And we are live with Maggie Johnson outside Breakup headquarters. Maggie, what is the latest on this stunning new development?"

"This is a Channel 6 News exclusive. I'm on location in downtown Baskin, where Manny Dogra, CEO of Breakup, is having a breakdown. The woman who has made her fortune writing breakup emails for a living—brace yourself, Alex—has nothing to write to her own fiancé. There you have it, folks. You heard it here first. No words from the Queen of Words, Manny Dogra. Looks like another royal is losing her crown. Back to you, Alex."

I looked back at the blank screen. Adam would be gone soon, our lives returning to missed calls and "good nights" from different time zones.

I slumped down in my chair, tired from the long day and my long thoughts. Another beep from my phone:

> Great to see you tonight, Manny. You looked stunning, but you already know that ;) See you in a couple of months. Don't forget about that favor.

Derek had been the best part of the evening. I only wish we had stayed longer. I took the business card he'd given me out of my purse but heard a ping.

You have 1 new email.

I swung the chair around and faced my computer screen. I opened my inbox, hoping it was Marie, apologizing in response to the hundreds upon hundreds of emails she must have received about the infamous cover.

Sender: Sammy Patel

I rolled my eyes. I glanced at the subject line as it screamed at me:

PLEASE READ THIS!

I stared at the email with its exclamation mark, its urgency marked with another exclamation mark, this one red.

I knew I shouldn't be opening work emails this late at night, or attempting to reply to them, especially after several glasses of wine plus the Rob Bombs. Nope. I wasn't going to open it. I swiveled around in my chair and took in the view again. If that Sammy Patel thought he could cajole me into taking his business, he had another think coming. Then I swiveled back again.

Dear Manny,

I need your help to come up with words so that I don't lose my girlfriend. I know that it's not something you would typically consider, but I don't have any other choice. Come on, you of all people must understand what I am going through.

Sammy

You of all people.

I sat back up in the chair and started to type, the words flowing out of me in a rush.

Sammy,

If I help you, I need something in return . . . please.

Manny

It seemed that no sooner had I hit Send than I received my reply.

ANYTHING. Just name it.

This was ridiculous. I was ridiculous. Dang, I could barely type, struggling to find the right keys under my fingers. Thank god for spell-check.

I need your help!

Send.

I knew better than to email when I was buzzed. I didn't even know what I was asking for. I leaned toward the computer and started typing again, but another email came in from Sammy.

Can we meet now?

Why not? I thought. The night couldn't get any worse, and I needed something more than a bottle of Jamieson champagne to numb the evening's earlier events. I put my fingers back on the keyboard.

Meet you at the Wallflower.

Send.

Chapter 9

Dear Breakup,

I've been working long hours in the hospital, and the resident doctor and I have been playing our own game of Operation. Only one problem: this game involves three people; my boyfriend just doesn't know he's also playing. How do I "pause" the relationship with him to see if this doctor/nurse relationship actually has a chance?

Janice

"Fire! That red dress is *fire*. Turn around!" Jay gave me the once-over, and then reached for me.

"This little old thing? Just my casual bar wear when I'm visiting Baskin's best bartender." It felt good to be hugged by Jay. "I was at a party at the yacht club. Adam's parents . . . it was their anniversary."

"Oh, is he with you?" Jay asked, looking behind me.

"Nope." I knew my disappointment was only too visible.

"Don't you worry. Come with me, and I'll make you one of those fancy drinks—as fancy as that dress you're wearing."

The place Jay worked, the Wallflower, was an upscale bespoke bar. Softly lit with charming vintage lamps, it was like a speakeasy from the 1920s, with antique bar carts and walnut Venetian glass mirrors. The best part about it, though, was that patrons had keys to their own private boxes that held expensive alcohol from around the world.

"And how is Mr. Derek Jamieson doing?" Jay asked as I trailed behind him through the room.

No matter who I talked to, the conversation always found its way to Derek. I didn't mind. He was just Adam's brother to me, but he was one of Hollywood's rising young stars to the rest of the world.

"He's great. He's working on a new movie with . . . ooh . . . um . . ."

"Zac," Jay and I said at the same time.

"How did you know?" I asked.

"Heard it on the radio the other day."

Of course he had. Jay was a pop culture junkie. He made it his business to keep up on all the celebrity gossip. He always asked if we had been involved in the latest celeb breakup, but even if he plied me with a glut of fancy drinks—which was nice—I always kept those matters confidential.

As we walked, I scanned the room for Sammy. From this morning's exchange I recalled he was tall, owned a green jacket, and was easily irritated.

It was a quiet weeknight at the Wallflower and the last customer left just as I sat down.

"Are you expecting someone?" Jay asked. "Derek?"

I threw him a look.

"A boy can dream, can't he?"

"I'm meeting a potential partner, I suppose you could say. I don't know what he looks like, though."

Jay measured out chilled vodka with a dash of orange bitters and handed it to me. He took his phone out from his shirt pocket. "So, who are we looking for?"

"His name is Sammy Patel. That's all I know."

Jay typed into his phone. "Geez, there are twenty-one Sammy Patels in Baskin alone."

"Who would have thought?" Certainly not me.

"Maybe he's a doctor or engineer. There's also a teacher and a—"

"Let me see." I took Jay's phone from him. I had no clue which one was my Sammy Patel. "I guess they could all be him."

"Can we narrow it down?"

"To what?" I pulled up Sammy's email to see if there was a signature attached. Nope.

"Maybe he's one of them?" Jay scrolled down the page through more Google images.

"Sorry to disappoint you both, but I am none of them," a voice declared.

Jay and I both looked up at the same time, bumping heads.

"Ouch." I rubbed my head.

Jay looked Sammy up and down, his eyes growing wide with approval.

"Can I grab a whiskey, neat?" Sammy asked Jay.

"Coming right up, boss."

I looked over at Sammy. A boss he was. At least he looked like one. He was wearing a gray suit with gray pinstripes and had loosened his collar as if he had just taken off his tie. His medium-length wavy black hair pushed to the side with no effort.

"Sammy?" I stood up.

"Oh, please, have a seat." As he sat down, he casually put his right leg on the footrest of my stool. Brown leather shoes. No socks. "I guess we both got the memo to keep things casual?" he said with a cheeky laugh.

"I was just getting back from a party—"

"With Derek Jamieson," Jay interrupted as he placed a silver bowl of mixed nuts in front of us.

"*The* Derek Jamieson? Aren't you fancy?" Sammy said, then admitted, "I actually know the guy."

"You do?" both Jay and I blurted at the same time.

"Well, I mean I've worked with him. He shot a few commercials for my family business. I mean this was way back when the guy hadn't hit it big. We've had a few drinks together at his family's estate. The, uh . . . Jamieson winery. Great place to get married."

Yeah, if I was ever to get married to a Jamieson. I thought back to the argument that Adam and I had. I could only imagine that when the priest asked if there were any objections, Adam's phone would be sounding off.

"How do you know him?" Sammy inquired.

"Work thing." I looked over at Jay to shush him. It wasn't the right time to get into the Jamieson connection.

"Hey, didn't I see you earlier today outside that food truck place?" Sammy asked as he reached for a handful of nuts.

"Yes. Let's just say I didn't exactly see you. I heard you, though."

At least he had the good manners to look uncomfortable.

"Yeah, sorry about that. I wasn't in a great mood, and I—"

"You also hung up on me."

Sammy looked for the drink Jay was preparing as if to distract himself from the embarrassment.

"I'm sorry. I'm not usually like that, but this whole thing has me so stressed. I know it's only a week, but it's going to feel like a lifetime with the Patel family, knowing how nosy they are." He was either a good actor, like Derek, or he was genuinely sorry.

"Don't worry. I know all about stress."

"So . . . where to begin?"

Jay handed Sammy the drink and slid farther down the bar, but close enough that I wondered if he could still hear what we were discussing. This was a potential client, after all, so I had to respect Sammy's confidentiality.

"Why don't you start with why you *really* need our services?"

"It's like I said." Sammy sighed and looked at Jay and me, drawing both of us into his story and making it clear that I didn't have to worry about Jay knowing anything. "I'm attending my brother's wedding, and I can't take my girlfriend. My younger brother, Sanjeev, is marrying into what's referred to as 'Indian royalty.'"

"Royalty? As in actual royalty?" Jay enunciated *royalty* as if he might recognize them from one of the reality shows he loved to watch.

Sammy looked at me. "Let's just say they're self-declared maharajas who live a life of heritage and privilege. Kind of like the Khans and Kapoors, but in this case the kings and queens of the diamond and aircraft industries."

I recalled both names from my various Bollywood conversations with Rajiv.

"If they find out the eldest son of their future son-in-law's family is dating and even considering marrying someone who's not one of us," Sammy said, pointing to himself and then to me, "they could call off the entire wedding. It's about reputation."

"But if you get married after—"

"That's just it. Anything that happens *after* my brother's wedding is considered suitable and out of their hands. No one is going to care about a misfit brother-in-law."

I saw Jay glance at me, and knew we were both trying to catch up with all the twists and turns to Sammy's story.

"That's why I need to break up with Lisa for a few days, so she doesn't find out about the wedding. When I get back, I can be with her and tell my family at my own pace. I can't bring that kind of shame to my brother right now. Patel disappointment I can handle, my brother not being able to marry the woman he loves—no way."

"So why not just tell Lisa the truth?"

"Would you ever look at my family the same way if you knew the truth about who my brother was marrying and their values? And if I lie about where I actually am, what if she sees pictures somewhere on some social media or something? It's not like I can avoid being in pictures of my own brother's wedding. How do you not get this, Dogra?" Sammy got up from his stool abruptly, almost knocking over the one next to him. "You know, I think this was a huge mistake." He reached into his pocket and asked Jay, "How much do I owe you?"

"You know what, thinking your attitude would have somehow gotten better since I saw you this morning, now that was a mistake." I raised my voice to be level with Sammy's.

"You're both getting worked up over nothing; let's just grab another drink." That was Jay. Always the peacemaker. Always the bartender.

"She's unreasonable with her judgments."

"I am not. It's my job to ask questions when I take on new clients."

"Is it your job to judge the answers?"

"Come on, you two . . . you're both just fueled up."

"Why don't you go home right now to your parents and tell them you're seeing someone who is *not* Indian and tell me how they react?" Sammy grabbed the fresh drink Jay had set on the bar as if it would help him cool off, and took a seat again.

"I don't have that luxury," I said as I got up. "My parents are dead." I started to walk away.

"Manny, wait . . . Manny . . ." I heard Jay scrambling after me as I stormed through the bar doors. "Stop!" Jay caught my arm. "Come here."

I fell into Jay's arms, the heaviness of the day weighing me down. The magazine cover, Adam's confession, and ultimately our fight—it was all too much for my intoxicated heart. Why wasn't I in the arms of the man I loved? Suddenly I was drunk, weeping.

"Oh, Manny, it's going to be all right."

"I just feel so lost right now." I told him the same things I had said to Rob just a short time ago and felt a sense of horrible déjà vu.

"Come back to the bar, honey. Hear Sammy out. He seems like a decent guy, and I think you both are just having an awful day. You have that in common."

"Jay . . . I miss my parents so much."

"I know. I know. Maybe getting to know someone like Sammy could help you with the . . . grief." Jay stumbled over his words.

"What do you mean?"

"Being friends with someone who is Indian . . . that may answer some of your questions about your parents. I know it's something you have brought up to both Rob and me . . ."

"You too, Jay?"

"Me too, what?"

"You're saying I'm not 'Indian.'" This time the air quotes were mine.

"No, sweetheart. That's not at all what I'm saying. Just come back inside. It's a little chilly out here for this dress. One hell of a dress it may be, but it's going to do diddly-squat to keep you warm."

Sammy was slumped over but quickly stood up when he saw me come back inside.

"Oh, Manny," he said. "I am really sorry. I had no idea about your parents. I've been out of line all day."

We both took a seat again as Jay headed behind the bar.

"Please forgive me." Sammy's voice cracked. "The whole day has been me shooting from the hip. I promise you, I am way more refined than this. I haven't seen my family properly in quite some time, and with this dark cloud hovering over my head, well, it's not an excuse, but it just brought out a Sammy I am not so proud of."

"Forgiven," I said with a little smile. "It's just that . . . you have to understand, some of your assumptions about me . . . I didn't grow up with this type of Indian life. There weren't any expectations for me to act in a certain way. I am sorry, Sammy, this is all unknown to me," I confessed.

Now it was his turn to look confused.

"My parents thought assimilation was the way. America— red, white, and blue, you know?"

"So . . . you've never been to an Indian wedding?"

"I haven't." I felt embarrassed.

Jay placed three shots on the bar. "These are called truce shots."

Sammy and I smiled, and the three of us threw back our lemon drop shots.

"I have an idea," I said. "What if I came to your brother's wedding with you?"

Sammy snapped his head toward me.

I had surprised myself, too.

"Oh, man, you really don't know. Do you have any idea what people would think?" he asked. "I can't bring you to the wedding."

"Wait, I think she's on to something," Jay exclaimed. "I watched this movie once where the main character went to her friend's wedding as his girlfriend and—"

We both looked at Jay, confused.

"Take her to the wedding!" Jay threw up his hands. "This is a no-brainer. You have something she wants. And she has something you want. It's like the big fat Indian wedding meets the little temporary Indian breakup."

"I don't know. I don't think I can do that," Sammy replied.

"Why not?" Jay and I said at the same time.

"They'll . . . they'll . . ." He paused. "They'll think we're together. You're a beautiful young woman." He lowered his voice. "Look, my parents aren't going to handle me marrying a non-Indian well, but at least I can talk to them about it while they scream at me in disappointment. Eventually they will ease into the idea, but I can't set them up for further disappointment by bringing you. They'll think I teased them with an Indian daughter-in-law. They'll want me to shack up with you."

"Nothing wrong with shacking up with THAT!" Jay said as he took a step back.

I shook my head in Jay's direction.

Sorry, he apologetically mouthed back.

"What I am trying to say is, you're single and Indian and so am I, and my family is waiting for me to get married, and suddenly you show up with me? Guys, this is Indian 101 here."

"No, look," I said, pointing at my ring. "I'm engaged." *To a non-Indian guy. Who thinks I'm not really Indian.* I could easily pick up the values, the beliefs, and even the traditions in a week with Sammy. This was the perfect way to prove to Adam that I wasn't just any shade of color he picked for me.

"Look, you can say I'm attending the wedding with you for . . ." I looked around and saw a sign hanging over Jay's head: OPEN FOR BUSINESS. ". . . for business!"

Sammy seemed intrigued.

"Business, huh? What would you need from me?"

"For starters, your girlfriend's name would be helpful."

"Lisa Donahue."

I started putting notes into my phone.

"And where is the wedding?"

"Marble."

"Perfect. I know a lot about the winery business." I thought back to the endless conversations Mr. Jamieson had tried to entertain us with about the perfect barrel and grapes. From the purple that produced the red wine in a Malbec to a Grenache, I had heard it all. "If anyone asks, we're looking to buy a vineyard to start a new winery. An Indian winery! And I tagged along with you to see how Indian weddings are celebrated in Marble. You know—our future customers."

"She does know a lot about wine." Jay motioned to a wineglass.

"Cheers to that," I said.

Sammy nodded, as if he were easing into the plan of taking me to his brother's wedding as a potential business partner who was working undercover to get the lowdown on Indian 101. I was sure if I asked Rajiv he would know a Bollywood movie with this exact plot.

"I like this idea. It's a new market, and you, my *engaged* friend, are coming with me to my brother's wedding as research for our new wine business."

"Yes!"

"Just like that movie I mentioned," Jay added.

Sammy and I looked just as confused as we had earlier.

"Please, Sammy? Will you do this for me if I help you with Lisa?"

"For real? You—*I*—send a temporary breakup letter to Lisa,

and in exchange, all I have to do is show you how to be a Patel at my brother's wedding? Kind of like a . . . class?"

"Exactly! A class where along the way, I get taught how to wrap a sari, greet family members, and celebrate being Indian. That's all you have to do."

"Be the naughty, nutty Indian professor," Jay chimed in.

We both ignored him.

"Show me your family customs, teach me a few traditions, and tell me the value of what being Indian means to you." I put my hand on his shoulder. "Please, Sammy."

He sat back as if to consider my proposition.

I put my hand out. "So, do we have a deal, Mr. Patel? After all, anyone who knows Derek Jamieson must be a decent guy to hang out with for a week."

"We have a deal, as long as I get my girlfriend back," Sammy insisted as he shook my hand.

"A deal is a deal," I told him, then asked, "By the way, what's the difference between being a Patel and just being Indian?"

Sammy got up and gestured to Jay for the bill. "Now that's a question you should have asked before agreeing to the deal!"

Chapter 10

Dear Breakup,

It started off as boredom. I joined a dating chat room for singles between the ages of twenty-five and thirty-five. For the last three months, I have been carrying on a relationship with an attractive twenty-nine-year-old woman who thinks she is "dating" a thirty-five-year-old man. The truth is, I am a seventy-year-old man with four grandchildren and two great-grandchildren. How do I break up with her before it's too late without telling her she was catfished?

Roger

"Manny, I had the best date last night!" Anjali was beaming from ear to ear. "He actually sent me a picture of the cork he snuck into his pocket from the bottle of red we shared, which *I* didn't have to pay for.

"Speaking of late nights," she went on, "it looks like you slept here, and you've missed your breakfast with Adam, Laura, and Jake, but not to worry; I've already sent over some fresh flowers and told them you had an unexpected client emergency."

"Ummm, yes, I figured—"

"And why on earth is that guy Sammy Patel downstairs waiting for you? He says you have a flight at eleven this morning. It's not on your schedule. I checked your calendar twice. And it's nine o'clock now."

"What? Damn!" I jumped up from the couch, a sudden movement that wasn't a good idea for either my tight dress or my throbbing head.

"What's going on? You look hungover, you're still wearing last night's dress, and the man you couldn't stand the sight of yesterday is waiting downstairs to board a plane with you. You, *we*, need to get our shit together." Anjali paced around the room cleaning up the mess from last night. "He also sent an order of fresh coffee and bagels for the entire staff, which I rearranged and created labels for from left to right, starting with everything bagel and ending with jalapeño. It's not just any coffee, it's that premium, expensive stuff. The one you have to dump most of your paycheck on. The nerve of this guy, trying to bribe us into taking the case . . ." she continued.

I was barely listening to her as she babbled on. But she was right about one thing: I did need to get my shit together. Desperate times, desperate measures, and all that. There was only one way I was going to make that flight.

"Code Red, Code Red!" I yelled at her in a panic. "Anjali, I am calling a Code Red. Now!"

"Right now?" she blurted as she pulled out her red tablet.

"Yes, right now!"

She sprang into action and started texting.

"Meet you in the green room in ten," I said as I marched to my shower.

There was no time to think about why I shouldn't be going away. Meeting Sammy last night had made me feel more excited about being part of something than I had in a long time. And it was only going to be a week. What could go wrong in a week?

After a quick shower, I threw on a change of clothes, grabbed a glass of water, and marched my way to the boardroom, my hair still wet. I heard doors slamming, papers swirling, and footsteps running down the sunlit hall, which also boasted more windows than walls. Another Adam design rec.

"Code Red!" my staff shouted as they grabbed their tech. I looked at my phone. Four missed calls from Sammy Patel. None from Adam, but Anjali had told him I had an emergency, so . . .

I called to Anjali, who was darting to the meeting room. "Can you please call Mr. Patel and tell him I'm on my way downstairs? Then I need you to go back into my office and pack a week's worth of clothes. Anything that looks like I could wear it to an Indian wedding. I am sure there are some bright after-work-appropriate dresses in the back of the armoire."

Shock didn't begin to describe the look on her face. "I'll explain later," I said. "Please *go*."

I walked into the boardroom, wondering why we had decided to hold Code Red assemblies in the green conference room. It was packed with key staff from sales, marketing, and partnerships, everyone eager to find out what was happening.

"Who is it?" Rob asked. "Hang on. I just got a text from Jay. It's Ben, isn't it? Or wait, he thinks it's Lindsay or Jessica."

"Rob, you know better than to text when a Code Red is in play."

"I didn't tell Jay there's a Code Red. I just asked him which celebrity is on the brink of breaking up. Those are most of our Code Reds. Jeez."

"Everyone, please have a seat."

I also took a seat and cleared my throat. "Today . . . the Code Red . . ." Everyone leaned into the table, ready to once again spring into action. "The Code Red is being used on . . ." Someone coughed. "On . . . me."

"I knew it!" Rob yelled as he smacked his hand on the table and leaped up. "Wait, what? You're Code Red? You're the crisis?"

It was as if all the air had been sucked from the room.

"It's that client from the last Marvel movie, isn't it? No, wait. It must be the client from that zombie show. You like that kind of guy. Dirty, hasn't shaved or showered in weeks. I just thought you would have told *me*, Manny—"

"Can we get back to business, Rob? I am not having an affair with a client. I'm using Code Red because this matter is urgent and, okay, yes, usually it's issued on a celebrity about to embark on a well-publicized breakup, but, sorry to disappoint some of you, it's me. I am heading out imminently to Marble with a client to help him with his breakup."

Feet shuffled under the boardroom table, accompanied by more furrowed brows than I had seen during Derek's fourth Breakup.

"All you need to know is that I'm taking off for a few days, and my flight leaves in a couple of hours. So, I gotta get going NOW!"

"What's going on, Manny? Leaving to do what exactly? Since when are we offering the Mile-High Club package?" A CFO about to lose his CEO for a week, Rob had every right to be exasperated.

"I'm helping someone, Sammy Patel, with a Timeout Breakup with his girlfriend, Lisa."

John from marketing jumped in. "Manny, you always insisted we don't do second-chance, pause breakups."

Katie, head of partnerships, waved the company handbook and reminded me of words I had written myself. "It's right here in section five of our values statement," she said. "'We shall not, under any circumstances, take part in or cause to happen any breakup that could be considered transitory, provisional, or pro tempore.' How am I going to tell potential partners or, better yet, our current ones that we are now offering the To Be Continued package?"

"I like that name. TBC, am I right?" Rob said, distracted for a minute. Then he regained his focus. "But we can't just start going against the company's values. What if a stakeholder gets wind of this, Manny? Breakup prides itself on being a one-stop shop for permanent breakups. Just imagine the type of clients we'd get if all of a sudden we let every Tom, Dick, and Sammy break up for a little while as they scoured the internet for something better. We might as well partner up with that new app . . . what's it called . . . Tie One On? Drink 'Em and Drop 'Em?" Rob seemed rightfully frustrated.

"How can we be going against the company's values when the company is *me*, and I wrote those values?" I asked. "Just trust me, guys. Have I ever let you down? This one is a special case, and it deserves the attention I'm about to give it," I reassured my staff, and I reassured myself.

Anjali popped back into the boardroom. "What she means is that she met a raving lunatic twenty-four hours ago, got drunk with him, and made some sort of shady deal that probably sounded better last night than it does now, in the light of day. Am I right, Manny?"

The room fell silent again.

Only Anjali could get away with such truth bombs. And Rob.

"The raving lunatic is actually a pretty decent guy, and turns out he's got something I could use in return."

"Okay, now we are getting to the good stuff. Do tell," Rob said, his interest piqued.

"There's nothing of that sort to tell, Rob. This one showers, from what I can tell," I grumbled, remarking on his earlier comment about my fondness for "dirty" men.

He sat back down and started tapping his finger on the table, a habit I found annoying on a good day. This was not a good day.

"Is this about the cover? I thought we hashed that out last night, Manny."

"The cover ignited something in me. An Indian fire, and it's raging out of control because . . . because I don't have any answers! Sammy, a client, has given me the opportunity to find some of those answers, and I can help him with something that I promise will still be true to Breakup."

"Are you sure I can't just take you down to the Tandoori Flame for some dinner to put out this fire?"

"Deep down inside you know I need to do this."

"I get that, but I don't quite get the other half of the story. The Sammy half."

"There's a lot more to our client's story than meets the eye, and it's rooted in culture and family customs. So, we—*you*—need to craft a letter from Breakup to his girlfriend. But the breakup has to be temporary!" I looked from Rob to some of the other staff, who were frantically taking notes. I imagined that Rob's iPad was laden with obscenities, most directed at me. I knew my plan didn't make much sense, but I also knew that it did. Sammy was my ticket to a few days of what I needed in my life, and I was the help he needed with Lisa and his family.

"Anjali is going back into my office to finish packing up my bags, and then I am going downstairs to meet Sammy," I said.

With that, Anjali hesitantly left the boardroom.

"But we don't know anything about this Sammy and his Lisa," Rob said.

"Her name is Lisa Donahue, and his name is Sammy Patel, like I said. I'll text you some specifics on the way to the airport, and you can take it from there. I trust you guys. Plus, we have worked with fewer facts before. Think back to that time we got that email from Tom's team? Now *that* seemed like a mission impossible, but we managed to do it."

Rob walked me out of the boardroom.

"Manny, are you sure this isn't just about the magazine?" he asked, concerned.

"It's more than that. Outside of this company, I just don't know where I belong. I guess our conversation last night really got me thinking, Rob, and this opportunity happened to fall into my lap."

"Manny, you belong here." He paused. "But for as long as I have known you, you've been this feisty yet curious woman, and until you have your answers, I know you aren't going to stop buggin' us all. So, get the heck out of here." He reached out to hug me.

"Thanks, Rob. Plus, Jay approves," I said and started toward my office.

"Jay? What?"

"He can fill you in."

He looked at me quizzically but returned to the boardroom to calm everyone.

In my office, Anjali sat on the floor with a suitcase, coordinating various outfits by color and best time of day to wear them. The label maker—the machine, not Anjali—seemed to be working overtime as she chipped away at her keyboard, also chipping away at what was once a fresh coat of nail polish.

"Manny, there is nothing in here that is remotely Indian. Like, nothing."

"It's all right. It's an Indian wedding in wine country in the late fall. People are going to be wearing shorts, long-sleeve shirts, and dresses. No one will even look at what I'm wearing."

She scratched her head. "I have to tell you, I've been to a lot of Indian weddings, and I have never seen anyone in shorts, no matter what time of year it is. At least in our family, the whole point of a wedding is to outdo all your cousins with the most exquisite lehenga or sari. What the heck else are you going to Instagram?"

"It's one of those small weddings. A small California Indian wedding," I said, hoping there was such a thing. "We'll probably have Indian food, and I'll meet some Indian people and listen to some . . . who is that big UK rapper who was just on the morning show the other day . . . M.I.A., and no one will even notice what I'm wearing."

"I don't know about this," she said under her breath.

I sat down next to her. "You know, yesterday, when you said, I love being Indian! I want to find something I love."

Anjali stopped packing and looked at me.

"All my life, I never really gave my cultural background much thought. I was curious at times, sure. I'd watch *Slumdog Millionaire* and have this urge to be Freida Pinto dancing at the train station. Or when Kamala Harris talks about her Indian roots, I wonder about mine." I put my hand on my chest. "I know I'm Indian. I just don't know what that means."

"Manny, you don't need to explain it to me. Go find your inner Indian goddess. We'll spill tea when you get back, Lakshmi," Anjali said in her empowering, you-go-girl voice. We both grinned as she zipped up the suitcase. "It's the best I could do with what you had."

"Thanks, Anjali." I headed out of my office, passing the boardroom.

"Manny, hang on one second." Rob jumped up from his seat and walked over to the door. "You're *really* going to do this?"

"I am *really* going to do this."

He turned to the team, who were also still in the boardroom.

"Manny is going to do this, and we're going to take care of everything here." A pause. "I said we are going to do this!" he said louder.

"Yes! Yeah, we are!" they shouted back.

"We got this, Manny."

I started toward the Breakup exit to the sound of what was now chanting.

"We. Got. This. We. Got. This."

Great. But do I got this?

Chapter 11

Dear Breakup,

Is there any hope in hell you can help me break up with my insane in-laws? There must be a way to keep your sanity and your husband and never see your crazy mother-in-law again.

Please save my soul.

Mindy

"Mr. Patel is just over by Aja Raja, Ms. Dogra. I'm Sammy's driver, Jenson. Pleasure to meet you." Jenson pointed me in the direction of Rajiv's truck.

Sammy was wearing another beautifully tailored suit. He was dressed for business—*and this is business*, I told myself. His hair was longer than I had remembered, and he seemed to have grown a little stubble overnight.

I watched Sammy and Rajiv share laughs as if they had known each other for months, a far cry from the morning before.

"I see you two have finally met . . . properly?"

"Oh, my goodness gracious, Ms. Manny. Met we have and Mr. Patel came all the way from home and give me this beautiful gold elephant. So sorry he was for yesterday he told me. I will put this right here, inside the Aja Raja. So shiny, so good-looking, so beautiful . . ."

I had a feeling Rajiv wasn't talking about the elephant statue anymore as he eyed Sammy up and down.

"Sammy, that is so sweet." I turned to him, caught off guard by his generosity.

"It's no trouble. After all, it's the least I could do for that scene I caused out here, which, again, I am so sorry for." He lowered his head in humiliation.

"No scene and no more sorry, sorry," Rajiv said. "But you know we do like the other scene here. Especially the scene of man and woman becoming lovers." Rajiv sounded amazingly animated for so early in the morning.

I grabbed Sammy's arm. "Why don't we end this scene? We're going to get out of here, Rajiv. We have a business meeting to attend."

"Oooh, I like business. Minding my business, I don't like that," Rajiv then said under his breath, but loud enough that we could hear. We walked away from what was quickly turning into the makings of a ladoo love connection, as I am sure Rajiv would have affectionately branded it if he could.

"Bye, Rajiv." I waved, as did Sammy, as we made our way back to the car.

"Here, have this. I thought you could use one of these." Sammy handed me an Aja Raja coffee. "It's just the way you like it," he added. "Dunkin' Donuts style," he teased.

"How did you . . . ?"

"I caught him coming out of Dunkin' Donuts and changing out the pot for you. He said that Indian coffee was just for you."

I looked back at Rajiv. He was smiling from ear to ear, holding his hands together as if in prayer.

"So, you managed to make amends with Rajiv?" I asked. No need to make this too easy for him.

"Ah yes, about that . . . Like I said, not my finest moment. I am really, really—"

"It's okay . . . we all have those days."

"He's quite the friend, isn't he? Admires your work. Did you know he has every one of your magazine covers plastered inside his truck? It's like wallpaper back there. He refers to you as his little sister."

My workday ritual beginning with Rajiv's coffee and stories had become deeply meaningful. My father and I used to share a cup of coffee every morning before he set out for his long day of work, and that tradition carried on with Rajiv now. He had also opened his home and family to me, and I'd taken on the role of Manny Auntie to his three daughters. It wasn't until I met Adam that those visits started to dwindle. Adam came with me to dinner at Rajiv's one evening (the amount of finagling that took!), but he'd spent most of the night on his phone with an "important client." After that, Rajiv began collecting the phone numbers of eligible Indian men.

"He means a lot to me, too. And there's never a dull moment around Rajiv."

"You ready for a not so *dal* Indian wedding?" Sammy asked, laughing at his Indian food pun.

"Very funny. I like the way you *roll*," I added.

"And she fires one back just in time to get the Secret Indian Sting underway."

"I'd say it's more of an operation?"

"Operation Indian?" he offered.

"I like it!" I said, jumping into the car as Sammy held the door open for me, extending a hand to Jenson to indicate that he had this.

"Then Operation Indian is off to a great start. We're actually on time."

"Why wouldn't we be?"

"Oh, you know that old joke about Indians and time."

"Which one?" I asked, as if I knew more than one.

"I'll be there at late o'clock sharp!"

"That's cute. I hadn't heard it."

"Really?" Sammy said, a little surprised. "It's a standard Indian joke. One of many."

"I guess I haven't heard as many Indian jokes. Not much in the way of Indian stories at all, as a matter of fact."

"I guess if you're not interested . . ."

"It's not that. I tried to ask questions, but I was always shut down by both my parents, really."

"But as you became older, you could have looked into it yourself." Sammy made it sound so easy.

"You don't get to judge my family or me, the same way I don't get to judge your family or you," I snapped. He had touched a sore spot.

"You're right, off-limits."

We sat in uncomfortable silence for a few minutes. I wasn't ready to share with Sammy yesterday's revelation by Rob about why I might have been shut down. I needed more time to think about it, and this wasn't the right time. This was the time for Operation Indian.

"Music. I think we need to get ourselves in the mood." Sammy took his phone out and set up the Bluetooth with the car speakers. "Jenson has gotten used to my eclectic taste in music, driving me around all day."

"What do you like to listen to?"

"Huge R & B fan. Soul, funk, jazz, and . . ."

Suddenly the back seat was filled with a familiar song, and Sammy was jiving to the beat of the music.

"Now this is our theme song," he said, setting his phone down.

"Even I know this song." I tried to dance along with him as we listened to Panjabi MC featuring Jay-Z.

"We may need to work on those moves a little," Sammy kidded.

"Are *you* going to teach me, Professor Patel? So far most of the moves I have seen have come from your mouth."

He shook his head in shame again as the music started to lower.

"So, wanting to know more, it's because of something some jerk said?"

How did Sammy know that? And did he know that *some jerk* was my fiancé?

"Rob mentioned it on the phone," he continued. "He called right before you came down, wondering what my intentions are with you on this trip."

"Sorry about that. Rob is also my best friend, and he's a little overprotective . . . Even if you did work with Derek in the past, he doesn't like the idea of me taking off with a next-to-complete stranger."

"I get it. He's trying to look out for you. Trust me, I am not complaining, I get the benefits of it."

"I guess you could say that it feels like there's a piece of me missing. But I know it's out there, so this week I'm searching for it."

Just not at a Jamieson winery, I thought as we passed a large billboard with Derek's face on it, reminding us the winery was only five miles away. "I think I've always felt it. Some portion of it, at least, but . . . I suppose it's easy not to pay attention, you know. Instead, push it to the side with other distractions?"

"I do know," Sammy replied, with a gravity that surprised me. "Look, if you think you can find the missing piece by partying with my family for the next few days, then you are more than welcome." He pointed to his heart. "You just want to know who you are in here."

That's exactly what I wanted to know.

"Your fiancé has great taste, by the way," he said out of nowhere.

"Come again?" I was suddenly aware that I was in a locked car with a virtual stranger.

"Your ring," he said, gesturing to my hand.

"It's actually a family heirloom. Jamieson family. My fiancé is Derek's brother," I admitted.

"No way," Sammy responded with wide eyes. "Small world."

"And you don't seem to do so bad for yourself!" I shifted the conversation, gesturing to the town car and looking suitably impressed.

"Family business with lots of perks, including a driver. All jokes aside, though, I help run it."

"Jay and I only got to 'teacher' and 'engineer,'" I said, referring to us scrolling through all the Patels in the Baskin area.

"Bombay Accessories—it's our business. Ever heard of it?"

"Of course! My mom used to shop there all the time. She loved staging houses with your merchandise. Those little wooden Indian elephants." I thought back to the gold one Sammy had given Rajiv this morning.

"My idea," he proclaimed.

"My dad used to tell her that she was spending all his American dream money on elephants."

"One of our more expensive items in the store."

"Figures," I said. "Mom had great taste."

"So, then, what was your dad's American dream?"

I was caught off guard by the family questions. Adam rarely asked me anything about my parents.

"I think all this was his American dream," I said, gesturing out the window. "He wanted us—me, especially—to have everything, and for the most part I did." I thought back to Rob's words last night. "There are just a few things I'm missing," I said as I looked back at Sammy.

With our airplane seat belts fastened, Sammy got down to business and gave me intel on the week ahead. I knew the names of every important auntie and uncle and what every cousin did for a living. I even knew why cousin Shalu had stopped speaking to cousin Parveen. I guess I would be upset, too, if a family member had chosen my pandit-picked astrological wedding date as theirs.

The Patels were well established in California and India, for both their business acumen and their community sense. The family's American branch garnered real respect for how they supported family who'd stayed behind in India. Oh—and they were nosy. Sammy warned me again that meeting a "business partner," especially one who was Indian and female, would be more than enough to get his family's hopes up.

Sammy was the oldest cousin and the one everyone was holding their breath for, the one they wanted to get married already. Like all eligible Indian men, he had begrudgingly gone on countless dates arranged by his numerous aunties. The very aunties I was about to meet.

"There was this time Seema Auntie set me up on a dinner date," Sammy told me. "When I went to meet up with the date, I noticed a large suitcase off to the side. She was ready to move in after dinner. We didn't even get to the dessert before she started asking me the square footage of my place."

"Let's give her props for bringing only *one* suitcase!" I laughed.

"She said the rest would arrive from Bhopal with her family once we were married. And by the way, she insisted her sister needed her own bathroom."

"You are making that up."

"No. True. All true, I swear," he said, putting his hand to his heart. "Oh, oh!" he continued. "Then there was Banita. Look, I like a good meal, too, but when you finish your dinner before I do and start eating off my plate—on our first date!—we, no, *you*," he corrected himself, "may have a problem."

Nothing had worked out—no surprise there—and all the set-ups had only resulted in resentment on his part. Seema Auntie and Reena Auntie weren't the only family matchmakers ("culprits" was the word he used), but they were the most relentless. He continued with his lesson.

"Remember," he reminded me, "every older man is your *uncle-ji*, and every older woman is your *auntie-ji*." I took notes. "First name and then *auntie*. So, Monee Auntie-ji, Pardeep Auntie-ji, Nanoo Uncle-ji. Get it?"

"Got it. Except, what is *ji*?" I typed everything into my iPad as quickly as I could.

"It shows that you respect the auntie and uncle. Hence why I didn't use it on Seema and Reena Auntie," Sammy said, grinning. He went on to try to explain the wedding itinerary, but the more detailed he got, the more lost I became. Baraat, bhangra, bindi—I never made it past the *b*'s. Maybe I should have taken Rajiv's suggestion: "You should give a watch to *Band Baaja Baaraat* on Netflix," he had suggested. "It has the most universal of acclaim awards." Whatever that meant.

"I know this is confusing." Sammy could see my typing had slowed down. "But these traditions have been passed through the generations. It's important to respect them—and each family respects them differently."

I gave a little yelp. What had I gotten myself into?

"Hey, it's going to be okay," he said gently. "Honestly. You have me, my sister Manisha, and about fifty cousins, give or take a few, to help you out. Plus, you know there's this handy little thing called Google," he said.

He must have seen the panic on my face.

"So, you're engaged to a guy whose dad used to be a big-time Western movie star? And he's Derek Jamieson's brother?"

It sounded funny when Sammy said it.

"I also did some research," he confessed.

"This Google thing you were telling me about?" I joked. I stared down at the chart I had created on my tablet and said, "You're so lucky to have all these people in your life. I'm sure Lisa would be thrilled to be in this hot seat right now, next to you," I added, immediately wishing I hadn't.

"Probably not," he admitted. "She's not much of a family person. She doesn't even want to have kids, apparently—" Sammy stopped suddenly, as if realizing he was saying too much. "I haven't really seen my family in about a year."

"Why?"

"Lisa used to hate being without me, although it seems these days she's a lot happier with me going away for business. What I mean is, she wants me out there promoting the stores and getting new stock." Sammy's response sounded like an out-of-office reply. "You know, she grew up an only child with just her mother. She's good with alone time. This big family thing is a lot for her to take in. And she can't stand bhangra or any of the music that goes along with it."

"You've been dating her for years, and you are just finding this out now?"

"I guess you could say we were a little preoccupied with other things in the beginning of our relationship, and until recently, I didn't realize just how different we are. But different can be good," he quickly added.

He sounded as if he was reassuring himself more than me. What was Sammy and Lisa's relationship really like, given what he'd just said? In the few hours we had spent together, he couldn't stop talking about how important his family was to him.

"So, is that the real reason she's not here?" I asked.

"No, it's like I told you yesterday. It's already bad enough that as the older brother in my family, I'm not married. I don't want to attract any more attention to my family during this wedding." Sammy's words became less audible. "It's not just the dancing, Manny. Or the music and what you see on TV. There are a lot of expectations."

"Like marrying an Indian woman?" I was irritated at the thought and may have rolled my eyes at "Indian woman."

"I can't wrap my head around how this is not sinking in with you!"

"It sounds like some after-school special. What 'Indian' lesson am I learning here, Sammy?" I demanded, and then lowered my voice when I realized other passengers were staring at us.

"Oh, so now *you* have morals and lessons to be learned?" Sammy lowered his voice, too.

"What does that mean?" I asked through clenched teeth.

"It means you run a business where you charge people to do their dirty work for them."

"Oh, please, you were the one begging us for our services."

"Services that prey on people! I walk into your office, you

make me look like a million bucks, and suddenly I don't feel like a bag of shit anymore because I *paid* you to give my ex closure. Maybe I just needed a friend to talk to. Someone who might actually get what I am talking about?"

"We have that package, too. It's called the BFF Breakup package. If you had really done your research, you would know that about me. I also hate to be the one to point this out to you, but I have been the 'friend' listening to you for almost twenty-four hours! And it's been the same outcome: one large order of a temporary breakup."

"With a major side of attitude. Which I don't remember ordering. Look, Manny, let's stick to reality. Indians are expected to marry Indians. We *all* know that."

"*I* don't know that, and I will go out on a limb, since Lisa is not sitting here with you and I am, that most people don't know that. Look, I think there are other things I'm going to learn this week, and about your family, too, and I realize I just need to be considerate of that." I shifted my focus from Sammy's family to my own. After all, my mother had been forbidden to marry her soul mate due to some small village squabble. "Don't worry," I continued, more coolly. "I won't mention anything more about Lisa until you're ready to discuss it with your family. And I'll make sure this is simply a temporary breakup, Mr. Patel. All business."

"You're right. It *is* business, Ms. Dogra. And may I remind you that sometimes you just gotta mind your own?"

Chapter 12

Dear Breakup,

Is there a way to break up with yourself? Hear me out. I am an asshole, and I miss my girlfriend so much. I shouldn't have sent her angry text messages accusing her of cheating on me. I was insecure. Can you break up with me, so I know what it feels like to hurt someone the way I hurt her? This isn't a joke, even though it may come across as one. Please, trust me. I want her to know that I would do anything to get her back. Including hurting myself the way I hurt her.

JT

Sammy led the way to the baggage claim. I followed close behind, imagining meeting all his aunts—*aunties*, I corrected myself—wondering how they would feel about me, an Indian woman who knew nothing about being Indian. He and I had gone over the background of Operation Indian after we had both cooled off. We didn't quite know the winery company name or the other logistics yet, but we figured the questions wouldn't get that far. After all, everyone was there to celebrate, not focus their attention on me. At least, that's what I hoped.

"You all right, Manny? I am sorry about getting so upset. I'm a little nervous about this. I'm also nervous about how Lisa is going to react to our break."

Suitcases were beginning to drop from the chute onto the baggage belt, but I shifted from staring at them to looking at Sammy. "I can only imagine how difficult this is for you. So, truce?"

"Complete with a truce shot later?"

"You got it. As for Lisa, are you sure you don't want to read the email that goes out to her?"

"Nope, I trust your team. I really want to be here for my brother this week. I don't want any distractions. As long as it's just a break, I can worry about Lisa and me as soon as I am back home. That's why I hired you."

"Gotcha."

"By the way, about tonight. It's strictly the cousins going to a dance club. Wear what you would wear on a night out."

"Okay," I said. That would be easy.

Our bags dropped onto the belt at the same time, and as they came around the carousel, Sammy took off his blazer, tucked it under his left arm, and grabbed both suitcases in one quick snap. *Wow. This guy works out.*

In the taxi on the way to the hotel, I asked, "Hey, why Marble for an Indian wedding? Not exactly the first place I'd think of."

"It's become a Patel annual event of sorts, I guess you could say," Sammy replied. "About ten years ago, my cousin Harvir got married here, and since then, well, getting married in Marble has become its own custom. The rokas, sangeets, and mehndis take place here. Getting the entire family together to celebrate . . . it's what we all look forward to. You know what I mean."

Actually, I didn't.

The Machisino Hotel was exactly how I had imagined it. Sammy didn't know, and there wasn't any point in mentioning it, but Adam had designed the resort. The large lobby and windows were reminiscent of the Breakup office and, along with the modernist floor tiles, contributed to a clean, light-filled feeling of openness. It was luminous. Only Adam would have dreamed this up. Speaking of Adam, I needed to call him to tell him I was fine and that we were okay. *But are we?* I wondered.

Sammy handed me the key to my room.

"If you need anything, shoot me a text," he said.

"Thanks, but I'll be fine. We're both here for a couple of reasons, a couple of contractual reasons. Remember, you've commissioned the services of Breakup, and we are committed to providing those services. In return, you're supplying your duties as a trusted chaperone for the week, someone who will show me your version of Indian culture. I will make sure Anjali sends you a transfer for all the money you've spent so far." I wanted to reassure him that this was a business trip, and I would be writing off the expenses on my own Breakup tab.

"Nonsense! Consider it payment for services rendered."

I put away my phone.

"You'll take this elevator since we are in different wings of the hotel," he said, pointing to the elevator closest to me. "I'll take the one to your left. Your baggage has already been dropped off in your room. I'll meet you down here at seven."

My room was as grand as I had expected. Sammy had gone out of his way to ensure I would feel comfortable for the week. As I slid open a large glass door to the living room from the foyer, I was greeted by a slight breeze that blew through the vintage-style window coverings. The sound of my high heels echoed on the tiles as I entered the room. One large brown leather sofa faced me, and another smaller one was off to the right by a door into what I could see was the bedroom. Strategically placed in the center of the room was a coffee table, on top of which was a tray with a perfectly crafted charcuterie board and a note. I read the note.

WELCOME TO THE BEGINNING OF A BIG FAT INDIAN
WEDDING. SEE YOU AT YOUR FIRST PATEL PARTY TONIGHT.

I placed the note back down and realized the table matched the one Adam and I had.

Adam! I took out my phone from my purse. Three missed calls from Adam—unusual for him. I read his text.

Missed you at breakfast. Off to Berlin. See you
in a week. Good luck on your business trip,
CEO Dogra. Use those new AirPods.

I was thankful for the excuse Anjali had made up to account for my sudden departure. I looked at the message again. No mention of our disagreement. *No, it was a fight.* He knew I was upset, or maybe he refused to see how I felt about his refusal to see color. I cringed at the thought of his words playing back.

See you soon, I typed back.

Chapter 13

Dear Breakup,

My boyfriend is constantly reminding me of how heavy I am, even though I have invested in a dietician and trainer—for myself not him!

This week, he hit an all-time low and has started to put sticky notes on food in the fridge that he thinks I shouldn't be eating. *Don't eat me, Chubbs!* Talk about a motivation *not* to lose weight. I want to break up with him and keep my relationship with food while I drop the 170 pounds of dead weight that's been hanging around me way too long. I'm ready to lose it.

Lainey

The phone woke me. I turned over and reached for the unexpected call.

"Manny, small bump in the road." It was Sammy. "Did you bring anything you could wear to a Bollywood party tonight?"

I headed over to my suitcase, knowing the likelihood of anything Bollywood-ish would be kinda *unlikely*.

"Let's see. Jeans, a bright red top, some colorful dresses for the parties. That's about it."

"We gotta get you something appropriate, and we need to get it now."

"What?" I said, still groggy from my nap. "I thought you said the cousins were getting together at a local club?"

"They changed the theme. The ladies have to wear their best Bollywood."

I went back to the edge of the bed. "Okay, give me an hour or so and I'll meet you downstairs."

"An hour? I can give you five minutes. And that's pushing it," he said.

So push it I did. I made it out the door in record time to meet a grateful Sammy in the hotel lobby. After a quick cab drive we arrived at our destination.

"And this is Little India," Sammy proclaimed.

All I could manage was, "Wow."

The street looked like the pictures I'd seen of the bazaar in Rajiv's hometown. A collection of clothing stores and restaurants embellished with paintings and sculptures lined the busy street. The smells, sounds, and scenes of food and patrons zipped by as we quickly headed to our destination. The brilliance of the Marble sun reflected off a store window that held the most glamorous displays of sequined fabrics and garments.

Sammy pulled me inside the clothing store.

"Hello, Uncle-ji," he said.

A large man looked up from the needle he was trying to thread.

"Yes, what can I help you with?"

"Your favorite color is purple, right?" Sammy asked me.

"How did you—"

"Research." He winked at me.

"Can we please try on that one, the one on the right, and that one in the back?" Sammy pointed to various garments hanging from the walls, gowns in colors I had never seen before that were embedded with dazzling beadwork, stitched to perfection. Some had floral patterns, while others had lace, but all were elaborately decorated. Matching accessories—chandelier earrings, choker necklaces, bangles, and hip chains—hung from the shelves next to the skirts, as did shoes and mini clutches. The place was straight out of a fairy tale.

"Can you believe it's all handmade?" Sammy asked, turning to me.

"Suman, you get for this man and his wife," the uncle said as he turned to one of his sales associates.

"No, no, no, not my wife," Sammy corrected him.

"Shame," the older gentleman said as he walked away. Suman, the store associate, brought the three garments over.

"Fitting room in back." Suman led the way through racks upon racks of Indian clothing. No two pieces looked alike. He closed the dressing room door behind me, and I grabbed one of the heavily beaded garments to try on.

"So, what did you wear to the other Indian gatherings you would go to?" Sammy asked on the other side of the door.

"What do you mean?"

"You said you have never gone to an Indian wedding, but what about your extended family? Birthday parties, celebrations, Indian friends?"

"There weren't any," I admitted. Somehow with a closed door between us, I felt free to talk about my past without feeling judged. "Like I said, we never did any of that stuff. My parents were both only children, and so there was no immediate family. And we never had any Indian neighbors or friends."

There was a longer-than-anticipated silence on Sammy's end.

"So, what about Indian guys?"

"What about them?"

"Your website bio says you went to Baskin College, full scholarship too, to their MBA program. You must have dated one or two in the business program you took."

"Let's say I dated guys more like Jason Priestley and less like . . . you."

"Then you missed out," he teased. "And what about Mr. Adam Jamieson? What's he like?"

"He's smart, he's a hard worker, he's . . ." *He's a jerk*, I wanted to say. I was still angry and couldn't think of anything else. "Maybe you'll meet him someday. What about Lisa? You must actually worship her to possibly give up your family."

I heard Sammy take a deep breath. "I don't know if I had a choice."

"Huh?"

"I guess you can't choose who you fall for. It's been quite a ride with Lisa. I don't want to hurt her."

"What do you mean, hurt her? And what's up with her out

of the blue deciding she didn't like the idea of you seeing your family?"

"I guess it went something like that. You just wake up one day, and the person decides . . ." Sammy trailed off without finishing his thought.

An image of Adam flitted through my mind again. *At least Sammy wakes up to someone.*

"Before my mom passed away, she told me to find someone who . . . who would make my heart dance. Apparently you're supposed to be able to hear love in your heart." Something Rajiv often said. "I guess you have to ask yourself, does Lisa make you dance?"

"Lisa can't stand dancing, so not a fair question. Speaking of dancing, you better make sure you can move around in these outfits you're trying. The Patels were born to get down."

I zipped up the side of the garment. "Ouch!" I had zipped up too quickly and pinched my skin.

"You all right in there?"

"I think so. This is heavy."

"Heavy because of beadwork, madam," Suman said.

"Come on, let's see it," Sammy said, a little too eagerly.

"I don't know. There's no mirror in here, and I feel a bit uncomfortable coming out and showing you and—"

"Manny, get out here! Stop fussing around. You wanted the whole Indian experience. This is all part of it. Dressing up and owning what you wear!"

"Owning it. All right. I'm coming out and owning it." I unlocked the latch and slowly opened the door.

Sammy got up from the chair he was sitting in as I walked

out. I felt a strange compulsion to hide, but I turned to the mirror beside him.

"Wow. You are beautiful, Manny Dogra," he said. "The dress It's gorgeous, and it makes you look as pretty as a . . ." Sammy stumbled over his words as we both stood in awe over what we saw in the mirror.

The gorgeous purple garment dropped down to the floor like an elegant gown fit for a mermaid. The pearls and customized embroidery added rich textures to the full-length skirt. The long see-through sleeves added a touch of sexiness that Jay would have gone mad for.

"Needs a little cut from the bottom. Easy," Suman said, sliding to my feet and pinning the bottom of the skirt.

"I don't even think we need to try on the others," Sammy said, still staring at the gown.

"No, no! This is the one, madam." Suman continued pinning.

"Yes," Sammy agreed. "This is the one."

"I think so, too," I admitted.

"Madam, you take off and we cut for you and make right size, right now."

"Sure thing."

"That was fast," Sammy declared.

"I'm not a fusser when it comes to shopping. When I was younger, I wasn't much of a shopper either. But I loved spending time with my mother, staging houses and picking flowers. Fresh flowers were her favorite."

"Is that why you have so many flowers in the Breakup office?" Sammy asked.

"I'm glad you were able to see past your intense fury and notice something nice," I said, only half joking.

"Sorry. I waited until the last minute to get this all sorted out, huh?"

Sammy continued to talk as I went back into the fitting room to change. And then it happened.

"Ouch!"

"Manny?" That was Sammy.

"Madam?" That was Suman.

"Sammy . . . Suman . . . the beading, a pearl . . . it's caught in my hair, and I'm . . . oh gosh, I'm stuck."

"What do you mean . . . stuck?"

"Madam . . . stuck?"

"My hands are stuck in the sleeves, and a pearl is caught on a pin in my hair. I can't shake it off."

"Madam, try to do this . . . how do you say—"

"Wiggle. Wiggle your way out, Manny. Suman is suggesting you slide your arms out."

"I'm trying, and I can't even manage to do that. I'm really stuck, Sammy."

"Can you find someone to help her?" Sammy asked Suman.

"Sir, all woman have break time for hour."

"An hour?" Sammy and I both shouted.

"We don't have an hour! Manny, can I come in there?"

"No!"

"I promise I won't look. I'll have my eyes shut . . . you can face the other way."

"Fine. Close your eyes. Close them tight and come in here. I swear if you even open them for one second!"

"What are you going to do, hit me with one of your arms that you can't really use right now?"

"Sammy!"

"I won't. It's not like I haven't seen this *stuff* before."

"You haven't seen *my* stuff, and let's keep it that way."

I heard Sammy push his hand over the top of the dressing room door to unlock it.

"Okay, I am coming in. Eyes closed."

I turned to the wall so that my back faced Sammy.

"I am reaching my hand out to see if I can find you. And I am slowly stretching it out . . . and oh, there you are." He was laughing now.

"This isn't funny, Sammy."

"Not even a little bit?"

"Not even a little bit!"

"Okay, Miss Dogra. I am sari, I mean sorry, you got tangled in your sari," Sammy said in a voice that I could only guess belonged to one of his uncles and laughed again. His hands worked their way up to my head and felt around until they reached the pearl that was stuck to the garment.

"There you go. Let me loosen this up and we can slide this off."

"Hurry up, Sammy. This is so embarrassing."

"Okay. It's unpinned and now we are sliding the top off."

"Your eyes better be shut."

"They are. I can't see a thing. And we are done." Sammy grabbed the garment.

The door to the fitting room snapped open. I shrieked and jumped into Sammy's arms, my chest digging into his.

"Sorry. I help," said an older lady who had apparently just come back from her break.

"I think we got it under control. Thanks, Auntie-ji," Sammy said. "Manny . . ."

"What?" I managed to say as I pushed my face into Sammy's chest, hiding my humiliation.

"I think the coast is clear. You can let go of me now."

I realized my arms were wrapped around Sammy's back.

"Hi," I said, feeling the warmth of his back on my bare arms.

"Hi," he said softly.

I lifted my head and looked up at him.

"Hey! No fair," I said.

His eyes were open.

Chapter 14

Dear Breakup,

I recently made out with my neighbor, who also happens to be the president of our condo board. It started off innocently as we caught up after I missed a town hall meeting, and then suddenly one beer led to his tongue in my mouth. I quickly put the makeout session to a stop because not only did I have a feeling it wasn't right, but my dog started humping my arm while the neighbor was trying to hump me.

The next day I received a text apologizing for what he had tried to do, and he's asked me to no longer attend condo meetings. It makes him uncomfortable! Can he do that? I didn't do anything wrong, so why am I being banned from the meetings? How do I get the neighbor/president to unban me, or is my only option to move away?

1-800-his junk was all over me,

Jenna

I'd long heard the expression "love is in the air," but in Marble I could really feel it. The town was noisy with tourists, mostly young adults, romancing the evening away with local wine and long kisses on the cobblestone sidewalks.

I looked at my watch. Seven p.m. I'd usually be in the office at this time, going through client emails and setting everything up for the morning. Not tonight. Tonight was business of a different sort.

I quickened my pace to keep up with Sammy, who was walking fast in what I presumed to be the eager anticipation of seeing his family.

"I still can't get over everything that's lined up this week," I said. "But why isn't this party on the list?"

"This is the type of night you really don't want your parents to witness. Dirty martinis mixed with dirty dancing and a side of dirty jokes. Not exactly an Indian parent's wish come true," he teased.

"It sounds like a lot of fun," I said, not sure if I really remembered how to have fun outside of photo shoots, brainstorming Breakup packages, and a few too many late work nights at the office or the Wallflower. Fun used to be catching up with my parents.

"Indians are always down to celebrate. But between you and me, a lot of this wedding stuff is show-and-tell. You know, showing off to the other families. My kid got married before your kid. Our wedding will be bigger and better than yours. It can get as competitive as cricket."

"Really?" I thought back to my father glued to the TV and blaring obscenities at the screen when India's cricket team was playing.

"Just my observation. Don't get me wrong, the wedding traditions are fun, but they're pretty elaborate. It's mostly for the parents, I think. Ask around tonight. I'm sure my cousins would tell you they have no clue what the traditions actually mean. Guaranteed you'd get a blank stare."

"But you seem to know."

"It comes with being the eldest son. You get a new car, and your mother blesses it with some organic oil, while the local pandit shows up to pray that it stays away from the prying evil eyes of others. You get a promotion at work, and your parents want to know your boss's astrological sign to make sure the stars are aligned for a salary bonus for you and your future wife. Although, now that I think about it, with you, I could just make half of this up."

"Oh, really? It's one thing for you to be sure of yourself, Sammy. But how can you be so sure of me?"

"All right, we have a few minutes before we get to the club. A quick game of true or false?"

"Sounds better than truth or dare."

"Before you get married, you're expected to eat a spicy mirch, aka chili, to ward off all evil on your wedding day."

"That's easy." I thought back to the string of dried spices that Rajiv had hanging in his truck. "True!"

"I am sorry, Dogra; you are already out of the game!" Sammy said in a talk show host voice.

"What? No fair. Let's try again."

"Okay. How about: if you bite your tongue while talking, someone is probably talking shit about you."

"That sounds like a false."

"Nope! It's true! According to Mama Patel, that is."

"Why do I get the feeling that the Patels have their own set of old wives' tales?"

"Now *that* is true!" he said, laughing. "Not bad, Dogra. You got one out of three. The odds are in your favor tonight."

"I hope something is in my favor. Right now, I feel like an oddball in this outfit."

"You insisted we walk over because you were feeling a little nervous," Sammy reminded me.

"Nervously trying to remember everyone's name. Gimme a break!"

"I'm sorry, you're right. I'm still getting used to the idea of you basically needing a crash course in all this, when right now you look like you could be a Bachchan family member."

"I'll take that as a compliment—that's the look I was going for," I said with more conviction than I felt. Thanks to Rajiv, even I knew that the Bachchan family was one of the most influential Bollywood families in India.

"Manny, this isn't just about a crash course in all things Indian. It's about having fun and making it your own Indian experience. Remember, different strokes for different folks. These are just the Patel folks' strokes, get it? And try not to get caught in your clothes."

I blushed. At least I think I did.

"Speaking of clothes, what's with . . ." I gave him a head-to-toe appraisal. He was wearing a white linen shirt with splashes of green, a dark gray linen blazer, and dark jeans that were just short enough to expose his sockless feet. (I was getting the feeling he didn't like socks.) He looked good in a classic, yet trendy sort of way. I looked like I was auditioning for the cast of *Bend It Like Beckham*. "How come the guys don't have to wear Bollywood gear?" I asked as we navigated the streets of Marble.

"No one cares what we wear."

"Oh, good. A double standard. At least some things transcend cultural boundaries."

"Hey, I'm all about building bridges," Sammy said, a smile taking over his face. We walked a little more, past the Marble clock tower and the town hall, then ducked into a side street lined with small family-owned shops. At the end of the street was a nightclub, a large brick building that looked more like a warehouse than anything else. Music was blaring loudly on the patio, where patrons were eating dinner and enjoying what looked like expensive drinks. I couldn't remember the last time I had been to a nightclub.

"My man, Sammy!" The bouncer, a large Indian man in a black T-shirt and jeans with a matching black beret, leaned in to give Sammy a hug. I couldn't picture this teddy bear of a man wrestling down rowdy patrons. The line in front of us was long, but the bouncer hustled us up to the stairs right by the main entrance.

"This is my business partner, Manny," Sammy said by way of introduction. The bouncer's eyes grew wide with excitement—or possibly suspicion.

"Nice to meet you, Manny." He took off his beret, exposing his bald head, and bowed slightly.

"Nice to meet you, too . . ."

"Arnie," he said. "So, you're here on business, eh?" he asked.

"That's right," I said. Short, sweet, and to the point. Well done.

"Every year a Patel gets married, and every year I look forward to seeing this guy." Arnie grabbed Sammy by the shoulder and pulled him in for another hug. "I'm like their unofficial security. Now, if only this guy would get married already," he said, with a sidelong look at me.

Sammy started to massage his neck.

"He's mine for this week," I replied. I tugged Sammy back from Arnie's hug. I was glad for the darkness of the club's entrance. My cheeks were getting redder.

"Ooh, okay," Arnie replied. "I like this woman." He looked over at Sammy, who laughed nervously, as if afraid of our cover being blown.

"After you, Aishwarya," Sammy said.

We made our way to the main room. The music was pounding much as it did in any other nightclub, but we made our way through people on the dance floor and arrived at a clearing where a group of late-twentysomethings were sitting around inside a marked-off area.

"That's us," Sammy said. "Every year we hire Arnie to help us with any security issues. When you have fifty cousins, something is bound to pop up."

Before I could respond to him, I heard a high-pitched voice.

"Sammmmmmmeeeee." A voluptuous woman in a revealing black-and-white polka-dot sari launched herself at him, cleavage bouncing, hair swaying. She then swung her thick arms around both of us and smothered us in her breasts.

"Manisha! Looking as covered up as usual," Sammy said.

"Sammy, my gorgeous single brother." She said this a little too loudly, I guessed so that all the single ladies could hear. "I missed you so much," she gushed, then locked her eyes on me.

"Manisha, this is Manny, my business partner," he said.

The strobe light centered on us for a quick second.

"O-M-G, this outfit is fabulous. Turn around. Ouch!" Manisha touched my sheer sleeve as if it was heating up. "Business? I am guessing you didn't give her that," she said, pointing toward my ring.

"No, I'm engaged to someone else," I managed to say. "It's so nice to meet you, Manisha, finally. I have heard so much about you—about your whole family, in fact."

"We actually haven't heard anything about you, not until that email this morning." Manisha turned to her brother. "Why have you been keeping THIS a secret?" She pointed up and down at me as if I were a drink the bartender had been keeping from her.

He just shrugged.

"But we're used to our brother keeping secrets from us. Come with *me*." Manisha grabbed my arm. "I'll be your hostess with the mostess for tonight." She gestured up and down her body, lingering on her wide hips. "The MOST-ESS! Now, let's meet everyone!"

Sammy leaned in to whisper, "Good luck."

"You have the tiniest little wrists I have ever seen on a grown woman. It's like, what do you even eat all day, air and more air?" Manisha said, chuckling to herself.

"Oh, I eat . . ."

"Sit." She directed me to an empty seat, then poured some champagne, quickly sipping hers as it overflowed the glass.

"Okay, so, from left to right." She turned her attention back to the group. "These are the Patels. That's Anil and Anita, surgeons from Vancouver. Ricky and Nyla flew in from India on their *private* jet. Shalin and Jameela are programmers. Also, very boring—their careers *and* them. That's our cousin Benny in the pink see-through shirt. He's totally in the alamari, the closet, but it's not as easy to come out yet in our family, among other things. But you never heard it from me." I had a feeling there were many secrets you never heard from Manisha. "That's Priya, the pretty, skinny, and tall one." Manisha rolled her eyes and took a sip of a drink that was suddenly almost half gone. "And that," she pointed to the couple directly in front of us, "well, that is our brother, Sanjeev, and his fiancée, Needa."

Needa was as elegant as Sammy had described, with a long black braid pinned to the side of her head. She was glowing in the dark club light as she sipped on her champagne. This royal glow, I imagined, followed her everywhere.

There were indeed a lot of cousins. I couldn't imagine Adam even considering any kind of family reunion before our big day. Would Derek still be looking for a signal to find that party invite?

"Here, have more."

I hadn't noticed my glass was empty until Manisha topped it up.

"So, you're doing business with my brother? That sucks," she said. "You're so cute." She pinched my cheeks and smiled.

"Ooh," I said in surprise and faint pain from how hard she had managed to squeeze my cheeks.

"I've always wanted a sister-in-law. Don't get me wrong, Needa is totally cool, but she's so royal and regal, you know, in that white-gloves-up-to-the-elbows kind of way. I want a sister-in-law I can get down and dirty with. I wanna dance to a Pitbull song, not the latest rendition of *My Heart Will Go On*. Booooor-ing," Manisha said all in one breath. "You sure it's *strictly* business?"

"Yeah, we are totally business, but I can get down to a Pitbull song," I reassured her.

"Hell yeah!" She lifted her champagne glass. "Cheers to that, girl," she said.

"You have such a big family. Sammy did warn me, but now that I see you all together it just feels so much bigger." I looked around the roped-off VIP section at the cheerful and very styl-ish Patel cousins as they took turns taking pictures and pouring drinks. I felt like an impostor.

Manisha laughed. "Oh, come on, Desi standard practice hav-ing a million cousins. Priya, Sanjeev, Sammy . . . Deena . . ." She continued to laugh. "No Manny yet."

She spent the next while filling me in on every one of her cousins. The ones who liked each other, the ones who couldn't stand each other. And if it sounded as though everyone *loved* Manisha, it was only because she had made it a point to tell me that.

"I'm like neutral, you know. I don't gossip and stuff or like talk about people behind their backs." She jumped up from her seat. "Okay, way too much talking going on here, and not enough drinking and dancing! This is a mutha-freakin' Patel party!"

"I need to use the restroom before I have another drink."

"Right over there. See—where Sammy is," Manisha said, pointing to her brother on the club floor. "Hurry back. I am going to request a PB song just for us!"

Luckily, the restroom wasn't as busy as the dance floor. I took a look in the mirror and reached into my purse to touch up my lipstick. Even if I actually had to pee, I was afraid I was going to need more than one night to master the art of moving around in this heavy dress.

"Hi, I'm Needa. You're Sammy's friend, right?"

Needa was even more beautiful up close.

"Oh, hi! Congratulations. Yeah, business friend, that's me . . . uh . . ." I felt foolish crashing their celebrations without ever having met them.

"Manny, right—I knew the family business was doing well, but I am so happy that Sammy is also venturing into . . . remind me again?"

"Wine . . ." Phew. I had almost forgotten, too.

"Wine." She raised her eyebrow. "Regardless, I am so glad you're here. Sammy seems in great spirits since we last talked to him. Not that we get to see him anymore outside of work. You know, the last time we saw him at a family gathering, it was . . . hang on, let me think. It was at least six months ago! Can you believe that? We still do virtual stuff, but we went from seeing him all the time to all of a sudden, he has no time for family parties, gatherings, reunions. What's the point of being Indian?"

That's exactly what I was here to find out. The point of being Indian.

"The family business keeps him so busy," I offered.

"*Family* business keeps Sanj busy, too. But it's always work, no time to play with Sammy. Dinner invitations, family vacations, or a night out—nope. He has no time."

"Thankfully, he's here now." I didn't know how else to respond.

"Won't the addition of this business also keep him busy? Turmeric wine, was it?" The word *wine* rolled off her tongue in disbelief as she stopped reapplying her lipstick and locked eyes with me.

"Turmeric. Yeah. That's a great flavor," I said, but I gagged at the thought. I knew I wasn't making much sense as I was cast in Needa's detective spell. She was sharp. I had to give her that.

She went back to reapplying her lipstick. "Although frankly, I prefer the sound of this new venture to him spending all his time chasing after wooden elephants. If this new side of things means bringing you around and we get to see him, I am all for it."

Needa didn't believe I was here for business, that much was clear. But despite that, there was something about her I liked.

"You're a pleasant surprise, and I usually hate surprises." She looked over at me and smiled. She finished up washing her hands and headed to the restroom exit, saying, "This purple is radiant on you, by the way! Back at home I used to get custom couture delivered right to my doorstep, days before any runway saw it. Anyway, hope you packed a lot of saris and lehengas for the next few days!"

Was that advice—or a warning?

Chapter 15

Dear Breakup,

We met online and talked for five months almost every single day. We were planning a trip to finally meet each other because we live on different coasts, when suddenly, POOF! The man I had been swooning over just disappeared. I woke up one day, and I was blocked on everything! Help, I need closure. Now!

Tina

I couldn't afford to get sidetracked. This was a business deal, after all. With the club music thumping behind me, I moved to a moderately more private area of the bathroom to call Anjali.

Pick up, pick up, pick up!

"Look who it is, Bollywood Boss Babe herself."

"Who? Rob? Why are you answering Anjali's phone?"

"You know she has you in her contacts as Bollywood Boss Babe. BBB. Triple B. I like it . . ."

"Aww, really?" I made a sweet face into the phone, surprised by Rob's find, then refocused. "Okay, anyway, why are you answering Anjali's phone? What the heck have you done with her?" I peered closer at my phone screen. "Are you at the Wallflower? Your Triple B, also the CEO, is away on an emergency business deal, and you're partying it up?"

"I took the team out. Keeping morale high during Code Red . . . and celebrating Anjali's new pormo . . . promotion."

"Great, you're drunk! Rob, I need to speak to Anjali on *her* phone and I need an update on the breakup—"

"Where is that Smottie?"

"Who?"

"Sammy and hottie equal Smottie, Manny, sheesh."

"First of all, he's a client, and second of all, NO referring to him as Smottie."

"Suit yourself, but when you look like that you get a nickname."

"Oh, do you now?" Jay jumped in on the call. "So, what kind of nickname do I have?" He turned to Rob and then back to the phone. "Because right about now I have a few good names for you. And, honey, I'll even give you a hint, they all start with *ass*."

"Oh, boo." Rob leaned in and gave Jay a kiss on the cheek.

"Can we get back to me for a second?"

"Aww, our Manny is feeling left out." Jay made kissy faces at the screen.

"Yes! I mean, not left out of your little lovefest. I have my own."

"Oh, you do now, do you?"

"I don't blame her." Jay gave a sidelong stare at Rob. "Smottie is cute," he teased.

"Smo . . . Sammy is inside with his family. And *my* lovefest is Adam, not Sammy."

When was the last time Adam and I had made love?

"How is Sammy, by the way?" Anjali jumped into the call, trying to squeeze her face and her fancy drink into the screen. "Hi, Manny!"

"Anjali, thank goodness! How are things going with Lisa? Can you give me an update on how the temporary breakup is coming along?"

"Manny, not to worry. We've sent the temporary breakup email," Anjali assured me.

"Yup, Sammy is a single Pringle, at least while he's away with you," Rob jumped in.

"Rob, where do you even come up with these things?" I asked.

"Yeah, where the hell do you come up with these one-liners?" Jay yelled from behind the bar, where he had gone back to making drinks.

"Guys, I need you to listen to me! Are you capable of doing that during happy hour?"

Suddenly the door to the bathroom swung open and a couple of clubgoers laughed their way in.

"Did someone say 'after hours'?" one of them asked. I didn't recognize either as a Patel.

"Sorry, no, no, no . . ." I shook my head.

"Bummer," they replied in disappointment.

"Over here, ladies!" Rob's face moved in closer to the screen so that most of his nose covered it.

The girls gave a look of being creeped out and continued to the stalls.

"Manny, what kinda club are you at? You sure this isn't Miami? Those girls were hawt."

"She is definitely not in Miami," Anjali added as she squeezed her face back into the frame with Rob and straightened the phone.

"Guys, can you please listen to me?"

"We are listening," Anjali said, slurping up the dregs of her margarita.

"So, there is nothing more to do with Lisa?"

"Nope. All done. In fact, done and overdone. Like that burnt chicken Jay's mother made last week," Rob squawked.

"I heard that, too. Someone's about to get cut off soon, and I don't just mean from the drinks," Jay warned Rob.

"Okay, great. So, the temporary breakup worked!"

"Yuppers," Rob added.

"Okay, now, listen up. I need your help!"

"What kind of help, Manny?"

I could see Rob raising an eyebrow in the background.

"I have no Indian clothes for the rest of the week's activities."

Rob leaned in closer to the phone. "Sure looks like you were on a Mumbai mission with a shopping trip earlier today. Is this on the Breakup corporate card?"

"Yeah, just like your drinks are tonight!" I sassed back.

"Good one," Jay chimed in.

"Wow, Manny, that outfit has major Miss India vibes. I love it on you!"

"Thanks, Anjali. Sammy took me out earlier since we were in a bit of a pinch for tonight's party."

"Jets off to Marble, lavish shopping spree from what I can see, and staying at the most expensive hotel in California. I'd say we got a Masala Mama on our hands. Shouldn't Sammy be your Dosa Daddy?"

"ROB!" Anjali, Jay, and I said at the same time.

"He's actually paid for all of it," I continued. "Can I remind you that this Masala Mama, aka your boss, is also handling company bonuses this year? So unless you want a stocking stuffed with margaritas, I would suggest you help me out."

"Okay, we're listening," Rob said.

"There's no more time for me to shop. It's a full itinerary from here on out. I can't show up wearing jeans and dresses, and everyone else is going to be wearing Manish Malhotra or some other Indian designer that I've never even heard of."

"Manny. We got this. You got this," they chimed simultaneously.

"My cousin Aliyan can help." Anjali lowered her face to the screen. "He's the stylist we used for the event a couple of years ago. Remember? He's actually a Bollywood stylist!"

Somehow I got the notion that if I needed a dentist, Anjali would have that, too, covered in her Rolodex.

"I'm going to send him your hotel info in the morning. Do not worry. Do. You. Hear. Me?" she shouted into the phone, sounding a bit tipsy herself. Probably the most disorganized I had ever seen her. "He will send over everything you need for the rest of the week. Manny, do you hear me?"

"Yes, thank you, Anjali, I heard you." The first time. "I should get going. Sammy's probably looking for me."

"Manny, go have fun! Live a little. You're in this sexy ensemble, go bust a . . ."

Rob looked at Anjali for help.

"Bhangra move," she added.

"Yes. Do that! That's what you wanted, right? Fire, flame . . . what did you say before you left?" Rob paused, seeming unable to recall the conversation.

"Manny, Rob is right. Go have fun. We love you! Just be sure to send us videos of everything."

"Errrything," Rob growled into the phone.

"I love you guys, too. GOOD-BYE!"

The club was even busier when I headed back to find Sammy. He found me first.

"Manny," Sammy said, swinging me around. "Having fun yet?"

"Yes," I said, throwing him a big smile. He was so happy. And I was somewhat relieved that Anjali would be calling her cousin for help.

"Come on, let's get out of here. There's a week of these parties."

"Whatever you say, boss."

"Pleasure doing business with ya," Arnie said with a wink as we left.

Another doubter who didn't buy our cover story.

"You okay to walk back in those heels?" Sammy asked as we crossed the road.

"Totally fine. Trust me, these are nothing compared to the stilettos I usually wear to work."

I followed close behind him. Once we were away from the club, I could see that Marble had settled back down to being a peaceful postcard town as evening dragged into night. Most of the tourists had retreated to their hotel rooms.

"Let's walk over there." Sammy gestured to a children's play-
ground glowing in the streetlights. "So when are we going to slip
away again to get you a . . ." He hesitated. ". . . a more appropriate
wardrobe to take you through the rest of the week? It was a bit
rushed this afternoon—"

"Actually, I think I may have it under control."

"Oh?"

"I have my ways!" I grinned at him.

"You do, do you?"

We sat on the swings, letting the wind gently sway us back
and forth. We seemed a million miles away from Baskin, when
really it was just a three-hour flight. And only a day before,
Sammy was an infuriated stranger who was pestering me and my
staff to take on what seemed like an all-too-impossible case. And
now the hothead was suddenly the charming life of the party, a
caring brother and cousin who just wanted to respect his family's
values. *Who was the real Sammy?* I wondered. *The furious street
freak or the sweet Smottie?*

I leaned back on the swing as I took in the magic of the night.
Sammy's silhouette was backlit against the glow of the moon,
and suddenly I had a feeling that something big was happening
in this small town. But this was not my small town. And I already
had my something big in Baskin.

A chill ran through me, and it wasn't the Marble wind.

"You know, this very moment is grounds for a Breakup email,"
I said, an attempt to course correct.

"What do you mean?" Sammy asked.

"Dear Breakup," I said. "My boyfriend let me almost freeze

to death on a crisp autumn night as we both stared at the stars and I clung on for dear life in the chill of the Marble air. What happened to chivalry? Is it dead like this relationship?" I smiled at him. "That's what I'd get in my inbox."

"Ha, what a knockout, Manny. How do you manage to not be so jaded with all these clients looking to you for a breakup?" Sammy said as he took off his jacket and placed it on my shoulders. "Better?"

"Yes, much. And to answer your other question, by making deals like this," I reminded him. And myself. "I guess I look at my business as a way to be kind for people. There are a lot of unkind people out there, and even though hiring us may seem like the easy way out, it's not. The easy way out is just dumping someone without explaining why."

"Also known as ghosting," Sammy chimed in. "Something I picked up from the radio this morning. Man, you must get all kinds of requests?"

"We do." I thought back to the client who wanted to dump her partner because he had no body odor. She said no smell was worse than a smell. "What about you and the Patel business? I do know a lot of people across North America who rave about all your stores."

"A few years of banking and I decided I wanted to really help take the family biz across the country. It had always been my dad's dream to go international. Marketing, sales, new partnerships— that was all me. Now we can't keep stock on our shelves. I know it's not the same as the feeling you probably get helping someone through a tough breakup, but seeing people's smiles when they find the perfect gift for a loved one or add that last pièce de résistance to their dream space is all worth it for me. It's that look on someone's face when you've made their—"

"—made their day." I finished his sentence as I thought back to some of the thank-you emails I received on a daily basis.

"Yeah . . . their day . . . it's not about my day. Although the money is good, too. Right, Dogra?"

"Right, Sammy, the money isn't so bad for either of us."

"But at the end of the day, it's my way of being kind to people."

I knew what Sammy was talking about. Although Breakup was a business that catered to some ruthless clients, at the end of the day, working there meant knowing that you had made someone's day by giving them the closure they needed or the relief they felt when they got invaluable dating advice. I knew exactly what Sammy was talking about. "By the way, what do you think of the idea of a turmeric wine?"

"Sounds nasty." He faked a gag.

"I may have led Needa to believe it was on our list of ideas for our new wine business."

He couldn't stop laughing. "Why not add a butter chicken one, too? You know, a little flavor for the person who is in *curry of a hurry*."

Now I was laughing, too. It did all sound so gross.

The trees moved slightly in the breeze as if swaying to the sounds of our conversation.

"How did we get all the way here? You would think we were still teenagers running around hiding from our parents."

"Sammy, you kind of are hiding from your parents—in fact, your entire family. From what I saw and heard tonight, they have really missed you."

"I've missed them, too.

"They all seem so accepting and warm. I can't imagine they wouldn't just want what's best for you and Lisa."

"It's a little more complicated than what you see sometimes."

"Don't I know it." I scuffed my shoes in the sand.

"Have you ever had this feeling that if it wasn't for someone *rescuing* you, you're not sure where you'd be right now?" he asked.

"Yeah, I have." I thought of Adam and how he had stuck around through all my phases of grief in the last couple of years. Although we actually never talked about how I really felt, Adam was my first boyfriend after my parents had passed, and he had been quick to rescue me whenever he detected any kind of sadness in my words. He knew all the right distractions that kept me busy: endlessly sending me business goals and financial achievement reminders, and helping me project Breakup forecasts that eventually had me so knee-deep in work, I had no time for anything or anyone else.

"But I'm not sure it's the best feeling," I said slowly. "I mean, at the time, it sure does feel good to be tossed a life jacket." I slipped off the high heels I was wearing and pushed them to the side, and then shifted some sand around with my bare feet.

"Humans can get into dark places, and sometimes the right person comes along and helps you out of that dark place," Sammy said.

Or takes you into another one unknowingly.

"Those earrings look stunning on you, by the way."

"From my mom." I missed saying that word out loud. To her.

"What was she like? I mean, if you don't mind me asking."

I didn't mind. "She was cute. She was quiet and cute." I smiled.

"So, the opposite of you."

"Very funny." I inhaled deeply. When was the last time I had really described my mother to anyone? "She was a woman of few words, but you knew when she was there. You felt her presence. She was so generous, so sweet, giving, loving . . ."

"You really loved her. I can see it in your face."

I looked at Sammy, and he smiled into my eyes.

"The truth is, I am not sure I always saw love on her face. In fact, I found out that she didn't have any other choice but to marry my father."

"Every Indian family has their own traditions, values—even skeletons in the family closet. At times they may not make a lot of sense in the world we live in today, but back then maybe it made sense to her." Sammy took a moment. "I guess in a way, we're all forced to do things we don't want to." He trailed off again, lost in his thoughts for a moment, and then he went on. "What about looking at it from a different point of view?"

"What do you mean?"

"Instead of being disappointed with your parents for not showing you the motherland ways, maybe—and hear me out for a second—maybe we can be thankful for all that they did show you. After all, that helped make you the exceptional woman you are today."

The wind picked up as we sat in comfortable silence, pondering what he had just said.

After a moment or so, he let out a little chuckle again.

"Now what's so funny?"

"I don't know, Dogra. You tell me. I'm sitting here in Marble, California, on a child's swing that I am clearly way too big for, and I just can't help but laugh."

That was all it took. Sammy and I both started laughing hysterically again, as if we'd known each other for years.

"Speaking of funny," he said when we finally managed to stop laughing, "you seemed to find Manisha's jokes funny. I don't know how you were able to talk to her for so long. Correction, I don't know how you succeeded in getting a word in while *she* talked for so long."

"Let's just say I know a thing or two about hearing people out." I gave Sammy the sort of pointed look I usually saved for Rob.

"I deserved that one. Hanging up on you wasn't exactly . . . mature."

"Truth. I actually enjoyed meeting her and the rest of your family. Even if your sister does tend to speak for the entire family. By the way, I was so overdressed compared to her tonight."

"Nonsense. Manisha tends to do that—show up in one outfit and then boom, outta nowhere she's in something else. The outfit you saw her in was probably her tamer one of the night. The less blinged-out one." He shook his head.

"Somehow that doesn't surprise me." I giggled.

"You made an effort tonight, Manny. I was watching you from across the club," Sammy confessed.

"It was effortless." And it had been. I was surprised by that.

"You've got a little . . . leaf in your hair."

"Oh."

"Here, let me get it." Sammy pushed his swing closer to mine, combing his fingers through my hair to remove the leaf.

"You should leave your hair like this." He tucked my hair behind my ear. "You've got these big brown Indian eyes. You should show them off to the world. The world needs more Indian Manny."

I looked at Sammy and his own big brown Indian eyes.

The world did need more Indian Manny. So did I.

Chapter 16

Dear Breakup,

When I started dating my girlfriend, I had my ex-girl's name tattooed on my arm. It was in code, so I lied and told my new girl it read "love." I really didn't think it was going anywhere with her anyway—I thought she would be a rebound. But, of course, I fell in love with her, and now we're set to get married. How do I tell her that my tattoo is actually a nod to my ex, and that she also has a matching one?

Kim

The text alert jolted me awake.

Breakfast?

I looked at my phone. Eight a.m. How could Sammy think about breakfast? I was still half-asleep trying to recover from the bottomless drinks Manisha had insisted on pouring.

Meet you downstairs in 30?

Make it 20. We'll be leaving the hotel for breakfast.

Where are we going?

It's a surprise. I'll see you soon.

I got dressed quickly after the briefest of showers. A little mascara and some lipstick—Dior 999 in Matte—and I was all set.

By the time I came down to the lobby, Sammy was leaning up against the concierge desk, wearing loose white linen shorts and a salmon-colored golf shirt. He was talking up the hotel staff and looking more at ease than I had ever seen him. He turned as I made my way toward him.

"Ready to go?" he asked.

"Ready as I'll ever be."

We went outside, and he led me around the corner to where the rack of vibrant cruiser bikes was waiting.

"Pick a color!"

"How about that one over there, the purple one?" I pointed to the bike next to him, not even sure if I could take on the challenge of a bike ride. The last time I had been on one was a casual ride through the Jamieson vineyard, but I had a feeling this was going to be more than a sip-and-ride tour, or as Derek called them, a slurp-and-stroll tour.

"You really do like purple, don't you?"

"It was my dad's favorite color. Or maybe it was just his practical color. Remember how Steve Jobs used to wear black turtlenecks all the time? My dad did that with purple golf shirts. He couldn't play golf worth much, but every morning he got up and wore a purple Lacoste shirt."

"Then how about we take the purple helmet, too, in honor of your dad," Sammy said and tossed it at me.

"And flatten this hair?"

"Better flat hair than a flat head! Now come on! Follow me. And stay close." He jumped on a bike and started pedaling.

A midmorning breeze wavered through the streets, catching a few townies on their way to work. Work? When was the last time I had even checked my work email? I trusted the team to have everything under control, despite their happy hour break, but I remembered that this week was also work for me.

"Just over here." Sammy pointed to a small building surrounded by several large oak trees. We jumped off our bikes, leaned them up against a tree, and headed toward it.

"I know my brother's wedding is supposed to show you one side of Indian-ness, I guess we can call it, but I wanted you to see another side, too."

He opened one of the double doors of the building, the gold color of which had a warmth I had never quite felt before as it shone in the bright sunlight. We went downstairs, where we entered a large open kitchen crowded with men, women, and children washing dishes, emptying baskets of food, and preparing meals. The open-concept area was filled with an organized chaos.

"What is this beautiful place?" I asked, looking around.

"It's the local Indian community center. People get together here to make food for locals who . . ." Sammy looked around. ". . . who need help."

I stood for a moment, taking it all in.

"Manny, a big part of our culture," he pointed at me when he said *our* and smiled, "for me, anyway, is giving back. It's not just the events. It's being grateful for what we do have and sharing it with others selflessly. It's called seva."

"Seva." *What a beautiful word.*

"Put one of these on." He threw me an apron. "Let's get to work."

Once we had our aprons on, he took my hand and led me over to a group of women who were kneading dough. I watched as he pulled a small piece of the dough from a larger section and put it in the middle of his right palm. "Roll it like this." He created a perfect circular ball with his left. "Come on, Dogra, give it a try."

I grabbed some as well and tried to form a ball, but mine fell flat. The ladies around us all giggled and smiled.

Sammy moved behind me and put his hands around mine, helping me create the perfect ball of dough. The ladies continued to giggle.

"Now, take it and put it over here."

As instructed, I tossed it in a large production line of other small rolled-out balls.

"Now that is what we call a round roti. You know, they say the rounder the roti, the better the wife," he said.

"True?"

"That's right, Dogra! True it is! I think, anyway. I could have sworn I heard an auntie once tell me that when she was trying to convince me to take one of her daughters out. She promised a long life of round rotis."

"Guess I am only going to make a good wife for half my life." I lifted up another roti that looked more shapeless than anything.

"Dear Breakup, My wife can't make round rotis—"

We both cracked up before he could even finish the sentence.

The rest of the morning was spent rolling dough and talking to volunteers. I heard stories about how the food they made helped feed five hundred families in Marble every year. I also watched the older ladies swoon over Sammy as he helped carry large pots that were too heavy for them. And I watched him goof around with young kids as their parents helped in the kitchen.

"He comes here a dozen times a year and helps us make meals," an older man shared with me.

"He does?"

"He helped create this center. It's changed the lives of so many families here."

I had no clue there was a center like this in Baskin. My family gave back, but our contribution consisted mostly of writing checks. It never dawned on me that I could donate by doing something like . . . well, something like this.

"You're a lucky girl. Most of the aunties are trying to set Sammy up with their daughters or nieces. He's a much-coveted single man," the man continued.

"Oh. We're just . . ." I was about to say "business partners," but the truth was, well, Sammy was becoming a friend. "I *am* a lucky girl," I told him.

At the end of the morning, as we left, Sammy stopped in front of a lady sitting behind a table with a pad and paper.

"Can we make a donation in honor of Dolly, Ronny, and Manny Dogra," he said to her.

I looked at Sammy, speechless.

"I noticed when you were taking notes on your tablet, your screensaver had a picture of your parents with their names underneath."

I still couldn't find any words. Instead, I hugged Sammy. Tightly.

"Okay, okay. I need my arm to write this check," he joked. He signed it and handed it to the lady. She smiled at the both of us.

"So, what did you think?" he asked as we made our way outside.

"I . . . I don't know what to say about anything. This program you got off the ground here, the donation . . . Sammy, I am just so impressed by your generosity."

"I was here a while back and I saw the need for this. It's not just me, it's everyone here today who makes this paying-forward happen. As for the donation, it was a tribute to your parents. It's your first visit here, but they helped in Baskin. I was looking through the community center files last night, because I knew I recognized their names. I was on the board about five years ago. They used to donate to the center there all the time."

"They did?"

"You didn't know that?"

"No, not at all."

"Yeah, hang on." He pulled out his phone and looked at a file. "Ronny and Dolly Dogra. Baskin Indian Community Center members."

"What? Members? For how long?"

"I don't know, Manny." Sammy started going through his email. "I'm pretty sure from day one."

I felt light-headed.

"Are you all right?" he asked as I tightly gripped the handle of my bike.

"Yeah, I am. It's just . . . I had no idea. I thought all these years they didn't want to have anything to do with their roots."

"Maybe this trip is also about getting some insight into a side of your parents that they weren't necessarily hiding, but that maybe they were just waiting for the right moment to share."

"Yeah, well, that moment was taken away from them and me when they died."

"Manny, I can't even imagine your loss. I can only offer up that coming out here with me may not just be about discovering what being Indian means to everyone else, but what it could mean to you and possibly what it meant to your parents. Even if they hadn't shared that with you, yet."

I looked down at the leaves on the ground and crunched some under my shoe. I was overcome by a wave of emotion at the notion of not knowing my parents as well as I thought I had.

"Don't look at it like they were keeping a secret, Manny. Secrets hurt people."

I realized Sammy thought he might have upset me.

He went on. "This was doing the opposite. Their donations

were helping the community thrive with food, education, and extracurricular activities." We stood in silence for a few minutes. "Maybe we should head back so you have enough time to prep for the rest of the wedding's activities, Manny. It's getting late."

The ride back was a blur to me as we sped through the streets of Marble. I couldn't believe my parents hadn't mentioned their support of the community center. Why had they kept it a secret? And it was a secret, no matter what Sammy wanted to call it. I could have had friends like Anjali and Manisha. Friends who looked like me. I could have met Sammy earlier. I could have known who I was. I imagined what Maggie would make of the news in one of her TV reports.

"This just in. Manny Dogra's whole life has been a lie! It was just revealed by our sources that Ronny and Dolly Dogra, her PAR-ENTS, were members of the Baskin Indian Community Center. Manny, what are your thoughts on this breaking news?"

I imagined a blank stare as I looked into the camera. My mouth open with no words coming out. Just a sea of thoughts floating about in my mind. I was mad. I was sad. I was angry.

No comment.

Chapter 17

Dear Breakup,

I was excited when I started a new relationship with Don a few months ago. I even took him to my best friend's wedding. Turns out, Don is a terrible dancer, and, unfortunately, his dancing in the sheets isn't any better.

How do I tell Don that we are not part of the same rhythm nation?

Lindsey

I sank into the bed and propped my head on one of the giant hotel pillows. I thought about what Sammy had told me, the Baskin Indian Community Center, and my parents. All that time. Why hadn't they told me? Why hadn't they—

"Knock, knock!!"

I nearly jumped out of my skin.

"I can hear you breathing," came a voice from the hallway.

I took a breath into my palm to see if that would register on the volume meter. I headed to the door and looked through the peephole. There was one giant brown eye looking back at me.

"Girl, open the damn door. I don't wait for anyone."

I did as I was told.

"I'm Aliyan."

"Aliyan?" I repeated back, trying to recall why the name sounded so familiar.

"Hel-lo . . . Anjali's loud and proud and incredibly stylish cousin." He whisked past me with four rolling clothing racks following, each propelled by an eager-looking assistant.

"You must have seen my work in *USA* magazine, *We Weekly*, *Much TV*, *MTV*, *Bollywood News Now*." He counted them all off on his fingers. "Oh me, oh my, look at that, I have run out of fingers," cousin Aliyan said, laughing at the joke I was sure he had made many times before.

"Set up in the living room," he ordered the handful of young men and women navigating the rolling racks. They rushed to get organized like bees buzzing around a flower.

Aliyan was a tiny man, but what he lacked in height he made up for in style. His orange blazer resembled the dried magnolias on Rajiv's truck. His bright pink shirt looked as soft as cotton candy, and his skinny red leather pants looked like, well, skinny red leather pants. Topping it all off was a large red hat. Aliyan's outfit may have outweighed him, but he stood tall, king of all he surveyed.

I watched as the living area in my suite was transformed into a temporary dressing room filled with all manner of garments. Some were covered in shiny gemlike beads, some with sequins, others with lace, all in the most resplendent colors. With every outfit came bracelets, shoes, oversize earrings, and purses. The room makeover was big and beautiful: my very own Little India, organized with labels and color coded. *Organization runs in the family*, I thought.

Aliyan placed his purse on the glass coffee table and his hat on top of that, revealing a shock of perfectly spiked hair. He put one hand on my shoulder. "We have a lot of work to do," he said. "I picked up the reception itinerary from a very charming bell-hop, and you have an event this evening, tomorrow another full day, and yup another one and yup, typical Indian-style packed days. This is a lot of pressure on me." He began to pace. "But when Pri married Nick Jonas, there was a lot of pressure on me, too. I can make this work." Having patted himself on the back (figuratively speaking, of course), he clapped his hands while his team continued working.

I sat down and sipped the fruit juice I had poured for myself. My panic from the night before was calmed by the pop-up shop Aliyan had created just for me. When Anjali said she would get her stylist cousin to send over Indian clothes, I had no idea he would be coming with them.

"I'm not sure if you recall your last styling with me, but I tend to wear straightforward things," I spoke up. "Simple."

Aliyan whipped around from the window he was looking out of, as if offended by that word. "You're going to an Indian wedding, Mintu."

"It's actually Manny."

"You need an Indian nickname. You're like a cute little breath mint. Fresh. My little Mintu."

Mintu. I'd never had a nickname before.

"Now back to what I was saying. There is no room for 'simple' this week. There's no such thing. What kind of Indian are you?" Aliyan must have seen the look on my face. He came over and sat down on the edge of the coffee table. I wasn't at all worried that it would break. He weighed less than me and was barely five feet two.

"Mintu, don't worry. You're in beautiful hands." He waved his in front of me as if to show me that he had once been a hand model, too. "Anjali trusts me to take care of her boss, and I will. I just don't do 'simple.'" He leaped up and waved his hand about again, this time as though he were holding a fake magic wand. "Let's start with your eyebrows."

I touched my brows in what I can only describe as a gesture of ownership. I had been going to the same aesthetician for years.

"We need to thread those suckers."

"Thread? I . . . I usually wax."

"Not anymore! These are bottom-barrel brows. Clearly your fake waxer needs new glasses." He gestured to my upper lip.

"Seriously?"

"A few, tops. Well . . ." He leaned a bit closer. "A few dozen. Girl, your upper lip is hairier than mine. You got a mustache, like my auntie Babu."

"Oh my gosh, I do?" I covered my lip. "Please thread it, then."

I guessed if I was going to immerse myself in all the traditions, it should include the traditional art of hair removal. The old me waxed. The new me threaded.

A larger Indian woman took my juice and placed it on a small table, grabbed my hand, and pushed me back on a recliner. She reached into her pocket and out came a spool of thread.

"Hold," she said.

"Hold what?" I asked.

"Like this," she directed, and showed me how to stretch the top part of my eyebrow.

Her hands pulled two pieces of thread across my lower forehead quickly and painlessly, and just like that, I was smooth and hairless.

Aliyan handed me a mirror.

"Thank you. Oh my gosh! They look so full, and there is actually an arch." As I was admiring my new brows I got a glimpse of the living room clock. "Aliyan, I completely forgot, but I have to meet the groom's sister for lunch."

"Oh, Mintu, why didn't you tell me this earlier? I could have enjoyed the day at the hotel spa getting a rub-dee-dub down while you got busy with the sista!"

"I am so sorry. Let me throw on some jeans—"

"Jeans?" Aliyan stared at me. "You don't *just* throw on some jeans like you don't *just* get invited to a last-minute lunch. Here, put on these leggings and this cute kurti. Trust me, this isn't going to be a ladies-who-lunch episode." He handed me what looked like a long blouse that stopped right before my ankles. The yellow cotton with white embroidery was as bright as the Marble sun. "We always dress to impress, Mintu. Always."

I pushed past the rolling carts and turned around.

"Thank you soooo much," I said. "Mintu thanks you sooo much." I blew him a kiss that he swatted away.

"The last time I took a kiss from a girl, I choked on a samosa after. Now, if you want to send any of those lovely brown boys I saw in the lobby my way, that's another story."

That was my cue to leave.

I headed down to the lobby, where I saw Manisha first. She was wearing similar attire to mine, but her blouse—kurti—was more of an Indian dress, and it showed a lot more cleavage. So, Sammy liked to show his ankles, and his sister liked to show her boobs. *I guess if you've got it, flaunt it.*

"Manny!" She charged at me. "Wasn't last night sooo much fun and O-M-G this kurti? Where did you get it? It must be another designer from India. I need your list on speed dial ASAP. You better not plan on outdoing my outfits. I got my eye on you!"

Before I could answer, she had whisked me away through a corridor leading to another part of the hotel.

"So, the girls and I were thinking . . ."

The girls—plural? I started to panic.

I listened, wiggling my arm ever so slightly, loosening the grip she had on me. If she was taking me to a room to interrogate me, I needed to be ready to make a quick getaway.

"We have this surprise for Sanj and Needa tonight. Like an engagement party surprise." Manisha waved her hand across the automated door at the entrance to the Grand Hall. "She's here," she shouted into the hall.

"Manny, are you going to dance with us?" Deena flipped her long braid to the side as she blurted out the question. Several more people moved closer, and suddenly I was surrounded by seven cousins in a Jamieson-style circle, except there was no talk of yachts and vacations but instead more pleas.

"Manny, please," from one cousin.

"You just have to; we're down a person," said another.

"Shhhh! I haven't asked her yet," Manisha said, looking irritated at most of them.

"Dance? What dance? No. No. *No!*" I started to back away. "I can't dance."

"Oh, we saw you dancing in your seat last night at the club," Manisha reminded me.

"That was at a club, and we were all having a good time and . . ." All eyes were on me as I stumbled over my answer.

"Come *on!*" Deena's sister Ali put her arm around my shoulder as if to hold me in place. Patels had some serious grip. "We'll put you in the back, and no one will even notice you."

Before I had a chance to consider this solution to *their* problem, Manisha said, "We all love dancing, no matter how bad some of us are. And it's our present to Needa and Sanj. Unless you already got them a present."

I hadn't. In fact, I had completely forgotten to add that to my list. In the frenzy of Code Red, I never thought to ask Anjali about a wedding gift. Now I felt foolish, although I was sure the way Anjali express shipped Aliyan to me, she would be able to do the same with a wedding gift. But when I thought about it, this involved more than a gift to Sanj and Needa; I needed this for me. I wanted to gift me with this dancing present.

"Would Priyanka Chopra ever turn down a dance? What the hell. I'm in."

The cousins charged forward and hugged me.

"YES! I knew you would say yes!" Manisha grabbed her phone and put on some music. "Okay, sit," she commanded. "It's not complicated. Just watch us first. You'll get the hang of it."

Within minutes, these lovely and very outgoing women were dancing rhythmically to the music coming from Manisha's phone. A mix of Indian pop it may have been, but it was like nothing I had ever heard coming from Rajiv's boom box. It was similar to something you'd hear on a Top 40 chart, but with an eclectic Indian spin that included hip-hop lyrics. Like Drake, but in Hindi. I was surprised at how much I liked it.

The dance that went along with the song had been perfectly choreographed to each beat, with every single shoulder shimmy in sync with each handclap. I didn't know where to look. The way the cousins moved their bare feet on the cold hall floor, with hip swings and thrusts perfectly timed to each beat, was captivating. The women turned around, and with a few quick jumps in the air came the beautiful sounds of the bangles that covered their arms. With a toss of their hair, they were finished.

"Wow! You were so good," I said. "All of you. Like professionally good." I looked at Deena, whose perfect posture and lean body made me suspicious about just how much time she spent dancing. "How am I supposed to keep up with you guys?"

"Manny, it's so easy," Ali encouraged. "Think of all the times you've had to bhangra. It's pretty much the same thing. Then, add in our moves."

All the times I've had to bhangra? If only I had watched Rajiv more closely, or asked his wife for a dance lesson after dinner.

"I don't know, guys. You all have been practicing for weeks."

"Two days," Manisha said. "It was a last-minute decision. Plus, I'll send you a link later. Rehearse with us, and then go back to your room and practice." She looked at her watch and back at the dancing troupe. "Don't worry, the hotel staff is bringing us lunch. We're gonna practice for the next few hours. Now, again from the top!" She reached for her phone and put the song on a repeat cue.

Deena grabbed me and brought me to the back of the group. "Look, you can dance behind me. All eyes are gonna be on Manisha and her big—"

"Mouth! Which is about to go cray on you, Deena, if we don't get this right," Manisha scolded her cousin.

"Whatever," Deena muttered under her breath.

I tried to follow and quickly found myself wondering why I hadn't opted for dance classes over baseball as a child. The moves were much more challenging than they looked.

"Okay, not bad," said Manisha.

No, not bad—*horrible*.

"Let's try this a few more times."

"Come on, Manisha, I think we all get it by now," Deena complained.

"A few more times for Manny."

Yes. Please. For me.

"Besides, what else do you have to do? Swipe through Dil Mil matches?"

"Come on! It's a whole new set of matches in Marble," Deena reminded her.

"That can wait. You can cater to your hungry ladoo loins later." Manisha rolled her eyes. "Practice now and play later."

Deena dropped her arms to her sides in a weak protest, but it didn't work. We continued to practice until my own arms felt like noodles.

Finally, Manisha said with a confidence I felt a boost from, "That was great. We are so ready for tonight!"

Everyone gathered their phones and purses and headed toward the lobby.

"See ya tonight! Don't be on Indian Standard Time. We're up first," one of the girls said and laughed as we headed toward our rooms.

"She means don't be late," Manisha whispered as she walked by.

"I knew that," I replied as if I had grown up with Dogras around me arriving late.

The exact opposite was actually true. My father used to remind me that punctuality was a sign of respect, and who was I to waste anyone's precious time?

And there's no time to waste here, I thought as I sprinted back to my room to practice.

Chapter 18

Dear Breakup,

My boyfriend decided to have "the talk" with me at our favorite park. As he was breaking up with me, I started to cry and, well, local parkgoers started clapping because they thought I was crying tears of happiness. You see, Steven had gotten down on his knee to pick up my tear-filled tissue, but everyone around us thought he was proposing! Realizing what was happening, he decided to pop the question and take back the breakup.

Can he do that? Can you take back breakups and turn them into proposals? If so, should I accept? After all, it is slim pickings out there.

Denise

I had a little skip in my step as I made my way back to my room. I was going to dance with Manisha and her cousins. In front of everyone!

I thought back to the pictures I had found of my mother in traditional suits and saris, pictures she had hidden in her closet. A young face, with not a single drop of makeup, but still so bright and beaming, with a smile as cheerful as the clothes she wore. She was a beautiful woman with a secret love, one who had her dancing and posing for family photos at weddings and parties. I thought about her setting off fireworks as she imagined her own wedding to the man she loved. I couldn't recall any parties where my parents danced. I couldn't recall ever seeing my mother as happy as she was in those photos.

I started to choke up thinking about the last few days I had spent with her, in what became her last home, the hospital. A woman who suddenly opened up a secret vault she had kept locked for many years. My eyes started to tear up, but I pushed the thoughts away. I had work to do. I got back to my room and turned up the music to rehearse. The dance was so much harder than it looked.

"What in the name of the drag queen goddesses are you doing?" Aliyan stood outside the entrance to my bedroom, hands covering his mouth.

"Umm . . . I am dancing, um . . . bhangra dancing."

"Oh, honey, that is a bhangra NO."

"I know. I'm awful." My earlier excitement entirely gone, I slumped into the chair next to my bed. "Sammy's sister asked me to dance at the party tonight. I don't know what I am going to do. There is no way I can go."

Aliyan put his purse down on the chair next to me and tucked in the spare room key I had given him so he and his team could come and go.

"I'm going to cancel. I'm coming down with something. *Cough. Cough.*" It was a feeble attempt, but an attempt none-theless.

"Oh, no, you don't. You're not getting out of this that easily, Mintu. Get up."

I did as I was told.

"Now, watch me."

It was the most spectacular thing I had ever seen. It was like the music was moving to Aliyan, not the other way around.

"Now you try. The key is to put all that energy into your hips and that fabulous booty. It's like steamy sex in the air flowing through your hot body. From the moment you clap, bring that sexy back into your waist and down to your feet and back up to your arms and that sexy smile."

Aliyan's dancing was certainly the X-rated version of what we had practiced earlier.

"Think of our dancing as replacing a romp session on-screen. It's the closest thing to making out in a Bollywood movie. BW movies equal no eggplant emoji."

He continued to sway his hips from side to side as his arms followed close behind in the air. His eyes squinting, lips tight, chest out, he looked like he needed a hotel room of his own.

I tried to move with the combination of steps my mentors had shown me, but I ended up a big fat dance disaster. Hips swinging in a not-so-sexy way followed by the beads of sweat running down my face made me feel exasperated.

"You have *had* sex, right?" Aliyan looked doubtful.

I let out a louder-than-anticipated sigh. "Yes, but maybe not . . . Indian sex."

"Oh honey, that is indeed the best kind of sex." He looked like he was remembering something delicious, and his mouth broke into a mischievous little smile. "But I don't think that's your problem here. A little more *this*," he pointed to his waist, "and a lot less *that*." He looked at my waist as he returned his attention back to my attempts. "And one, and two, and clap, and three."

I tried to follow the beat and his directions.

"You know this dance is from one of the most popular Bollywood movies of all time." Aliyan danced and talked effortlessly. "The song is 'Sheila Ki Jawani,' featuring Katrina Kaif, the hottest BW actress—well, in my opinion, and, of course, don't tell PC that." He recognized my confusion. "Priyanka Chopra!" he proclaimed.

"Oh, yes," I said. "Of course, PC."

"And Katrina is half-Indian, you know," he said as we continued to the beat. "If that only-one-half Indian girl can dance, well, girl—you can do it, too."

A couple more hours of practicing, and then I jumped into the shower. When I got out, I found a black tote Aliyan had left for me. There was a note that said to follow his instructions and to watch Katrina Kaif on YouTube before I headed out that night. Aliyan was busy with a VIP client but promised me I'd have no trouble with the makeup tutorial he'd left for me.

"Your hair needs to look like *this*, and your makeup needs to look like *this*. Just press play on the iPad I left on the coffee table." I couldn't believe the number of channels devoted to the art of Indian makeup and hair. Aliyan had bookmarked influencers like Ami Desai, Farah Dhukai, and Deepica Mutyala who had turned hashtags like #bollywoodbridal, #bombaybrides, #indianmakeup, and #indianbride into empires.

The outfit instructions were easier. The sari was "ready-made," as Aliyan called it. It was flowing red with a matching beaded blouse secured with a few clicks and clasps. I wasn't about to get trapped in this one.

After doing and redoing my makeup, and watching the Katrina Kaif videos several times, I was ready to go. My mother's gold necklace was tucked under all the other jewelry, still giving me warmth, as it always did. I stood up and stared at myself in the long mirror attached to the antique bedroom armoire. I couldn't believe who was gazing back at me.

I looked Indian. I looked, somehow, more me. I felt more me.

I took a quick picture and sent it to Rob and Anjali. #operationindian

The backstage was buzzing with cousins when I entered the private entrance to the Great Hall. "There are so many people here," I said nervously to myself, or so I thought, when I joined everyone behind the black curtain.

"Not really," Deena responded. "They kept things small." Deena fixed her braid and looked at me. "Honestly, don't worry! It's just like all the other family weddings you've been to. Except this one has a royal presence." She rolled her eyes. "You'd think being *royal* would automatically entitle you to good-looking family members. How is a girl supposed to find her future husband here when there are no decent-looking men? Story of our lives, right, Manny? All these cousin weddings we have to go to every year, and we put so much time, effort, and money into getting ready for a dramatic entrance, and for who?" Deena headed toward a mirror as she continued to fuss over her perfect hair.

I felt like a fraud. All my excitement at looking Indian had vanished. What was I thinking, getting up in front of all these people and putting on a show? What did I know about any of this? Did I think I could learn enough to pass for Indian in a few days? Just because I had spent the afternoon practicing some dance moves and got into a ready-made sari after? I was completely out of place.

Manisha must have seen the beads of sweat building up on my face and the panic that was slowly starting to take over. "This is going to be so fun, Manny. Wait until Sammy sees you." She smiled with a little too much hope in her eyes.

"It's six thirty. MC Jungle is going to introduce us," one of the girls whispered excitedly.

An appropriate name for the DJ, as I felt I was about to be tossed into the Patel jungle, full of hungry animals who would eat me alive once they found out I had never danced in their—or any—circle before.

I pushed the stage curtain to the side and snuck a glance out. The house lights were dimming, and the tables were full of Sanjeev and Needa's family members. Sammy was making his way to the front table wearing a traditional long shirt and skinny leggings. And, yes, loafers with no socks.

The room sparkled with gold and red, and at each table was an elephant centerpiece. The couple's stage was decorated with an opulent backdrop and a velvet lounge chair where Sanjeev and Needa would take a seat for their party. This was Indian elegance.

MC Jungle got on the mic. "And without further ado, your entertainment for the night: the Patel cousins!"

I wasn't a Patel, and I wasn't a cousin, but at that moment, catching a glimpse of myself in a backstage mirror and thinking back to all the names I had written down as Sammy walked me through the Patel family lineage, I saw myself as a branch on the family tree. Even if the branch was temporary, it felt different from a Jamieson branch. A Patel cherry blossom growing up fast, even if it was only for this week.

The DJ put down the mic. The room fell silent as we walked onstage. Then Manisha said, "Hit it!" and the familiar track began. I channeled my inner Aliyan and started dancing. I looked over at Manisha, smiling, and Deena winked at me. I shifted and swayed like I had earlier in my room. The moves were all about timing. I managed to keep up with the Patel cousins, even though they had had years of practice and I had had one afternoon.

As I twirled around the stage, I caught a glimpse of Sammy. He was shaking his head and smiling. *No way*, he mouthed. I smiled back, really smiled back, feeling far away from my Baskin life and all the things I knew. My hands, my feet, and my hips were remembering the sexy air dance moves Aliyan taught me. For a brief moment, I was a full Indian version of Katrina Kaif. I was in a Bollywood movie. I was discovering my own Indian version.

The song ended, and we all hurried off the stage as everyone clapped. I even heard some whistles. I grabbed Manisha. "I can't believe I was Indian dancing," I said with a rush of adrenaline.

She hugged me. "That was your first time?" she asked slightly sarcastically and smiled. She'd known all along.

"I . . . you know . . ."

She hugged me again. "It won't be your last," she whispered in my ear.

I held her tightly, hoping she was right.

"Now, let's go out there and have some real fun."

The banquet hall was noisy as guests danced away to the DJ's songs. Those who weren't dancing were mingling, eating, and drinking. I still couldn't get over the number of people at the party. A few hundred at least. Would there be more at the actual wedding?

Sammy appeared at my side. "What the heck was that?" he asked and picked me up and swung me around, smiling. "You were so awesome out there, Manny. Floored. I am totally floored!"

"Oh my gosh, Sammy. It just happened. It was the greatest feeling in the world. Even though I thought I was going to vomit at the thought of it earlier today. But here I was dancing. *I* was Indian dancing." I realized I was still hugging him. I let him go and stepped back.

"I had no idea you had it in you, Dogra. You sure you've never been to any Patel weddings before? And this outfit, how did you find this hot sari?" he teased.

"Let's just say Priyanka wasn't using it tonight."

"Honestly, Manny, the way you were dancing up there, it was

like you were this different person. No, that's not right. It was as if you were yourself."

I felt a little thrill as I recognized the truth in what he said. I had always been Indian Manny. I just needed to go and find my *inner* Indian Manny, as Anjali would say. "Your sister actually asked me earlier today to be part of all this, and, well . . ."

"Who can say no to Manisha?" Sammy asked, laughing. "You might have, I guess, but then you'd have been the first."

"Yes, I couldn't say no to Manisha." I looked up at him. His eyes were overcome with pride, and so were mine. "I really don't know where all of that came from, Sammy."

He reached for my bangle-decorated arm, placed my hand in his, and put it on his heart.

"It came from here."

Suddenly I could hear my heart in the noisy banquet hall.

"Mom, Dad, over here." He waved at an older-looking man and woman on the dance floor.

"Can't complete Operation Indian without meeting the Patel parents," he whispered to me.

The couple headed in our direction. Sammy's father was wearing a black blazer and pants with a red silk tie. I saw where Sammy got his great hair. His mom reminded me of Manisha in both height and weight. Her sari was an embroidered yellow work of art with tiny beads and sparkles from head to toe. Her hug was as tight as Manisha's, giving me little room to breathe. She had her hair tied up in a small bun, and her bright red lipstick matched her polished red nails.

Sammy cleared his throat, and as his palm swept past mine to hug his dad, I felt a nervous shake come from him.

"Oh, beti, you were so good onstage."

"Mom, this is Manny, my business partner. Remember, I mentioned she was coming along for the week since we are doing some work out here?"

"Yes, Sammy. My, oh my, you are very sundar, beautiful, like your sari. And you are dancer? You are every proud mother's angel even if for business, I guess. I always say mix the business with pleasure," she said.

"Mom. She's business. Only business," he reminded her, embarrassed by his mom's joke.

She tugged on his ear playfully. "He never gets my jokes."

"Namaste, Auntie-ji," I said to her.

Sammy looked over in my direction as I greeted his mom in Hindi. He must have wondered where I had picked that up from, and I winked at him under the dim banquet lights. *Thanks, Aliyan.*

"Oh my, and she can speak Hindi," his mom said, impressed.

"Not enough, Auntie-ji. Manisha taught me a few words to get me through this week," I lied, not wanting to explain who Aliyan was.

"My Sammy knows lots of the bad words, so good you are learning from his sister. Maybe teach this scoundrel something, too." She turned to her son and rolled her eyes.

"This is my father, Manny." Sammy looked over at his dad.

"Namaste, Uncle-ji."

As Sammy's father looked at me, his eyes turned dark and he nodded quickly.

Had my Hindi greeting offended him?

Mrs. Patel must have noticed. "Are you with us for the entire week?" she jumped in.

"Yes, I am. If that is all right?"

"Yes, of course. The more, the better."

"Ruby, I see Mr. and Mrs. Ashok. We must go." Mr. Patel pushed past Sammy and me, and Mrs. Patel followed with a quick wave and wink at us.

"I am so sorry," Sammy said. "I have no idea what that was about. He's probably jet-lagged or—"

"No, no, it's okay. Not everyone is going to like my dance moves." I laughed nervously.

"Military. The Indian army did a number on him. Not exactly the most affectionate father out there."

"Did I offend him?"

"No, of course not. He's tired from all the planning that went into this wedding. You know what, let's not let the old man get to us, Manny. Let's grab some food and celebrate that hot performance!"

Sammy was right. And, as Aliyan would remind me, PC wouldn't have had it any other way.

Chapter 19

Dear Breakup,

I've been married to Kyle for five years, and our lovemaking is hitting an all-time low. Sure, we have sex, but half the time I can't even tell if Kyle is enjoying it because he makes no noise. The other day, I tried to tell him that sleeping with him was like sleeping with a dead corpse. He reminded me that all corpses were dead to begin with. I feel dead in this relationship. I need help with an email telling Kyle, loudly, it's over.

Jenna

My knowledge of the culture was expanding hourly. Sammy explained that the roka ceremony was like biting into a piece of gulab jamun at the end of the buffet. If the dessert smelled or even looked bad, the rest of the week was ruined. In other words, the roka set the bar for the soon-to-be-married couple, like an official announcement to kick off the week. I liked the word *roka* and how it rolled off my tongue, and was determined to use it in a sentence twice this week. The roka of Adam and Manny just didn't seem to have the right ring to it, though. Maybe I needed Rajiv to help me practice a bit more in case I decided I wanted to present the idea of an Indian wedding to Adam. I could only imagine the size of the headphones the Jamiesons would need to drown out all the *unrefined* party noise. But then again, that could probably wait, as it wasn't like an official anything had been set between Adam and me, and even when it almost had, it was quickly changed because of Adam's unpredictable schedule these days.

At this roka was the most extravagant variety of Indian foods. My mouth watered as I recognized some of the dishes I'd had at Rajiv's house. His wife, Rajna, had been a sous chef in India, and the few times I had accepted his many invitations she had spoiled me with traditional meals from the motherland. Aloo gobi, parathas stuffed with all kinds of savory veggies, and dal, my favorite by far. Adam didn't like to experiment with his food, so when he accompanied me for dinner, Rajna had whipped up butter chicken and naan, dishes popular in the West. He insisted he had had some childhood encounter with dal that didn't land so well. I tried to make light of it by comparing it to the first time I had tried root beer, which tasted to me like liquid toothpaste.

"Start here," Sammy suggested, after we had slowly made our way to the buffet tables.

The silver trays were labeled in both Hindi and English. It was a thoughtful gesture, and I felt better knowing that I wasn't the only partygoer who didn't know the dishes' names. The smell of flavorful spices jam-packed my nose when I raised a large spoonful of chickpeas—chana masala—to my plate. I ended with a helping of curry chicken and some basmati rice topped with saffron, and grabbed a few small pieces of naan and, of course, a gulab jamun. I could only imagine that my wedding to Adam would have a Michelin chef and five-course plated meal.

"Sammy, seeing everyone celebrating . . . I can't believe your family would ever care who you date. As long as you're happy. They all love you so much," I said out of the blue as we sat down at an empty table.

"Oh, Dogra, what's love got to do with it? Aren't those the famous last words of someone important?"

"Tina Turner! But, Sammy, please tell me you're being silly. Love has everything to do with it."

"No doubt all the Patels love me and each other. I guess with Lisa I define our love differently."

I thought about Adam and wondered how I would define our love.

"I thought the whole reason you reached out to Breakup is that you'll do anything for love, including lying to your family."

"Manny, I forgot to get raita, can I sneak some off your plate?" Sammy said, deftly changing the subject.

I pushed the yogurt closer to him. At that moment, the doors to the banquet hall burst open as more guests arrived. Dozens of young men and women in glamorous attire made a beeline for the buffet. From what I could see, everyone in the family was paired off except for Manisha, Sammy, Deena, and closeted Benny. Sure, Sammy was the oldest, so he felt the most pressure. I felt it for him. But I also saw a family who cared a lot about him. I couldn't imagine that they would have *disowned* him if he had brought Lisa instead.

Sammy leaned closer. "How's that email to Lisa?" he whispered to me.

"I thought you didn't want to know?"

"I don't."

"I understand. You still have control over the breakup, even though you're using our services."

"I'll read it before I head back to Baskin. For now, I'm really enjoying being here at my brother's wedding, with you."

I was enjoying myself, too. It was the most fun I had had in a really long time.

"Your parents look so adorable dancing together."

"Look who just passed them." Sammy pointed to the dance floor.

"Where exactly am I looking?"

"See the uncle in the white shirt with the red checks?"

I looked around and found the man next to Mr. Patel who Sammy was referring to.

"That's Jerry Uncle. Now look at Jerry Uncle's face."

I looked as closely as I could at the face, under dim lights and twenty feet away.

"His mustache. See how it's curled up at the ends?"

"Sammy!" I playfully hit him on his shoulder, as Jerry Uncle curled his mustache higher and higher each time he made a lap around the floor. "So what? It curls up."

"It's called art, Manny. The art of the perfect handlebar mustache. Cricket players and Bollywood actors and Jerry Uncle have spent hours upon hours on this masterpiece with

the help of the precise amount of wax, brushing, and the ulti-
mate twisting."

Sammy pretended to twist his nonexistent mustache.

"One day they'll be at an Indian handlebar mustache mu-
seum. Manny, I'm simply trying to give you a taste of *everything*
Indian. By the way, usually the groom and bride have separate
events, but Needa and Sanj combined everything so that the
families get to know each other. Most of the rest of the week will
be like tonight," he said, then added, "Kill two chirian with one
stone." He made wings with his hands.

"Ah, birds," I replied.

"That's Billa Uncle by the DJ booth. He's joined by one half
of my favorite matchmaking duo, Reena Auntie, off to the right,
just getting in. They're late. *Two hours* late, and their room is
right across the hall."

"Indian Standard Time," we both said at the same time.

"Look at you, Dogra!"

"Told you I was a quick student."

I hesitated and looked down at the huge pile of food on my
plate. The dancing earlier must have made me a lot hungrier
than I realized.

"Lisa and I met two years ago," Sammy said suddenly, his
tone somber.

"Yes?" I encouraged him. I had to admit, I was curious to hear
the story.

"I got myself into a terrible motorcycle accident, and she was
one of the nurses who took care of me."

"Sammy, I had no idea."

"She took care of me day and night. My parents were calling

repeatedly, and she made sure they weren't freaking out. My dad had just suffered a stroke the year before, and I didn't need to burden him with my stupid mistake of getting on a motorcycle in the rain. I had also taken on the family business expansion. She helped manage the business while I was on the mend."

I could certainly relate to that.

"She took care of everything for me and held everyone at bay so that Sanj could start planning his wedding and Dad could focus on getting better. And I didn't want Manisha flying all the way here and screwing up her new law practice."

I thought about what he said. More and more, I was seeing a totally different side of him than I had expected, to be honest, from that first view of him outside Rajiv's truck. I couldn't believe how selfless Sammy was, but yet I could.

"What about confiding in your mom, though?" I asked. Sometimes telling one parent is better than the other.

"My Jeh Uncle-ji died in a motorcycle accident a few years back. He was my mother's only brother. Her twin. She made me swear not to ever get back on a motorcycle."

Were those tears pooling in Sammy's eyes?

"Lisa spent all her time nursing me back to health, and, well, we eventually fell for each other. She made me realize what it felt like to be away from all this. That I could do my own thing without all the politics of a big Indian family."

"The politics, maybe. But what about all the family traditions that seem to put a smile on your face? Is that what you want, Sammy? To forever be away from Manisha and Sanjeev and your entire family?" I gestured to the party full of Patels. "They certainly wouldn't want that, would they? It'd break their hearts. And some of it's just tradition, so it isn't that important, is it?"

"Dated tradition," he replied. "Sure, Lisa doesn't want to be part of a big family; she doesn't want to be part of any of the rest of it, either. I may not have known that earlier, but I still owe her, you know. It's not her fault she's not into this." He looked at my outfit. "Any of it."

"So, no Indian couture for her?"

"I owe her my life, Manny. She's the reason I got through the weeks of pain and rehab and our family business didn't tank. She's probably the reason I'm here today. It's what she wants. And it's what she'll get. Let me just get through this week, Manny. Once Sanj has cleared the path for me, I'll just marry Lisa. Give her what she wants, and, well, my family will get over it eventually."

Just marry Lisa. I wondered why Adam hadn't *just* married me yet.

"Sammy!" I yelled. A couple of people at the next table looked over, so I lowered my voice. "Give her what she wants? So, limiting how often you see your family and the amount of love they have for you. You're just going to draw a line in the sand and say don't cross this to Manisha and Sanj and . . ."

"Boundaries are good, Manny. Patels could use some boundaries. Besides, like I said, I owe it to Lisa." He pushed his naan around his plate until it was too soggy to even eat.

"That was Lisa's job. To nurse you back to health. Your strength is how you survived and why you're here today. Your smart business skills are why the family business went international. The only thing you owe each other is the right to grow and go." With that I referenced one of our popular and often sold-out boot camps. "You both are on different paths now, and your priorities have shifted." I stopped for a moment. *Was I still talking about Sammy and Lisa?* "Look around you, Sammy. Everyone worships you. Manisha, Sanjeev . . . family is what you value. And it's all right if Lisa doesn't, but that doesn't mean you have to make your relationship with her work. She took care of you because she cared about you, yes, but sometimes the best care is also letting people go if they don't share the same beliefs as you do. No matter how much you think you may owe them." I grabbed Sammy's hand and placed it in mine as I brought it up to my heart. "A wise man once said to me, it's in here. It's what's in here that matters. Don't you want 'in here' to be the truth?"

Sammy stared at me. "Manny . . ."

The music faded into the background as the voices at the party became louder, but Sammy was the only person I could hear.

He put my hand back in my lap and turned the palm facing up. "Henna. You need to get henna done tomorrow. You can't be mehndi-free."

I took a breath. *Had I not been breathing?* "Yes. Henna," I said softly.

Perfect. *Temporary* body art, just like this week. *Temporary.*

Chapter 20

Dear Breakup,

Every single time I set up a date with a guy, I get all dressed up and ready to go, but just as I am about to walk out the door and meet him, my narcolepsy kicks in, and I fall asleep. Sometimes I'll wake up to a missed message and the guy is waiting on me to show up. What am I supposed to say? "I just got up from a nap. See you soon!" and drool?

Is this normal?

Maybe I'm just not ready to date after my bad breakup?

Joanna

I heard a voice behind me as I made my way into the lobby of the hotel. "Done for the night already?"

"Sanjeev! Congratulations. What an amazing party, I mean roka," I said with excitement.

"This was all Sammy and Manisha. Who could ask for better siblings, huh?" the obviously proud and happy younger brother said.

"They both did an amazing job."

"As amazing as your dance moves! You guys killed it out there!"

I felt my face turning red. This was Sanjeev's wedding, and I hadn't even asked him if it was all right to join the rest of the Patels onstage.

"Manisha asked me, and I couldn't say no. You know, it's Manisha, and she's so convincing—"

"Manny, those moves . . . it's like you're a born Patel."

I blushed more.

"Drink?" he asked.

"Ooh, I was going to retire early."

"Retire early? That's a good one." Sanjeev led the way to the lobby bar. He was the spitting image of Sammy, but you could tell he was younger. Both had their father's full head of curly hair, but Sammy had a few more grays. Although Sanjeev brushed his hair away when he talked to me, just like Sammy had.

He seemed nervous, and somehow, I was feeling anxious, too. Maybe Needa had told him her suspicions about our "business trip" after seeing me in the club's restroom.

"Can't wait to get out of this kurta later tonight. I still can't master the art of not sweating through these things," he added, loosening the collar on his long turquoise shirt.

"You and me both," I said, although part of me felt that I could have slept in my sari. I felt so proud to be in it.

We sat down at the bar.

"Two glasses of white, please. Let's do a chardonnay," he told the bartender. "I could use something drier with that spicy food I just took down. Or is there another wine you can recommend, since you're in the business?" Sanjeev asked me.

"A white chard this time of year is perfect," I answered, sounding like Mr. Jamieson.

That drink couldn't come soon enough.

"Thanks again for letting me wedding crash this week, Sanjeev. I spoke to Needa last night, and she's not only stunning but also graceful and intelligent. I really like her."

"She mentioned, too, that she got a few minutes alone with you. That's what I love about her, always going out of her way to get to know everyone around me. Her genuine curiosity and the effort she puts in with my family and friends. She's always showed up for me."

I thought back to the efforts I had made with the Jamiesons. Despite the dull, often unrelatable, and sometimes offensive conversations, I still always tried. And I always showed up. Between dinners, anniversary parties, and trips, I was girlfriend of the year. Too bad Adam never had time for Rob and Jay.

"And anything for my Sammy's business partner, right? I mean, that's what you are here for, business."

Was it my imagination, or did Sanjeev sound a little wary of Sammy and me being business partners?

"Manny, did he ever tell you the story about how Needa and I met?"

"No, but I'm curious."

"It was four years ago. Sammy and I had traveled to India to find some new stock for the family business. We used to do a lot of brother trips." Sanjeev fiddled with his wineglass.

"Brother trips. That sounds nice."

"We decided to stay in Mumbai and went out with a few family friends for dinner. I was talking to Sammy, when I looked across the room and there was Needa, sitting alone while her friends were dancing. I told Sammy I *needed* to talk to her. I was instantly drawn to her. So, Sammy did what any brother would do: he distracted her security guards so I could go over. Turns out her foot was in a cast. That's why she was sitting alone," he said. "For the next week, Sammy ended up doing most of the work on the trip, and I spent most of my time with Needa. I had fallen in love with her, and we decided that we wanted to spend the rest of our lives together. So we went to the local temple, and we got married after a week."

"What! You're already married?"

"Yup! We couldn't bear to be without each other and decided right then and there that we wanted to be committed to one another right away. So, what better way than getting married in India? Eventually she told her parents what we'd done, and I told mine. Now we're getting married again. She finished up design school in Mumbai, got her American visa, and now she's ready to take LA fashion by storm."

"Wow, that's incredible, Sanjeev. And her style is so impeccable. Count me in for a few Needa pieces when they hit the runway."

"Deal." Sanjeev smiled proudly.

"But what about Needa's parents and yours? How did everyone take the secret wedding news?"

"If anything, Needa's parents were more concerned about her moving to California. My family was simply happy for me. I think my mom was delighted. One of her sons was finally married. And this . . ." He looked around the hotel lobby. "Well, this is all for the moms." He chuckled, then fell silent. After a moment, he said, "You know, I have to say, when my brother mentioned he was bringing you, I found it a little strange."

"Oh, really?" I said, trying to sound surprised.

"I was just thinking, here I am about to marry the love of my life again, so why wouldn't my brother want to bring the love of his life?" He drained his glass and looked at me as if I had the answer to this question.

"Can I get you anything else?" the bartender swooped up to us and asked.

"No, thanks," Sanjeev replied quickly, and the bartender slid quietly away. "You know, Manny, we thought our older brother might want to bring his girlfriend, Lisa, to this wedding."

I suddenly missed those dull Jamieson conversations over the suspicious Sanj conversation that was going on now.

"I know Lisa has distanced us from Sammy over the last year. I used to talk to him every night and see him outside work, but these days, he doesn't answer most of my calls and he's not available to do anything outside work. The business is doing so great now, Sammy doesn't need to be *working* so much. The business is working on its own. I know he's just trying to keep . . ." Sanjeev hesitated. ". . . trying to keep Lisa a secret from all of us." He looked down as he lost eye contact with me.

Sammy's words popped into my head. *Secrets hurt people.*

Sanjeev's story also sounded all too familiar. I looked at my empty glass and spun it around as if this action would produce a few more drops.

Sanjeev looked at me with what I read as real sorrow in his eyes. "I miss my brother, Manny. I miss the Sammy who existed before he met Lisa. The guy who was first on the dance floor and last to leave a party, sure, but the brother who celebrated birthdays, anniversaries, and other family events with us."

I suddenly missed those things with my family, too. The things we did all together. I had a sudden urge to tell Sanjeev everything about Operation Indian, about the temporary breakup . . . but I couldn't do that to Sammy. I reminded myself he was my client.

"The way he looks at you, Manny. I want my brother to look at all of us like that again. To trust us, to know that we support him, like we did when he wanted to take the family business to the next level. We trusted him."

"The way he looks at *me*?"

"He trusts you. After all, you know about Lisa, and you're meeting us all for the first time but are keeping it a secret for my brother. That's trust."

Trust. I had forgotten what that felt like, what that even looked like with Adam anymore. It was more than just second-guessing leaving my laptop with Adam ever again; it was the calls from Derek that Adam declined in plain sight these days, and the Berlin project that had him so busy our wedding had no date in the near future. Losing my trust in Adam was not like the emails Breakup received about a cheating partner, an online catfish, or a client who watched her house being repossessed as her husband gambled it away; this lack of trust felt lonelier. After all, it was me and my relationship, and I couldn't distance myself from it.

"Sanjeev, I . . . I don't know what to say . . . I'm merely Sammy's business partner."

He finished the last sip of his drink.

"Yeah, business. You said."

"I'm sorry. I wish there was something more I could say or do, but Sammy loves Lisa and—"

"Does he?"

"What do you mean?"

"If he's *so* into her, why isn't she here?"

Sanjeev and I were on the same page. I had just interrogated Sammy with the same questions.

"But Sanjeev, wouldn't Needa's family disapprove of Lisa? Sammy mentioned how reputation and honor are the foundation of Needa's family. Bringing Lisa here and letting everyone know they're a couple could have ended your wedding before it even began. Add that to telling your own family! Maybe he wanted to wait for the right moment to tell you guys he was dating someone non-Indian. Maybe your big brother was protecting you?"

Sanjeev sighed. "You're right. But if Sammy absolutely loved Lisa, wouldn't he fight for her to be here? I would have fought for Needa if for some reason my parents had disapproved of our marriage. I mean, of course they want their children to marry someone who can relate to all this." He tugged at his kurta. "But that doesn't mean they would have disowned Sammy. Family loves you no matter what. That's the Patel motto."

He was making sense. Way too much sense.

"Why haven't you tried to tell him any of this?"

"I have tried, but getting any alone time with Sammy this past year has been next to impossible. And right now if all I get is work time with my brother, it's good enough for me. But I got a fooling it won't be for long." Sanjeev paused and took a look at me as he leaned back and crossed his arms over his chest. "Especially with you in his life. As his new biz partner, of course."

My mind was a whirl of questions. Or maybe it was just the wine. Everyone was doing what they thought they should do. Only Sanjeev and Needa were doing what they actually wanted to do. Well, Manisha, too, I guessed. She didn't seem the type to let duty interfere with her desires. So, what about me? What did I want?

"I should probably head back into the party before my fiancée and our guests wonder where I am," Sanjeev said. "But before I go, Manny, can I ask you something else?"

"Of course." Like I had any place to hide right now.

"Why are *you* here? Don't you think there are loud whispers about my brother's 'business partner'?"

A little shock wave ran through me, and I looked everywhere but at Sanjeev, who suddenly got up, turned around, and hugged me.

"Love doesn't pull you away from your family, Manny. Love is family. But you only really get one Patel family per lifetime. Even if there are over a hundred of us in one family."

"A hundred . . . that's it?" I teased Sanjeev as I hugged him back.

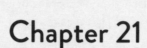

Chapter 21

Dear Breakup,

I wish I could afford your services, but I can't because they're so expensive! I guess my girlfriend, who refuses to take the hint that I have broken up with her at least a dozen times, will continue to be my girlfriend. I hope you guys are happy.

Not so rich,
Rich

I plopped down on the plush hotel bed, my mind a whirl of triumph and agitation. Just last week my life was predictable. I had a good sense of the shape of each day. I knew what to expect. So what if my relationship with Adam existed for the time being mainly through my iPhone, computer screen, and the occasional impersonal yet functional present? These days most relationships followed some sort of unorthodox formula. Didn't they?

That was a hard question and one that deserved an answer. Maybe—

Buzzzz.

Phew. Saved by the bell.

I answered my phone.

"Manny? Is that you? Wow, you look gorgeous! One second, let me patch in Rob."

The two of them crowded together on-screen, my very own double-trouble.

"Mannnny," Rob stretched out my name as he said it, "you are giving Padma Lakshmi a run for her money."

"How do you even know who Padma is?"

"Two things I know in life. Numbers and food. Padma makes a lot of money making delicious food."

"She's also a super-hot entrepreneur," Anjali added.

"As a very gay man, I will agree with that. The woman could make any apron look sexy."

"Okay, I am never wearing an apron again with your tongue wagging like that."

"What a most glamorous outfit. You managed to outdo the last one!" Anjali's eyes went wide.

"Isn't this beautiful? I couldn't have done any of this without the help of your cousin."

"I told you, Aliyan is extraordinary," Anjali said. "How's everything going out there?"

"Sammy's sister asked me to be part of their dance routine for the roka. You know, the engagement party."

"You mean dance in front of people? Live? As in bhangra?" I could see Anjali squirming at the thought.

"Yes, bhangra! Stop making that face. I practiced for a few hours, and Aliyan showed me how to 'have sex with the air.'"

"Wait, what? You had air sex?" Rob said, his interest in the conversation renewed.

"No! I mean he showed me how to make my hips look sexy while I'm dancing. Which is so much harder than it looks, Anjali."

"Sounds like my hero. I need to meet this guy," Rob said suggestively.

"So, let me get this straight, you got up in front of a bunch of uncles and aunties and did a Bollywood number?" Anjali asked. "Those aunties must have been all over you for your biodata."

"What's biodata?" Rob asked.

"It's what those auntie matchmakers collect to set you up with potential matches."

"Like a bio on any other app?" Rob questioned.

"Yes, except it's a bit more intrusive. Details on your height, skin tone . . ." Anjali said "skin tone" quickly, probably not wanting to conjure up Photoshop memories for me. " . . . salary and even weight."

"Damn. Now *that* is a Breakup business we need to get our hands on," Rob said. "Imagine an email to find out your 'biodata' was rejected because of your height. That's one hell of a Breakup from a matchmaker!"

"Rob, we are not selling this package, no matter how lucrative it sounds." I cracked up at the thought of having Reena Auntie as a client.

"Clearly you're in great spirits, Manny. Must be all that dancing?"

"Sammy loved my dancing. He was proud of me and smiling a lot."

"Like the big smile you have on your face right now?"

"Yeah . . . I mean, back to business! It's been a family affair over here. I spent some time with Sanjeev, Sammy's brother. Turns out, he already knows about Lisa!"

"No way!"

"Manny, are you serious?"

The phone lit up with two shocked faces.

"Yeah, and despite what Sammy thinks, no one would have a problem with it. Sanjeev said the Patel motto is family is love . . . or something like that."

"Wow!" Anjali paused. "Are you going to have Sammy read the email from today?"

"Not right now. I am going to let him focus on the wedding. That's the priority. His family has only seen work Sammy in the last year. They're finally getting a taste of the old Sammy before Lisa came along. I want to let them enjoy that for a bit longer. Any other updates on Lisa? Just in case Sammy asks?"

They were eerily silent. I checked to see if I had accidently hit Mute, but I heard Rob chomp on a slice of pizza, and I knew I hadn't.

"Anjali? Since Rob is busy right now."

"Manny . . ." Anjali looked at Rob with pleading eyes, but his mouth was full, and for once he couldn't say anything. "Manny, I don't know how to tell you this . . ."

"Tell me what?" I insisted.

"Manny, Lisa emailed Breakup last night asking for help in

calling it off with Sammy . . . permanently, not a break," Anjali finally spit out. "She didn't open our email. We had IT trace it back. Manny, I don't think she's going to open an email or take a call from Sammy ever again."

"What? Why would you say that? Tell me what happened. *Everything*."

"CliffsNotes. It's over for our man Sam." Rob had finally swallowed. "Lisa has moved on to someone else."

"Someone else?" I shouted into the phone. "Who?"

"No idea. And no, she didn't mention our email, she just went straight for the jugular," Rob continued. "And it gets worse."

"How the hell could it get worse from here?"

"I took a little stroll down Cheater's Lane, and Lisa had a moving van at the house this morning, filled with boxes and boxes and boxes. Honestly, I'd be surprised if she left a light bulb," Rob said.

Poor Sammy. This was going to crush him.

"I was camped outside for about thirty minutes," Rob went on. "I left when she put her key under the welcome mat, and then she and the new guy drove off into the sunset."

There's irony for you.

"She wanted to do this fast," Anjali stepped in.

"It's like she had the whole thing planned." Rob took another huge bite of pizza.

"I have to tell Sammy. I need to get him to myself . . ."

"To yourself, huh . . ." Rob managed to mumble. I got the feeling that he was about to make another alone-with-Sammy joke, but then thought better of it.

"Miss you, Manny," Anjali said.

"Miss you guys, too," I said, ending the call. I thought about what Sanjeev had said. I did miss them. *Like family*.

Except this was business, and I wasn't taking care of it. All this dancing and socializing was all very well, but . . . I had to put up some boundaries. I was getting lost in someone else's wedding, someone else's life. I had to fix this whole mess with Sammy—but first there was something else I had to do.

I called Adam.

"Baby . . ."

"Adam, I . . ."

"I was thinking about you."

"Really? That's good to know," I said.

"I'm always thinking of you, babe. Even when you storm out of our house. You know that, don't you?"

Did I?

"How is work out there? New client?"

I ignored the question. "Adam, all this week I've been think-ing about us getting married. Can we please set a final date? I have to have something to look forward to."

"A date?"

"Yes. Like a month and a day. You know, a *date*." We'd set dates before, but had always had to change them when some-thing else more important came up.

"Now? I'll be home in a week, and we can sit down and set the date with our calendars in front of us."

"Adam, who would be your best man?"

"I don't know. I haven't thought that far ahead. I'll pick some-one."

"How about your brother?"

"That's a definite maybe," he said. "You look really dressed up, Manny. What are you wearing?"

I looked down at my sari.

"I was invited to an Indian party . . . for . . . work." Even my lies were about work.

"And your makeup? You really don't look like yourself."

"Seriously, Adam, what does that even mean? Are there too many colors on this canvas for you to see?"

"I thought you'd let that go," he said. "Are you planning on bringing it up every single time we end up talking? Grow up, Manny."

"*Grow up?* Did you just tell me to GROW UP?" I shouted, much louder than I ever thought I was capable of.

"Yeah. That's what I said. I come home for one night and you go apeshit over a misunderstanding and take off for the night. And now you went from asking me to pick a wedding date to bringing up that stupid cover again. You were busy. I was trying to help. That's what fiancés do."

"Help? Are you kidding me? Helping me by making me look like a whole new freakin' person. Or are you just spending so much time traveling that you have actually forgotten what your fiancée looks like? And you know, it is not like you picked up your phone and called me, let alone chased after me."

"Come on, Manny. You have really lost your sense of cool lately. You want me to chase after you? I was tired from the long flight. I had work emails to get through. What the hell is going on with you, anyway? You seem to be pushing buttons just to pick a fight lately."

"No way! If I am pushing buttons it's to get something more out of you than work. Like . . . like sending Derek a message back."

"More than work? Why? We make a great team. That's why I love you. We *work* well together."

"That's why you love me? My work ethic?"

"No, I mean that is part of it, yeah, but no . . ." Adam struggled to find words that he didn't have. "What else do you want from me? This is who I am. I am never going to stop working. Just like you haven't stopped working since the day I met you."

"I had to because my parents died. I had to stop thinking about them all the time. I am more than just work, Adam. They were more than just work."

"They *were*, Manny. They aren't here anymore."

"So?"

"Look, this is taking a turn for the worse. All I am trying to say is, the more you focus on work, the less time you have to think about family and to reme—"

". . . to remember?" I didn't want to finish his sentence, but I did. "If I am not going to remember them, who will?" I asked.

"Maybe it's time to . . ."

"Don't you dare say it, Adam . . . don't you fucking say it . . ." I *trusted* that Adam wouldn't dare say it.

"Look, maybe they just need a folder for *our* shared inbox. You know, we can remember them when we've cleared out our other emails first."

And just like that, Adam compared my grief to clearing his inbox.

Suddenly I wished I had set an out-of-office alert before I made this call.

"Good night, Adam," I said and hung up.

Chapter 22

Dear Breakup,

I'm dating a loving, kind, and generous man. Most women would fall for not only his good looks and warm heart, but also his commitment to his family. The problem is, I can't seem to commit to any of that. I can't stand the idea of being with someone who needs to spend that much time with his family and wants to have kids of his own. I need your help breaking up with Sammy. I want to move on with someone else. In fact, I already have.

Lisa

No way could I let Sammy be ambushed by returning to an empty house. I sent him a text to see if he wanted to join me later in the day for a walk around Marble. I figured this kind of news was better done offsite in case an unpredictable Sammy came out again. After all, it was a matter of the heart. Just because it was a new day in Marble didn't guarantee the old Sammy might not make a return.

He was slow to respond. Knowing how the Patels loved to party, there was a good chance he was still in bed after a late night. I put on my robe and walked into the living room.

"Good morning, sunshine." A bright voice filled the room, and I screamed. As in, slasher film screamed.

"Oh, Aliyan," I said, recovering when I saw his smiling face. "Okay, new rule. Don't scare the living daylights out of me! For goodness' sake . . ."

Poor guy. He started pouring himself a drink.

"I forgot about the spare key." I rubbed my eyes. "How long have you—"

He looked at his watch. "About five minutes, honey. I snuck in while you were snoring away in your little Desi dreams. That must have been one hell of a sapna. You look a little garam and sweaty." Aliyan fake fanned himself down.

More like irritated and annoyed.

"I know it's early, but I need a strong one of these. How about you?"

My conversation with Adam trickled back into my consciousness. A stiff drink did sound good right about now.

"Honey, like I always say, it's Aliyan o'clock somewhere. Like wine o'clock, but *my* cocktails don't come cheap. By the way, I ordered breakfast," he said, gesturing to the table. "Eggs, fruit, but ban the bread. You've gotten plenty of naan all week."

"Don't worry. I've been dancing it off."

"I know," he said. "I've been sneaking into the parties, spying from the back. Like Bond, Aliyan Bond," he said in the closest thing to a Sean Connery voice he could manage.

"You have?"

"Like a proud drag mama. You're something else, Manny, hiding all that sexy back. You've got some moves. Here I thought you were some plain aloo paratha wrapped up in a gorgeous body just going to waste, but my gawd, girl, you are the mooli paratha of all parathas. You're everyone's favorite girl, we just never give it the credit it deserves."

"I'm a horseradish?" I asked, puzzled.

"Minus all that gas and bloating. What I am trying to say is that you are a gem!"

I made my way over to the breakfast table, helping myself to the buffet of breakfast fruits.

"Thank you, Aliyan. I mean, thanks for showing me what I can and cannot do."

"There is nothing you cannot do! And that is why I brought this!" Aliyan held out a studded black garment bag. I got the feeling a lot of things in his life were beaded. "One of my clients ended her engagement after she found out her fiancé was sleeping with one of the bridesmaids. Long and boring story because it doesn't include me, so I'll cut to the exciting end where you get to wear her custom Indian dress!" he squealed.

"I thought you picked something already?"

"I did, Mintu, but that was a couple of days ago, and today is today. Out with the old and in with the new! Squeeeeee!"

"Can I see?"

"Hands away!" he exclaimed. "I can't wait for you to wear this! But it's staying in here until the very last moment." He placed the large garment bag on the gold rack next to him. "And no peeking until the girls bring over the matching jewelry."

"Thank you so much, Aliyan," I said. "You've been very kind to step in here like this. You're worth your weight in gold."

"Gold, Mintu? No, no, no! At the very least diamonds are Aliyan's best boyfriend," he said, and pretended to toss back his hair.

"Oh, shoot! What is wrong with me?" I looked around the room, wondering where I'd dropped my purse. "Here you've been doing all this work, and I haven't paid you a dime. Please, tell me what I owe you for everything you have done for me so far?"

"Money? Oh, puh-lease. Let's not talk about something as vulgar as money." He waved a finger in the air, pretending to be disgusted.

"There's nothing vulgar about being paid for your services," I said, sincerely. "As a business owner myself, I know how hard it can be to accept your own value."

The pretend hair toss again. "Oh, I know my worth. Believe me," he said, sitting on the ottoman in front of me as I started to pick at the fruit. "I've worked with everyone. You name the diva, and I have suited her up. Freida Pinto, Archie Panjabi, Elizabeth Hurley—"

"Elizabeth Hurley?"

"You know she was married to an Indian man. The girl thinks she's got automatic Indian divatude!"

I laughed, thinking back to Hurley's time with Hugh Grant and the infamous scandal that rocked the celebrity world. A messy case. Breakup wouldn't have gone near it.

"You, though . . ." He leaned in and touched my knee. "There's something magical about you, Manny. The way your face beams when you try on all these garments. You're like a gay man drinking his first cosmo at a gay bar in the face of an unsupportive auntie. It's as if you're coming home to yourself at long last."

I didn't know whether to hug him or ask for a cosmo.

"You know," he continued, "when I came out a few years ago, Anjali was the only one who supported me. She was advocating for me at every function our family had. None of those aunties and uncles wanted anything to do with me." He pushed a hand past me as if to illustrate that's what they had done to him. "Shortly after that, I stopped receiving invites to family weddings, birthdays, parties—you name it. They all got 'lost in the mail.' But I knew better, and so did Anjali. Instead of attending the events, she'd always come to my bachelor pad. We'd have our own little party. When she told me that all you wanted to do was fit in and find your inner Indian, I thought, *That's all I've been trying to do for the last few years*. I wanted my family to accept me for who I am. I may not ever get that, but you, Manny, this is your chance to show everyone who you are. And girl, do it for you and do it for me!" He clinked his glass against mine.

"Aliyan, I know I couldn't get through this week without you. And one day, if I get married, you'll be there. I promise."

"*If* you get married. Has something changed?"

"No, no, I meant if I get married next summer. We may move the date sooner or later . . . that's what I meant."

"Mintu . . ." He became serious. "The best advice I ever got, which I will give you whether you want it or not, is, 'Only you know who you are, and no one else can change that about you.' No matter who you end up looking like on a magazine cover."

Not the cover again!

"How did you know about that?"

"Oh, honey, look at me. I am the queen of content. I know who is on what magazine on any given day! That cover looks nothing like the beautiful Indian woman who is here today. That cover is some whitewashed exec who has no pizzazz. Generic, no color! You are a freakin' rainbow of color! Do you hear me?"

"Yes," I managed to say as tears welled up in my eyes and Aliyan wrapped his arms around me tightly.

"Don't you ruin the morning with an ugly cry," he said. "That drink I made you doesn't need any extra ingredients, you feel me? Come here." He brought me in front of the long hallway mirror and stood behind me.

"Look at that nose—we both have that little bend in our noses. And your glistening brown skin and this wavy thick dark hair that shows off your glowing oval face. Of course you are Indian—your yellow undertones and those dark circles under your eyes are INDIAN all the way!" He chuckled. "Remind me to get you some eye masks tonight.

"Manny, your parents raised a royal princess worthy of any Roshan, Khan, or Singh—especially Ranveer. Yummy." Aliyan's hips softly swayed as he listed his favorite hunky Bollywood stars.

"Your face shouts *proud* as soon as you walk into a room. There is no doubt in anyone's mind that you are a lioness. Say it with me?" And with that, Aliyan roared for good measure. "Lioness?" he growled again, grabbing his phone.

"Lioness," I shouted back.

"I can't hear you, girl. Not over KP roarin'." He cued the music and started playing the chorus of Katy Perry's "Roar."

"I am a proud lioness," I roared back and started dancing with him.

Chapter 23

Dear Breakup,

Can you be friends with an ex if you still have feelings for him?

I'd like to be friends with my ex-boyfriend, but I'm hoping we'll get back together if we spend time together. Can Breakup coach me into getting back my ex as a friend first before I work on getting him back as a boyfriend? You must have a Breakup boot camp for that?

Jien

My thoughts turned to Baskin as I wondered again how Laura and Jake Jamieson would react if, all of a sudden, I roared and insisted on having a Patel-style wedding, with all the Aliyan beads/bells and Manisha whistles. I could just see the looks on their faces, questioning where I had learned such *unsophisticated* behavior as my bhangra.

Rajiv had told me that his own wedding celebration ended up spilling onto the street in his small town. Apparently that was common in India. Even the neighbors who weren't invited and ultimately crashed the party were welcomed by Rajiv's family. "With arms open!" he told me. "Everyone comes to this wedding, you know. It was the most joyous occasion for everyone, no matter who you are. Then we did the fireworks and the whole sky light up." His face itself lit up at the memory.

Rajiv often talked about his wedding. He had a large picture mounted on the inside of Aja Raja of himself holding his wife Rajna's hand. "Manny, this is no! Touching, no, no!" He waved one finger and pointed to the secrecy of the two of them holding hands under her beautifully laced red sari. "But I am romantic man. Mr. Romance. I sneak in and say *snap, snap* to photographer, and now we have this picture."

I looked through the photos on my phone of the last twenty-four hours. Rajiv was right, there was limited intimacy. But I could see the love in everyone's eyes. It was important for me to believe that people did still really love each other. I *loved* working at Breakup. I was beyond proud of my team. But maybe all the emails, phone calls, and pleas for help had left me a little faint of heart when it came to thinking about loving relationships.

My laptop indicated a video call coming in. I answered it.

"Rob, if this is a call to try to convince me to give in to filming a behind-the-scenes reality show at Breakup, my answer is still no. This is not going to be an office version of *The Hills*."

"Geez, Manny. I was just joking around. Remember the word F-U-N? Something you used to have when we talked about how cute we thought Brody Jenner was."

"Sorry. I am really sorry. I miss you guys so much. Being out here has made me realize just how much you and the team mean to me and have meant to me. I think I am just upset with Adam right now." *Again.*

"What happened?"

"Rob, do I ever talk about my parents with you?"

He hesitated as he shuffled some papers on his desk.

"Manny, you don't, and Jay and I don't push it. We kinda figured when you chose a steak dinner over your mom's passing anniversary that it was best we let you deal with the grief on your own."

I stared blankly into the screen.

"It's kinda become your thing. To work, and work and work and do more work with Adam, and over time I guess Jay and I figured we didn't want to step on any toes."

"You know what, I think the Breakup boot camps, new closure packages, writing Breakup emails from dawn till dusk . . . haven't left me with much time to communicate with anyone."

"Yeah, these things happen," he said unconvincingly. "Speaking of emails, listen to the one I got this morning—it was from a guy wondering if we could fake an email to his girlfriend to see if we could tempt her to cheat. This shit can be a lot, Manny."

"This *shit* pays for your apartment by the water and your Range Rover, so let's keep the shit coming," I said.

"Press release words from our CEO," Rob said, as he raised his hand in mock surrender. "I just wanted to check in to see how my BFF is doing?" He had turned serious.

"I haven't really had time to think about how I'm doing. I just know that I have never had so much fun and excitement with this much family since . . ."

"Since our trip to Florida with *our* families?"

"That was such a great time!" I thought back to our hilarious vacation with our parents.

"Your mom actually had her first drink that weekend."

"And her second and third and fourth and—"

"Yeah," Rob cut in, "she discovered her passion for screwdrivers, that's for sure."

"'Who knew orange juice could taste this delicious' were her exact words. You know, she ended up telling me about the love of her life on that trip? Dad had already gone to bed. After you and your parents headed back to the cottage, it was just Mom and me, and she looked over and said, 'I was once in love, too, Manny, but that was a long time ago. Not like dating now. You and Rob and the families hanging out. That's not how it worked in India.'"

"Did she ever tell you about the other man?"

"She met him at the local library, and they bonded instantly over books. 'I would sneak away in the afternoon when I knew my nani was about to take her afternoon nap,' she said. 'He would be waiting for me with armfuls of books he had picked out just for me.' She loved reading."

"Is that why your home was filled with more bookshelves than bare walls?"

"I think it reminded her of the library. The smell of the books, the notes that students had written in the pages of the overused novels. It was the only real reminder she had. She also told me that loving my dad was different. 'It's a circumstantial kind of love, sweetheart. I had to *learn* to love. *Falling* in love, when you get to choose it, makes you feel so full, you can hear love in your heart.'"

"That's how I feel about Jay. Sure, my song changes every week, but I get what your mom was saying. That's so sweet—"

"And heartbreaking?" I finished Rob's sentence. "The last time she saw him, he gave her this necklace." I touched the necklace around my neck.

"See, Manny, like I said, that probably explains why your parents never spoke about the dreaded past, doesn't it?"

"But it doesn't explain keeping things from me. Sammy told me they used to donate money to the Baskin Indian Community Center. Why didn't they tell me that?"

"Because it wouldn't have ended there. You would have asked to go with them and had so many other questions and—"

"And it was too painful for them." What Rob said was true, and it was all starting to make sense. "They weren't just trying to protect me from all the answers they couldn't give me, they were also trying to move on from that life in India that my mother had had."

"It's all so tragic. But they loved you so much." Rob suddenly seemed even farther away.

"My mother and I never spoke about any of it again, until her last night in the hospital. She told me that all the letters they had written to each other and exchanged in the library were hidden in a box back at our house. Rob, I went and read every single one. I don't think my mother ever got over losing this man."

"I can understand wanting to bury the pain of a lost love," he sighed, knowing what it was like to bury his own heartbreak. "Manny, you have to tell Sammy about Lisa." The story must have reminded him why I was really in Marble.

"I know," I assured him, "but he feels like he owes Lisa his life."

"What do you mean?"

I told Rob about Sammy's accident and how Lisa had nursed him back to health and helped him with work.

Rob drew in a breath, then looked straight into his screen. "Is this something you can relate to?"

"Why would you say that?"

"I . . . Jay and I . . . we sometimes wonder if you stay with Adam because you feel guilty and can't leave because he's been there for you since . . . the accident. You never really see him as much as you'd like, he doesn't seem to get *you*. And this past week, I feel like I've seen you be yourself more with Sammy than ever before. You seem excited talking about Sammy and what's happening in Marble. And you know I missed this Manny."

"Work is happening in Marble and I'm still the same Manny."

Was I?

"Sammy is a client. I am just excited for the client. I guess I am just on?"

"Turned on?"

"Rob!"

"Come on! That was easy! Look, all I am saying is this permanent smile you have on your face for this client, are you sure it's because he's a client?"

"Rob, you're being impossible." Suddenly the hot room felt like it needed a cold blast from the air conditioner.

"Well, maybe it's the Marble sun, but BBB has a triple-threat glow."

"The glow is because I'm also away from the office and you," I shot back.

"Look, I don't want to step out of line here, Manny, but as your gay ex-boyfriend and current CFO, I think the company forecast looks really bright."

I had a feeling Rob wasn't talking numbers anymore.

Chapter 24

Dear Breakup,

We have a strict "no dating coworkers" policy at work. But I've spent many long hours with Jon on the marketing team and have fallen in love with him. I really want to tell him how I feel. However, I am up for a promotion, which would make me Jon's boss. Can you help me fire Jon so we can be together??

Sandy

How many banquet rooms did this place have? Master Hall had been turned into a combination of hotel opulence and food truck kitsch. Strings of orchids and daisies draped the doors, which opened to an elegantly lit room infused with incense, candles, and exotic flowers. Bollywood music filled the air—Rajiv would love it here—and those women not waiting for a turn with the henna artists were dancing in the center of the room. In the middle of the stage, framed by a fiery orange-and-red backdrop, was Needa, being attended to by her own dedicated artist, who I was sure the maharajas had flown in from India. Perched under a trellised mandap adorned with lush foliage and pops of pink, white, and baby blues, she was—there were no other words for it—queen of the castle.

"Messy times call for undressy times," Sammy said as we slipped past guests into the busy room. "Although I feel like all Indian wedding garments are dressy. What do you think, Manny? Even the simple garments don't look simple, do they?"

I nodded, enthralled by the music, the scents, and the joyous camaraderie of these beautiful women.

"Hello? Earth to Manny? You ready for this?" Sammy waved a hand in front of my face.

"Yup, I am! Sammy, do you think we can talk after?"

"Yeah, sure, plenty of time to—" he started.

"There you are!" Manisha rushed over and hugged me and Sammy, and then extended her arm to reveal the most intricate henna art I had ever seen. And by "seen," I meant on social media.

"You're next," Manisha said, tugging me toward the mehndi table.

"I'll be with those guys," Sammy said, pointing to a large group of men gathered by the bar. "This is where the guys take a step back to have their own good time."

I watched as he headed over to his cousins, one of whom handed him a drink. There was loud laughter. Back slapping. Genuine affection. I could tell Sammy was respected. He was loved.

Manisha said, "Go for it. I'll be back in a flash," and vanished behind me as I took a seat and rolled up my loose sleeves. Thanks to Aliyan, I knew that the henna designs would crawl up my hands and onto my arms.

"What design would you like? More modern or traditional?" the artist asked.

"I . . . well . . . I'm not sure? How about . . . umm . . . this one?" I pointed to a stencil, and she got to work right away.

"He's so good-looking," a voice beside me said.

"Excuse me?" I turned to face a woman around my age sitting next to me. I didn't recognize her as part of the Patel family.

"Sammy! What I wouldn't do to have him marry me." She faked a shiver up and down her body. "I want to run my hands through that thick hair of his."

"Oh," I said, feeling violated for Sammy as she then licked her lips.

"Unless he's dating you?"

Wow. If looks could kill.

"They're business partners, Tina," Manisha said as she returned, nibbling on a sweet something she had found at the buffet that the hotel staff had just brought out. "Stop talking about my brother like he's a piece of meat at your father's deli."

"Whatever, Manisha. I've got to fend for myself. The population of Indian men in the US is at its lowest in years."

"It is?" I asked, surprised.

"Don't listen to Ms. Gupashap, Manny." Manisha plunked herself on a cushion on the floor in between us both, her big behind shoving Tina to the side—I assumed on purpose. "Ms. Gossip is her real name. She's also just hungry to get her hands on a husband. As if my brother would *ever* date someone like you."

"What the hell are you trying to say, Manisha Patel?"

The gloves were coming off.

"Well, we all know you have a flavor of the week. Last month it was Bobby, then Pramod and . . ." Manisha searched the room. ". . . and didn't you also try to get your hands on the newly divorced Nader Uncle?"

"Manisha, you're so disgusting. The things that come out of your filthy mouth."

"And the things that go into yours," Manisha whispered to me, and then said out loud, "Stop getting so worked up, Tina. I just came to sit down with my friend Manny, who happened to be getting the daily *Eye on Asia* breaking news from you."

"You're annoying, Manisha." Tina got up and left in a huff.

"Well, if she stopped drooling over my brother, I would stop being annoying. As if I want her as a sister-in-law anyway."

I smiled at Manisha. "Thanks for saving me."

"My brother has been in such a good mood over the last few days. I haven't gotten to see him much lately. Of course, me living all the way in London doesn't help, but I swear I have never seen him smile so much. He's always been so sweet, though; I am sure you already know this. There were days in law school I would be stressed, not sure I could keep up, and Sammy would talk me through all of it, staying up until all hours of the night."

Everyone seemed to agree that Sammy was really missed by his family, which made me think of the first time Rajiv and I met him and how I didn't miss his attitude at all. That fiery Sammy, spitting love angst like some teenage song, was now the smiling, loving, caring Sammy he always had been before he met Lisa.

By the time I was done with the henna, it was almost eleven

p.m. The brown paste had dried on my arms, hands, and palms, and it had flaked off, leaving a breathtaking design of yellowish orange and revealing yet another layer of Indian Manny.

"It always smells so horrible, but give it a few more hours," Manisha said, sneaking up behind me.

"Of course, yeah. The outcome is so worth that smell of, umm . . . hay grass, right?"

"Let me see," she demanded as she crouched next to me. "Oooh, did you ask for the butterflies?"

"I did." When I picked the design, I had thought back to a picture I'd seen of my mother in mehndi when she was a teenager, her palms decorated with small butterflies.

"Cool. Rebirth and change. I like it. It will be even more beautiful once the color settles." Manisha got up and headed to the bar.

"That's what the butterflies represent, my dear. A change. A change within you," the henna artist said.

She was right. I was the butterfly who had gotten my own bright new wings and was now shimmering with gorgeous colors.

I found Sammy loitering at the bar with a couple of cousins in a corner. "So, what do you think?" I asked, showing off my arms.

"I think you can check an official mehndi experience off your list," he replied.

"Have you been here drinking the whole time?"

"Don't be judgy, Dogra. Dodging auntie setups isn't easy."

I could tell he was a little drunk.

"Bhishma Auntie cornered me just a few minutes ago, threatening that if I didn't get on the train, it would be leaving without me." He laughed. "The train is her daughter."

"You are an auntie magnet." I laughed, too.

"And behind you, Raja Uncle offered me a large incentive to marry his daughter."

"Money?" I was shocked.

"A wing in their family mansion. He wants to make sure we all live together."

"I can't keep up with all these setups—or all these Patels, for that matter," I joked. I was exhausted and ready for bed.

"Warned ya." He peered at me. "You're tired. Let me walk you back to your room."

Great. This would be the perfect time to tell him about Lisa even if I was about to break client confidentiality, but this client was now a friend.

We left the ballroom and meandered down the hall.

"Check this out. This is where Sanj and Needa will be getting married." Sammy opened the door to yet another ballroom, this one with a large skylighted ceiling with moonlight streaming through. "Over here," he said. We followed a winding path through the small tables in the room, then looked up at the radiant sky full of stars.

"It's incredible."

"Well, when you come to enough Patel weddings in Marble, you make some magical discoveries," he said, turning to me, and I caught that same magic, but in his eyes. "That includes you."

I just stood there, caught off guard and silent, all thoughts of Lisa fluttering out of my mind. My heart was beating fast, and my mind was racing to catch up as I stared at Sammy.

I shook my head and looked back up at the stars.

"I know this trip hasn't been easy for you, Manny. I hope you found what you were looking for."

A few of the stars seemed to twinkle.

"Growing up, my father used to sit with me on our back porch as we stared into the sky and remind me that there is always someone out there looking at the same stars.

"I think your mother and father are out there looking at you right now, Manny, and just how beautiful, kind, and courageous—"

"Courageous or just kinda dumb to think I could learn how to do all this in a week."

"I'm still learning, Manny. That's the best part. There is nothing *planned* about it." He paused. "You know, every time you speak about your late parents, you light up."

Suddenly it felt like someone had punched me in the stomach. Adam had said those same words to me, but about work. But how could I have that same light for work and my parents?

"You've got this inner beam in you, but this outer light . . . boy, is it bright. I bet your parents had that same glow as you, Manny. Don't ever forget that, or them. If you're not going to talk about them, who will?"

No one, I thought. No one had been talking about them for a long time. I looked back at the two stars twinkling right before my eyes.

I had never forgotten about them. But lately, I had remembered out loud.

Chapter 25

Dear Breakup,

My best friend's boyfriend has confided in me about their rocky relationship. It's been months of me offering advice to him about what to do. Now I've realized that I've secretly been sabotaging their relationship with bad advice because I've started to fall for him. How do I tell him that I did a bad thing but am a good person, and that he should be with me?

Courtney

I still hadn't told Sammy about Lisa. Last night I'd found myself with a sky that was lit up just for him and me, not one that I thought should be darkened with a thunderous Lisa cloud rolling in. This entire trip, all I had heard from Sammy's family was how happy he'd been over the course of the week. Telling him Lisa had left him nothing more than a key and possibly a dried-up houseplant would kill him. But the team was right: whether you were crushed, lying on the floor of your living room and listening to Lana Del Ray, or eating M&Ms for days, this was our job. *Sammy* was a job. My job.

I would do it today, I resolved. No time like the present and all that. I'd see what Sammy had planned for us, and then work out the best way to tell him the truth. Nothing but the truth.

He was waiting for me in the lobby. Same charm chatting with the staff, same smile, same sockless Sammy.

"Where to, client?" I said. Best to keep it laid-back and remind him why we were here.

"Client. Right. Taking you to Little India to continue our . . . contract."

"Again? But I already have enough clothes!"

"No, we're going to celebrate Diwali. It's a weeklong celebration in Marble! Great way for the Little India small business owners to make some money, with it being tourist season. This time I am taking you to the West Side, Dogra. West Side Little India Dogra." He said, attempting to make a *W* with three fingers.

"But didn't Diwali end a few days ago?"

"Manny. What did we talk about?"

"Indian Standard Time." I chuckled.

"Yes! So let's go give those people some business and spend some of your money," he joked.

Little India had been transformed into an outdoor party, complete with pop-up food trucks that would give Aja Raja a run for its money. The Samosa Suite and Kulfi 'n' Kreme were busy serving up all kinds of delicious food. Flavored dosas and rich ras malai filled the mouths of hungry adults and children as they crowded around, dancing to the Indian hip-hop that echoed out of a large truck. A young DJ seemed to have taken the reins, so the music was a mix of what Sammy told me were popular beats by artists like Fateh and Mickey Singh.

But it didn't seem to matter what race you were or what you were wearing. Everyone was celebrating. Aunties and uncles were dancing in the street. Children were playing mini games of cricket and golf and guessing a large elephant's weight—any opportunity to take home an oversize plush stuffed toy. Others were learning to bead bangles, having their faces painted, or watching mimes put on a magic show.

"Wow, it's like a huge party!" I said. Ibiza, except it was open to all ages.

"Come here; I want you to try some paan."

"It's a leaf, Sammy!"

"Dogra, do you trust me?"

I did, wishing he could say the same about me.

"It's more than that," he continued, noting that the green leaves were filled with all kinds of ingredients, including masala with dashes of nutmeg and fennel seeds. He reached for one and said, "Open up."

I obeyed, and he popped the delicious treat in my mouth. The savory mild spices of paprika and bay leaves filled it with a taste I had never experienced before.

"Mmm. Delicious."

"Good. There's more where that came from."

We spent the next few hours eating chana bhatura and jalebis, and drinking mango lassis. I could just imagine Aliyan shaking his head at my carb overload. Every once in a while, Sammy would tell me we needed to work it off, so we would jump into one of the impromptu dance circles in the middle of the street, Sammy's smile as wide as his hands in the air as he danced. We didn't care who was watching because the truth was, no one was. Everyone was celebrating the Indian new year in the most optimistic and colorful way. People were throwing powdered paint at each other, bright reds and greens symbolizing love and fertility and new beginnings.

Sammy threw some red powder at me. "They usually save this stuff for Holi. The festival of spring or the festival of love."

"Are you trying to cast a love spell on me or something?"

"Yeah, Manny, the whole town wants to fall in love with you." He laughed and tossed more powder at me. Before I knew it, I had become a rainbow.

Something Adam wouldn't have seen anyway since he didn't see color, I recalled.

We headed toward the water to cool off from the day's hot sun and wipe some of the powder from our faces.

"Rajiv mentioned the other day that you had forgotten Diwali."

"That's why you brought me here?" I hit Sammy playfully on his chest.

We sat down by the large rocks that perched over the small lake. Sammy lay down on a flat rock, stretching his long legs so they were hanging a bit over the rocks toward the water. I lay down next to him on a smooth part of the rock.

"I've missed out on so much."

"One of the things about our culture is you can always come back to it."

"You can?"

"It's a welcoming culture. There's room for you here," he said, his eyes locking with mine.

I thought about the key under the welcome mat that Lisa had left behind.

"Someone sounds like they miss all this," I said, pointing to the splashes of color that covered my white kurti and thinking how to approach the topic of Lisa.

"I miss it, yes . . . but maybe I needed a break from it?" Sammy questioned his own answer, repeating what he had said the other night. "The setups and the constant asking of when I'm going to get married. It was a lot."

"Well, at least you had aunties trying to set you up. I have Rajiv, who thinks that I would be better off with an Indian man."

"I got the feeling that Rajiv isn't exactly an Adam fan," he said.

I tried to think of who was, and realized I couldn't think of anyone.

"Well, what do you think?" he asked.

"About?" I turned to Sammy as the sun reflected off the water and lit up the rocks like fireworks celebrating Diwali with us.

"Would you be better off with someone else?"

Sammy's question caught me off guard.

"I . . . I think sometimes we all need a break from our lives. It was nice just to get away." I took a deep breath. "Sammy, I need to tell you something, and I should have told you a lot sooner—"

"Manny, whatever it is, I am really happy right now. I haven't felt this alive since . . . well, since my accident. So please, can we save it for later? Happy Diwali, Manny."

Damn. I needed to talk to Sammy. Sooner rather than later. But he really did look *so* happy.

"Happy Diwali, Sammy."

Chapter 26

Dear Breakup,

I think I am in love with my best friend. I know this is so cliché, and I am so embarrassed to send this to you. We talk every night, sometimes a few times a day, and now I suddenly want to get married? Ugh. I hate the fact that I am writing an email to a breakup agency for help with this. I've officially turned into a millennial.

Dimple

It was the big wedding brunch before the big night tomorrow. I headed down to meet Manisha, as we had arranged the night before. But it wasn't Sammy's sister who waved me over to her table; it was his mother.

"Manny! Oy, Manny." I smiled and headed toward her. "Come,

Aja. Come over here, beti. Sit here beside me." I pulled out the chair to sit down, and Sammy's father stood up.

"I have an urgent call," he said abruptly.

"Oh, sit down. He is always Sergeant Downer until he drinks his whiskey. Just like Sammy, always too busy with this phone and that phone. Why they make so much money to spend on who?" Mrs. Patel asked no one in particular as her husband walked away. "Don't worry about him. Sit and kha. You need to eat. You have such a tiny waist."

She pushed a plate full of besan bread toward me. *So much bread on this trip*, I thought as I looked down at my bloated stomach.

"Oh, eat it, beti. No diet here."

I tore off a small piece.

"Wow, what a dance you put on. You surely are a Patel girl at heart, you know. Moving hips like that." She took a sip of her tea.

"Aw, thank you. Your daughter was sweet enough to ask me to join."

"Yes, but just like us Patels, you accepted the challenge."

Yes, I did! A small surge of pride rushed through me as I realized that I had risen to the occasion. It was nice to be part of something.

"So, you are doing business with my beta, huh? What kind of business?"

"Just looking at some vineyards. We were thinking about creating our own Indian wine label." I stuffed more bread in my mouth as if the more food I ate, the fewer questions she would ask.

"Hain? Wine? What a stupid idea. Who needs to drink more? To look like fool. No. I don't like it."

"You're right, Auntie-ji. It's not even worth looking into."

"Good!" She sounded satisfied. "You know, he is so smart. So good-looking, but sometimes does a stupid thing. Indian wine. Buying motorcycle. Crashing it in bad accident—"

At this, a piece of bread caught in my throat, and I started coughing.

"Oh, drink this." She offered me a glass of water. "Yes, beti, I know about the accident and how serious it was."

"I'm sorry," I said, as if it were possible to apologize for someone else. "He didn't want to worry you. How did you—"

"I am his mother, after all," she said with assertion. "Should know everything!"

I thought about my own mother.

"If you don't mind me asking, why haven't you told him? He thinks . . . well, your brother, I am so sorry about him."

"Why should I tell him?" She crossed her arms across her large chest. "He is my son, and he lies to me. Yes, Jeh, my generous twin, died from terrible accident, and I miss him so much, but I miss my eldest son, too. No. I will wait for him to tell me why he lied about buying a stupid motorcycle. If he is lying about this one thing, hai bhagavan." She dramatically raised both her hands to the ceiling. "Imagine what else he is lying about?"

Despite her theatrics, Mrs. Patel seemed genuinely upset. But Sammy had lied for a good reason. At least he thought he had.

"Whom are you engaged with?" she asked as she pulled her glasses to her nose and reached for my hand. "Let me see . . ."

I placed my hand in hers.

"Wow! So big . . . so *beautiful*. Like you. What prince you must be marrying?"

She looked at me expectantly, as if I were about to tell her I was marrying someone she knew, but I couldn't even say Adam's name. Suddenly the ring didn't feel like an engagement ring, and I didn't feel like a fiancée.

"Mom, are you giving Manny a hard time?" Manisha pushed my hand away as she sat down.

"No, no. She was only asking a few questions," I said.

"Okay, good. She gets a three-question limit." Manisha reached for a large piece of bread.

Her mother slapped her hand. "So moti already, why need to eat more bread when you are so chubby?" she scolded.

Manisha rolled her eyes. "Whatever. I already ate some," she whispered to me.

Mrs. Patel placed her hand to her forehead in another dramatic gesture. "If I have a limit of three questions for Manny, do I have more for my sweet betoo?" she asked Manisha.

"Ask as many questions as you want, Mommy-ji. Let's see how many I will answer."

Mrs. Patel made a face. "What a brat I raised. Spoiled brat."

"Not a brat. I already know your questions."

Mrs. Patel raised her eyebrow.

"Who are you dating? What does he do for work? When are you getting married?" Manisha rhymed off.

"So, can't a mother ask?"

"Yes, she can, but my answer has been the same for the last six months, Mommy-ji. No one, therefore no work, and therefore no wedding."

"I can't take this emotional turmoil right now," Mrs. Patel said. "My heart rate going up, as I can see on my watch of Apple.

I will deal with you after Sanjeev's wedding. I have two more kids to get married . . ." She got up and walked away, half-annoyed and half-happy that at least one of her kids was getting married.

"Bye, Mommy-ji." Manisha waved as she reached for some bread. "She's the best mom, but you know our moms, they always have the same question: When is my daughter getting married? So typical, you know? It's like you can't bring any guys around because they think he's the one! I swear, being an Indian woman is so hard sometimes. So thankful the food makes up for it." She took another bite. "What about your mom? Is she this way?"

I didn't want to spoil the moment, so instead I said, "Well, maybe she's concerned about you ending up alone?"

"Alone? Ha! If she could spend the rest of her life throwing these kinds of parties, she would. It's the only reason she wants me and Sammy to get married: more events to plan and show off," she exclaimed. "Actually, I am single, but I am also totally dating around. Please don't tell anyone. Especially her."

"So, they can't know?"

"Gosh, no. If they were to find out, they would demand to meet families, and I would be married off in a few weeks. I don't even know which one I really like yet. You know what it's like being a Desi daughter. So many questions, and they all end with when should we set the date? It's enough to drive a girl pagal." Her eyes widened.

"What are you guys talking about?" Deena came and sat next to Manisha. Her long braid from earlier was gone, and her hair was now in loose long curls that went down to her hips. She was beautiful. An Indian goddess.

"Indian moms and how crazy they make us," Manisha joked.

"Don't get me started. I'm avoiding mine right now. See that guy over to the right in the brown shirt? The one picking at his teeth?"

I spotted the young man sitting alone, industriously maneuvering a toothpick.

"My mother seems to think *that* is my future husband. He's an engineer, so you know, that's the perfect match, according to her. And he comes from a nice family."

"And he has a nice car," Manisha added.

"And his brother was top of the class." Deena laughed.

Manisha joined her, so I started laughing awkwardly as if I knew what was so funny.

"Imagine if my mom knew that I wasn't taking engineering courses at the university but am actually studying to be a dance instructor."

Deena was a dance instructor. No wonder she was the most graceful on the dance floor.

"She would kill you," Manisha replied.

"Why?" I asked.

Deena swung her head to look at me. "Um . . . because being a good Indian means growing up to be an engineer or doctor or lawyer, not a Bollywood dancer, even though our parents spend all day watching those movies. God forbid I get to star next to Hrithik Roshan."

"He's got enough leading ladies," Manisha reminded her.

They laughed again.

I thought about my father, who always encouraged me to be whatever I wanted. He would tell me that America is the land of dreams, and I could have as many dreams as I wanted.

"Manny, you are the smartest kid on this block," he would say while he was barbecuing on Sundays and my mother was tending our garden. "No one compares to your grades, your medals in track, and the outstanding work you do in the community. You can be anything in this country."

"Dad, sometimes I'm not even sure what I want to be."

"That's why money, the money we have in this great country, will give you the opportunity to attend any schools. Manny Dogra can do anything!" he would tell me as he grilled our most American meal of cheeseburgers. That was our family tradition.

"Look at poor Pinky over there," Deena said, gesturing to a cousin I hadn't met yet. "Can you *believe* she is even here? Like, I would never show my face at a family function again. She married an Italian guy last summer, FYI," Deena continued, suddenly lowering her voice. "Her mom says she's been getting these splitting migraines since their wedding, and she hasn't been able to leave the house."

"Wow, that's awful; maybe she should get that checked," I suggested.

"You're so funny, Manny. I love your sense of humor."

I wasn't sure what I had said.

"If I were Pinky, I wouldn't have come. Well, not since the wedding."

Manisha made her way to some more bread, adding butter this time. She looked around to see if her mother was watching her commit the sin of excessive bread eating.

"Poor Pinky," she said after taking another bite. "Her father passed away last year, and everyone says it's because she married *that Italian*."

"*So* much family shame." Deena made a face.

Maybe Sammy was right not to put Lisa through this.

"Oh, Indian moms, you can't live with them . . . and you can't live with them." Manisha and Deena cracked up.

"I have to get going before my mom finds your mom," Deena proclaimed.

"Byeee." Manisha turned to me after she left. "You know what, let's get out of here, too. Come with me. I want to show you the anarkali I'm going to wear tonight." We headed out of the ballroom, and she led me up to her room.

On the way there, I had a sudden urge. "Can I ask you something?"

"Sure," she said as we got to her floor.

"Your dad . . . I don't know. He doesn't seem to like me?"

"Really?" She stopped and looked at me as if she had never heard anyone say such a thing about her dad. "What makes you think that?" She continued toward her room.

"Every time I see him, he walks away. He doesn't speak to me." I recounted what had happened as I sat down for brunch with Mr. and Mrs. Patel, and how he suddenly had to leave as soon as I sat down.

"He's a man of very few words," Manisha assured me as she gave me a little pat on my back. "He spent his teenage years in the military, and I think something must have happened out there to keep him so . . . so . . . well, you know, his personality is kind of rigid." She went on. "My grandfather told us that he used to be this outgoing teenager. He played a lot of cricket and spent time on the family farm, then one day he came home and said he wanted to join the army."

"The army? Why?" I asked.

"I don't know, but he enlisted that very day, and when he came back three years later, he was married to my mother. She was a military nurse; they met after he was injured on the base."

The Patels seemed to enjoy the company of nurses.

Manisha stopped and gestured to room 815. "Right here. Don't be upset by it, Manny. His son is getting married. I am sure his head is in the clouds. He's a cool dad. He still gives me an allowance. Please don't tell my mother," she said, and used her room key to swipe us in.

Maybe she was right. *Maybe I'm making something out of nothing*, I thought as I followed her in.

"Sorry about the mess." She grabbed a pile of Valentino pumps and tossed them to the side like dirty towels, trying to clear a path. I could see where her allowance had gone from the Chanel pearls, Dior shorts, and skirts lying around. It also looked like she had shopped in Aliyan's private closet. She had the most extravagant wedding party outfits slumped over the backs of chairs. Her room was the same layout as mine, but it was way messier.

"Sit here," she gestured as she moved a few jackets off the couch and dropped them carelessly to the ground. "I always pack too much and anarkalis take up so much room, and yet here I am—I still have nothing to wear."

She moved a long black-and-white frock-style top with a fitted bottom to her bed. That thing was worth the overstuffed suitcase.

"Drink?"

I stared down at my watch. It was one p.m.

"Oh, come on, it's chug a jug somewhere." She giggled. "Plus, that brunch was so stuffy. Needa's royal family"—she said "royal" with a fake British accent as she rolled her eyes—"insisted we have an Indian brunch. I love Needa. Don't get me wrong. She and Sanj are so cute it makes me barf. Like, their kids will grow up to be models. Her parents are something else, though. You know, like the type of families that need to show off their money. Like, really show off their money. Not like our parents, who just want to show off their money to get their kids married." She laughed.

I didn't know. But I knew something about non-Indian families showing off their money.

Manisha opened a bottle of Moët and made a couple of mimosas once she found the orange juice in the back of the bar fridge.

"I used to be a bartender in college. My dad would kill me if he knew. Cheers!" She passed a glass to me. "Come." She grabbed my hand, and we made our way to the balcony, where she plopped herself on the large outdoor sofa. I sat on the wicker chair, moving it to the side so the sun wouldn't blind me.

"Okay, my turn."

I smiled. "For what?"

"To ask you a question." She pointed her champagne glass at me playfully.

"Okay? Go ahead."

"Well, two questions. That's my limit."

"All right."

"Your *big* engagement ring . . . tell me more. Who is the guy? Is he Indian? I picture you with a tall, dark, handsome Ranbir

Kapoor type. Before he hooked up with Alia Bhatt, because after that he just got way too beefcakey for me."

"Yeah, me too." I pretended. "My boyfriend, fiancé . . . His name is, um . . ." Why couldn't I say Adam's name?

"Sammy?" Manisha jumped in, sounding hopeful and mischievous.

"What!" I almost spat out my drink, startled that she would even suggest such an idea. "No!" My voice suddenly sounded higher than usual.

"I know, I know. Just teasing." She took a big gulp of her drink and sat back in the chair. "But I have to confess, I did think this whole biz partner thing was a sham so you could meet us and judge us. You know, see if you liked us?" She leaned her head back, as if disappointed.

"If I liked *you?*" I placed my glass on the table in front of me. "Why would I judge you guys?"

Manisha leaned in and filled it right back up. "Well, we can be a bit much. There are so many cousins, all the aunties, uncles, and us. And we all get along so sickeningly well. Loving each other is kind of our thing, give or take the few Tinas of the world."

I sat back and let the sunlight hit my face. What she was telling me made me very happy and sad all at once.

"I was kind of hoping you could be the bahan I never had. Sammy and Sanj had each other growing up. I really wanted a sis!" Manisha took a sip of her drink. "I could have been toasting with my sis every weekend." She waved her glass in the air like she had at the club. "Anyway, so then why are you really here?"

She had every right to be intrigued.

"Um . . ." I swirled my glass. How could I tell Manisha the truth about my "arrangement" with her brother?

She changed her position on the couch as if I were keeping her waiting too long.

"You know . . . like Sammy said, the . . . wine . . . business of wineries."

"But you're both already so successful. Why would anyone with your money and stature need to start *another* business?"

"What do you mean?" I took a dry gulp.

She jumped up from her seat. "Hang on. I'll be right back." She disappeared inside.

I gulped back what was left of my mimosa, wondering if she had even asked me up to her room to see her outfit at all. I needed to get out of here before she started asking even more questions.

"Manisha, I should go," I called out. "It's getting late."

"Oh, are we talking about *this* kind of work?" She came back outside, holding up the cover of *Beyond More* in a ta-da moment.

I was caught. Caught in a lie.

"How did you . . . where did you manage to find a copy?" Of the most-read magazine in the country.

"Honestly? That's really a question? Actually, I didn't even think it was you . . . you look so . . . you look like a white girl. Don't worry, no one else knows, not even Deena, and trust me, the second-best thing the Patels do besides dance is talk. If anyone else knew, I would have heard about it by now."

"Okay, thanks," I said, downing another mimosa.

"So, if you're the CEO of Breakup, what kind of business would you be doing with my brother?" Manisha was not letting this go. I might have done the same thing in her position.

"Client confidentiality," I said. "Ask your brother."

"Wait! What!" She jumped up again, and the magazine fell from her lap. "My brother is your client?"

"No . . . no! Not at all. Any client, as in our clients' privacy is confidential and so . . ." What was I even saying? The champagne had hit me, and I wasn't making any sense.

"Wow, this is getting juicy."

"No. It's not what you think. I have to go." I got up.

"I am not thinking anything," she informed me. "Look, I'm sorry. It is not any of my business, I suppose. As long as Lisa is out of the picture, I don't care."

I stopped at the door and turned around as soon as she mentioned Lisa's name. "What do you know about Lisa?" Panic rushed through me.

"What do *you* know about Lisa?" The lawyer in her had kicked in, and just like that, I was on the stand, crumbling in her courtroom.

I had to get out of here.

"Okay. I'm going now." I turned back around again.

"No! Manny, don't leave. I know everything about Lisa!"

I stopped dead in my tracks.

"Sanj and I have known about Lisa for quite a while."

"And—? Out with it." I had no right to interrogate Manisha, but I was going to.

"A friend of mine at the hospital told me about Sammy's injuries. I mean, I knew he was hurt, but I got the full lowdown from her."

I was stunned. What about patient confidentiality and all that?

"She thought I knew," Manisha continued. "Prisha called to ask if she could do anything to help, assuming Sammy had told us, which he had. He had just left out how serious the crash was. Poor Prisha. She could have lost her job."

These dear people. Such chaos, and all because they wanted to protect each other from hurt. Could this be another plot from a Bollywood movie I had chosen not to watch? I didn't have anything to say. Luckily, Manisha was happy to fill in the blank spaces in the conversation.

"She assured us that Sammy's injuries weren't life-threatening and that he had the best doctors and nurses . . ." Manisha cleared her throat after "nurses." "So we waited on the sidelines, knowing that Sammy was most likely holding back due to my dad's stroke. Not that it was easy for any of us. But we respected our older brother's wishes. Then you showed up, and I thought . . . hoped, actually, that 'business' was code for something else. But apparently I was wrong," she said, pointing to my ring.

"Manisha, Sammy hired me to help him break up with Lisa—" I couldn't believe I had said that.

"YES!" she yelled, pumping her fist in the air. There was that air drink wave again.

"No, it's not what you think. It's just for the week. He didn't want to bring a non-Indian girlfriend here because he was afraid that the family would disapprove and that Needa's family would cancel the wedding."

"A girlfriend who keeps him away from us!" she exclaimed. "And, yes, Needa's royal family." There was that British accent again. "They would have disapproved, and obviously so would some of the other Patels, but we could have all stood together like we always do." She saluted me like a drunken soldier with glass in hand. "So, is Sammy getting back together with her when he returns home?"

"Something like that," I said.

"But that still doesn't answer my question. Why are you here?"

"We made a deal. I would help him break up with Lisa, and he would help me by bringing me to all the parties with your family this week."

Manisha looked confused. "Why? There are a million weddings you could attend. Why choose this one?"

"Because there are a million Indian weddings *you* could attend. Not me. Look at the picture. Do I really look like one of you guys?"

She stopped, and before she could ask any more questions, she answered her own. "You made a deal so that you could see how it *feels* to be us for a week? Like test it out, like some car? Like, like Lisa did to Sammy by just testing him out until a new car came along?"

"What?"

"I *just* found out via text from a friend who saw Lisa running around town with some other guy behind Sammy's back, and now here you are, also lying to all of us."

When she said it out loud, it sounded horrible.

"What exactly are you doing here? The facts all point to you using my family and me." She said it in her most lawyer voice. "That's so . . . so disgusting, Manny."

"No, Manisha. Listen, I know how it looks and sounds, for that matter. I didn't even like your brother when he found me."

"Found you? Like he googled you and boom, you suddenly appeared?"

"Our services," I corrected myself.

"Oh? So my poor brother comes to you for help and your plan is to use him and us while he is so caught up with a woman who he *thinks* saved his life? And you don't even like him? No! No one does that to a Patel. Not even a wannabe Indian girl like you."

Manisha's words hurt more than I expected.

"Get out of my room, Manny. You're . . . you're a total b-word if that's what you did! You are exactly what that cover shows. A whitewashed bitch. I never want to see you again."

Tears started running down my face as I tried to leave the room.

The last time I had cried like this was the night I said good-bye to my mother in the hospital. The night I had lost the most important thing in my world.

Chapter 27

Dear Breakup,

Thank you for sending that email to my fiancé. It's been a year since we broke up after I registered for your boot camp. I took some time for myself in Italy, just like you suggested, found courage and confidence, and also found true love. I know, talk about a cheesy rom-com, but it was the Eat, Pray, Love moment I needed, and I couldn't have done it without you.

My ex, Carl, and I are still friends today because of your email, and as I sit here in a café in New York City waiting for my new fiancé, who has come back with me from Italy, I can't help but smile thinking that it all happened because of your email.

Lana

I sobbed into my pillow for ages before finally coming up for air. Staring at my room's ceiling was the closest thing to Adam I had right now—after all, he had designed it. It made me miss us. And there still was an *us*. Okay, so things had been a little bumpy lately. That happens in even the closest relationships. I couldn't blame Adam for saying the things he did about my parents, could I? It's not like I had done the best job of communicating my feelings in the last two years when it came to them. And I of all people knew that communication was the key to fixing most relationship bumps. This was just a bump, right? I wasn't going to throw away the best thing that had happened to me just because a few things had gone wrong. Adam and I *were* well suited. We were both passionate businesspeople and were both committed to our future. We just needed a little coaching, a little one-on-one consulting, a plan, as Adam would say, didn't we?

I had to get back to Baskin. This wasn't real life. Real life was my business, that and Adam. This . . . whatever this was, it was an Indian fantasy world. It wasn't mine.

As I pondered all that, I heard a familiar ping. It was a text from Sammy.

How are you doing?

Not feeling so great, I responded.

Coming to see you, he quickly responded.

NO! I texted back. I'm fine. I just need a night to myself. You Patels have tired me out with your parties.

Indeed, they had. But they had also been so generous and welcoming and kind. Every single one of them—except for Mr. Patel.

There was a pause before Sammy messaged me back.

> All right, all right. You're off the hook for the rest
> of the day. But tomorrow is the big night!

Sammy sounded so cheerful. A far cry from the man who had sent those frantic messages a few short days ago. He had held up his part of the bargain. Now it was my turn—and I was bailing.

I got up from my bed, preparing not for the quiet night I told Sammy I needed but to gather my things. Enough was enough. It was time to go home. The Code Red chaos should have been my first sign that something wasn't right. And that panic. Why had I been so desperate to find answers to questions I probably should have insisted on asking when my parents were alive?

Never mind that.

Time to pack. My unbelievably inappropriate things.

How on earth had I thought I was going to glide through an Indian wedding with some Reformation jeans and my Shopbop dresses? I brought over the suitcase that Anjali had packed for me. That's when I noticed the small white envelope stuck to the bottom of the case. I opened it to find a handwritten card.

Dear Manny,

I am so proud to be part of a company that is run by a strong Indian woman. Yes, you are Indian. You were always Indian. Please don't forget that while you are on this journey this week.

Love, Anjali xx

Had I always been Indian? Maybe Anjali was right. I didn't need a week away with Professor Patel to prove to anyone who

I really was or wasn't. My parents did the best they could, given what they had. I needed to stop being so hard on them, and ultimately on myself.

I gathered my things and wrote a thank-you note for Aliyan. I left it on the garment bag and the gold rack, and then headed out. When I got downstairs, the lobby was empty—not a Patel, not an auntie, not a wedding guest in sight.

"Leaving so soon?" I heard a booming voice behind me just a minute later.

I turned around and faced Mr. Patel. "Mr. Patel. I mean, Uncle-ji. I . . . um . . . didn't see you there." In my haste I had somehow missed this towering man. Tall at six feet three, he was just as handsome as his two sons. Except his handsome features were much more intimidating.

"It looks like you are in a huge hurry to get out of here." He looked down at my suitcase. "The business is not going well?"

"Oh, no, it went well, so that's why I can head back home now."

"Before my son gets married?" he asked, seeming not at all pleased.

"No. I mean, yes," I stammered.

"I thought this is why you came here. For the business?" He stepped in closer to me.

"Yes, but the business was a success, so now I can leave?" I continued to fumble through my words. "I need to get back to my other business?" I was uptalking like some intern.

"One person doesn't need so many businesses."

"You're right, Uncle-ji. I mean, Mr. Patel." What was appropriate here? I couldn't recall.

In the week that I had been here, Mr. Patel had dodged any

opportunity he had to speak to me, and now, as I was trying to escape, here he stood in front of me. I scrambled to find answers to his questions.

"I'll abandon it as soon as I get back to Baskin."

"Abandon Sammy?"

"Yes. No. Business. I will *quit* my business with Sammy."

"You're not making any sense."

I was losing this interrogation fast. I was losing all the court battles today.

"Come with me." He gestured to the outdoor garden.

I grabbed my suitcase.

"You can retrieve that later." He nodded to a pimply-faced concierge, who leaped up from behind the desk, seemingly as afraid as I was.

"Yes. Of course." I followed him.

"Such wonderful weather on the West Coast. Clean air." He took a deep breath.

I also took a deep breath, afraid that I would get into some kind of trouble if I didn't.

We made our way out into the back garden, which was filled with guests having afternoon tea. He was right, the air was fresh and clean. I followed close behind.

"You are a slow walker," he observed.

I wasn't, actually. In fact, Adam often accused me of walking too fast. "Yes, sir. I am," I agreed, though. Now I was calling him "sir"?

"Like your mother or your father?" he asked.

"Like my mother," I said. My mother was a slow walker, but it was because she loved the smell of fresh flowers. Her pace always slowed if she saw a flower she wanted to pick and take back home with her.

"Have a seat."

He pointed at a white wicker bench at the back of the garden. We sat all alone, as if Mr. Patel had planned everything with the staff, insisting that this space be left empty specially for us.

He cleared his throat and sat back.

"My son is fortunate," he started.

"Yes. Sanjeev is marrying a lovely woman. He seems to adore her," I agreed, though he didn't seem to hear me.

"He also has a very big heart. Sometimes I worry it is so big that he can't handle it. He sees people for all the good they do, not the bad. People can be bad, Manny."

"Sanjeev does seem to have a big heart."

"Not Sanjeev, Sammy."

I furrowed my brow, confused as to why he was telling me about Sammy's big heart.

"To have such a great business partner come to spend time with his family on such a special occasion. This must be an important business trip for both of you. To come here and meet all of us on this big day for all the Patels," he continued.

A bed of flowers lay before us, perfectly lined up for an outdoor wedding: white roses mixed with purple tulips, green hedges set back along the garden fence. It reminded me of the Jamiesons' vineyard. Adam and I didn't want to get married there—we wanted something new to both of us—but in the end, it turned out to be our only option. We had changed our wedding date so many times that each of the venues we had chosen before had given us our deposits back and asked us politely to find another place.

"Yes. The timing worked out that way," I lied. "I am so thankful that you included me on this special occasion and that your entire family has opened their arms to me."

"We are like that. The Patels have big, big arms and big, big hearts." He touched his own heart. "You know they don't teach us Indians much about love. Old traditions from the homeland ask us to marry for other things—family, endowments, wealth. Love can come after, if it needs to at all."

I thought of my parents, knowing that love didn't even come after they married each other. Respect. Companionship. Friendship. But not love.

"But sometimes you are lucky," he continued, "if you find love and it finds you."

I realized I was one of the lucky ones.

"I was lucky. I found love. The true love of my life." Mr. Patel lowered his voice.

I pictured Mr. and Mrs. Patel and imagined that, outside of this week, they probably showed a lot more affection and love.

"Beautiful she was," he reminisced.

She's still beautiful, I thought, and then imagined his wife as she must have been when she was younger, as pretty as Manisha.

"Back in those days in India, love was more complicated. If you fell in love with the wrong person, it could be quite complicated. I am lucky to have found love in those complicated times, even if it hurt me much later." Mr. Patel stared straight ahead, hardly moving as he told his story. "My son thinks he is in love, but she is not the right person. She is not a good person."

"I think Needa is a lovely girl, and Sanjeev loves her very much, Mr. Patel," I tried to reassure him.

"Not Sanjeev. I am speaking about Sammy," he clarified again as he looked at me.

Manisha must have told him about Lisa. She must have told everyone by now.

"It's okay, beti."

It wasn't okay. Sammy had every right to know, and for some reason, I couldn't bring myself to tell my client what he needed to know.

"I am not a dumb man. I am old, but not dumb." He chuckled to himself as he reached for his pocket.

"Of course, sir. I wouldn't ever think you were dumb."

He pulled out his cell phone. "Sanjeev showed me these pictures a few months ago."

He leaned in and started to go through the photos on his phone. It was Sammy with a striking blond woman. They were at the beach, at a party, at the grocery store. "This," he pointed at the picture, "is not my Sammy in love. My Sammy doesn't love this Lisa."

Everyone knows about Lisa!

"*This* is my Sammy in love." He opened a new set of photos of Sammy. He looked so happy. He was dancing and smiling. I realized they were all from this past week. All his cousins were in the pictures, and the girls looked so stunning. All the Indian girls looked . . . I stopped on one picture, an Indian girl beaming next to Sammy.

"Mr. Patel, that's me . . . That is *me!*" I choked back a few tears. How had I not recognized myself?

I looked at the picture again. My arm wrapped around Sammy's. Both of us smiling. All those Patel cousins trying to get into one picture. We must have been cued by the photographer to cram together.

"Beti, you look as pretty as your mother." He started to tear up, too.

"Yes," I said. "Just like my mother."

Wait, how did Mr. Patel know that my mother was pretty? I turned to him. And then I saw it, the gold around his neck. Mr. Patel was wearing the necklace my mother had given me.

I reached for the chain that was tucked under my shirt. It had been hidden most of the week under the chunky jewelry. But it was still there. I was still wearing it. Mr. Patel wasn't wearing *my* necklace, he just happened to have the same one as me. My mother had insisted the necklace was a gift from the man she fell in love with, the only man she ever loved.

A loud gasp escaped my mouth. My head started to spin.

"You're . . . that man . . . You?" I asked, unable to put words together.

"Yes, beti."

"That's why you haven't spoken to me this whole time?" I cried as I got up.

He gestured to the wicker seat. "Please, sit back down."

"You're who my mother was in love with? She shared the stories about you and her . . . in the library . . . all those letters. She loved you so much." I fell back onto the bench.

"I loved her, too," Mr. Patel managed to say. The man who

lit up talking about my mother was a far cry from the man who wouldn't even look at me earlier this week. "It was much different back then. I wasn't good enough for your mother. Not according to her family. When she married someone else, I left for the military, heartbroken."

My heart was pounding in my chest as I thought back to Manisha's story of her dad suddenly announcing he was joining the army. All the pieces of the story were finally coming together. "Mr. Patel," I said, trying to catch my breath, "my mother never talked about my father the way she spoke of you."

He held the chain around his neck.

"Did you ever see her in Baskin? Did she ever see you?"

"No, she did not. She came to the community center one day, and I recognized her right away. I never went back, knowing she could be there again. What was left to say or do? We both had our children, our families, our broken hearts."

"Mr. Patel, my mother died a few years ago."

Sammy's father put an arm around me. I tucked my head into his shoulder and sobbed.

"I know, beti. When I read about it in the newspaper, my heart broke again. I had lost her twice."

He started to cry, too. We held each other.

"Beti, Sammy loves you as much as I loved your mother. I see the look he gets in his eyes. I see it, and I feel it because I was once a young Sammy. Look at how my son is smiling in the pictures with you. Look at how you are holding him. That is how your mother and I were together before we were ripped apart from each other."

What was he talking about? Feelings between Sammy and me?

"No!" I got back up on my feet and wiped the tears from my eyes. "I am engaged, Mr. Patel. I have to go. Right now."

As I rushed toward the hotel lobby, I heard him implore, "Manny . . . Manny . . . don't turn your back on love. Not the way I was forced to."

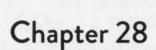

Chapter 28

Dear Breakup,

I came home to find my clothes outside our apartment again, because my girlfriend was upset that I left the toilet seat up. I can't handle this anymore. I need to break up with the PSYCHO without having my entire wardrobe on display for the neighbors to see. They don't need to know I wear Joe Boxer underwear.

Artemis

I felt like the star of my own Bollywood movie, and not in a good way. Rajiv had often shared the plots of his favorite movies, and after a while I wondered if he was watching the same movie but with different actors, since they all seemed to center on falling in love with someone your family didn't approve of.

"Manny, it is the best three hours of life, you cannot compare for anything," he would say. "Sitting and watching love story through music, dances, and changes in clothing attire. You must spend some time seeing one. You have not lived a proper good life without seeing Shah Rukh Khan cry into lap for the one woman he cannot have because he is poor man. Which is what I call hot irony since he the man is richest Bollywood actor."

Suddenly, sadness crashed over me as I thought of my mother and Mr. Patel unable to be with each other. All these years he had kept the chain around his neck as a reminder of my mother, and she had done the same. And just as my mother had told me to follow my heart, so had Mr. Patel.

I peeked over the edge of the balcony in my room. I missed my mother. I missed my father. They may not have loved each other, but they had always loved me. A quick nap to ease this heavy pain, that was what I needed. But first, I grabbed the garment bag that Aliyan had placed on its own rolling rack in the living area. I put it on my bed as if it were a person, hoping to receive some sign about what to do next.

"Mintu, you getting everything ready for the big night?"

I turned my puffy face around to find Aliyan standing in the doorway as if he had just read my thoughts.

"Oh, what is wrong, Mintu, honey?"

"Aliyan, I can't do this anymore. I am not going to the wedding reception. I'm just trying to be something that I'm not."

"Oh no, no, no, honey. You are certainly not returning to Baskin without going to Sanjeev's wedding."

"What's the point? So I can play dress-up for the night like I have been all week? Adam was right to say the things he did about me. All of a sudden I am Indian in a week?"

Aliyan looked at me for a minute, and then said, "Put your clothes on and grab your shoes. We are going out!"

"Now? I can't. Anjali has booked me a flight out tonight, and I need to get on it."

"Well, you can get on it tomorrow morning. You owe me a night out. I have had zero fun time with you. This week of wardrobe fittings and soap opera plot twists, and I don't get one drink outside this damn hotel with you? No, girl. We are going now!"

"I don't know. I'm not in the mood."

"Change that mood like this Dior mood ring gifted to me by Mindy Kaling and put these on." He handed me a pair of jeans and a long-sleeve pink shirt. "Go!" He motioned into the other room. "I will meet you downstairs in ten minutes. We don't want to see the devil of Aliyan come out, girl." He made fake devil horns on top of his head. "Do as I say!" he ordered.

I managed to get ready and head downstairs, where I found Aliyan waiting in his car outside the front door.

"Get in," he said and pulled the top down, and we drove away from the resort.

"Where are we going?"

"I want you to meet some friends of mine. I think it'll help you figure out what's in here." He pointed to his heart.

All these people who are so confident of their hearts, I thought. I had no idea what was in mine, except that it felt empty and broken.

We drove to the other end of town and pulled up to an old, abandoned building.

"Where are we?" I asked. Suddenly I felt nervous.

"Don't worry. You're safe with me." He jumped out of the car and waved at me to follow him toward the decrepit brick building, which looked as though it had lain empty for years.

"Watch your step," he said as we entered the place and went downstairs through a narrow staircase that got darker and darker as we descended. He finally turned on the mini ring light that was attached to his phone. "I usually feel my way around, like I did with Jonny's body last night," he growled, "but since you're here, let's do things the safe way."

I could hear music and muffled voices as we moved down the hallway at the bottom of the stairs. Aliyan grabbed my hand and kept me close. We approached a large door, and he knocked out some secret code: two quick knocks followed by three more, and then another two. As we waited for someone to answer, I noticed that the dark hallway was full of cobwebs and dirt.

"It gets better on the other side," he said, sensing my discomfort. "Promise."

After what felt like a few minutes, the door swung open.

"Alllllllllliiii! Come in!" A tall Indian Deborah Cox hugged Aliyan and ushered us both in. "You made it. God, I thought you'd be working on that princess all day."

Aliyan cleared his throat. "Stevie, meet the princess."

"Oh gosh, well, foot in my large mouth!" he said. "I am the fabulous Stevie, and you must be our little Mintu. We have heard sooooo much about you."

All the men in the room were dressed in drag like Stevie, their outfits even grander than the ones Aliyan had brought me over the week. The drag queens had perfected the art of looking like RuPaul, Whitney Houston, and Barbra Streisand, and added

their own flair. Bangles chiming on bronzed arms, beautiful turquoise, bright red, and purple bustier tops, and the shortest of
decorative skirts barely covering the longest of glitter-sprinkled
legs filled the room.

My eyes widened with excitement.

"Do you like what you see?" Stevie asked in a mischievous
voice. "You can always borrow anything we're wearing for your
own closet. Although, honey, where are your hips? Indian girls
have hips!"

"Well . . ."

"How is anyone supposed to grab this rail gaddi?" he said as
he shook my hips back and forth.

"He means train. A rail gaddi is a train, honey, and happens
to be one of the most overplayed Indian wedding songs." Aliyan
shot Stevie a look.

"Oh, shut up, Aliyan. You and your celebrity client stories are
overplayed."

"Manny, these are my friends, my Indian friends." He brought
my hand to his heart. "This is where we get to be who we are.
Without judgment."

The music started back up again as an announcer welcomed
"Ms. Naaaannna" to the stage.

Aliyan found my hand, and we followed Stevie to the front of
the dance floor.

We watched Ms. Priyanka Bollywood drag dance to a track.
Aliyan was dancing and singing next to me. "Come on, girl, move
those small hips like I showed you."

Stevie started moving my hips for me again, and soon I was
dancing along with Aliyan. He looked so happy as the music

blared and the disco lights dropped black-and-white bolts across the dance floor, beads of sweat settling on his face.

"Let's take fifteen," the DJ announced.

We headed toward the back of the room and sat at a high-top table.

"Wow, Aliyan, what a great place."

"Most of these men have been cut off by their families, so we have our own little family here. If there's one thing we know, it's that there is no one way to be Indian. That's what you need to keep in mind. No one can tell you how to be you, Manny. Gay, straight, stylist to the stars, the CEO of a successful public company . . . it doesn't matter."

"Aliyan, back at home I just disappeared into my work. I was too busy solving client problems, and I guess I didn't even realize I had any of my own because I was buried so deep in work." *And not in the arms of my fiancé.*

"I think you did, Manny. But you're so kind and generous, you just pushed your problems to the side to help others—while others might have helped themselves."

I thought back to Adam and all the times he had promised to make time for us.

"But I—"

"No buts. Unless you're talking about that cute little butt of yours and how you've learned to shake it."

Ms. Naana came over to our table and gave Aliyan a double kiss.

"And you must be Manny? As much a sight as Aliyan said you were." He came over and hugged me. "Wow. You are an Indian goddess. Smiling from ear to ear like Parvati."

I looked at Aliyan, confused.

"Parvati is the Hindu goddess of love, beauty, bravery . . ."

"Honey, I could smell Indian and goddess on you from that stage," Ms. Naana said. "It's in your soul. In your blood. It's in your heart and it's bursting out for someone." A quick wink and she was off to the bar.

I looked around and realized something. That while dear sweet Aliyan might have brought me here because I was a little lost, now I was ready to find my way again.

Chapter 29

Dear Breakup,

My girlfriend dumped me for her best girlfriend. Apparently, she's been gay all her life and "used" me to confirm her sexuality. How am I supposed to get over that? I need your help getting my confidence again. Enroll me in your boot camp NOW!

Mitchell

I headed back to my hotel room, ready to reschedule my rescheduled flight. I wasn't going to go home yet after all. I wanted to stay for the wedding. But first, I had a job to do. I texted Sammy to meet me in the lobby in a few minutes. I started down the hotel stairs ready to tell my client some things I should have told him a few days ago.

Sammy was charming the concierge with his big smile, but made his way over to me when he saw me.

"Are you feeling better, Manny?"

"Oh yeah. Just a stomach bug. Thanks for meeting me down here." I took a deep breath. I had to come clean about Lisa. I was the CEO of a thriving business and, as Adam always said, I needed to take my personal feelings out of the business.

"Do you wanna get some air in the back garden? I could use a walk," Sammy suggested.

"No!" I said a bit too loudly. I didn't need a reminder of earlier events with Mr. Patel. "Let's take a walk through this way." I pointed to another exit, and we made our way out to a beautiful path beside the hotel and walked toward the middle of the garden.

"My favorite thing as a kid used to be camping outside in our backyard and listening to the crickets," Sammy said.

"Really?"

"Yeah, Manisha and Sanj hated it, so it was the only time I got to myself."

"I guess I never thought about wanting alone time, being an only child and all."

"Trust me. Those two were very obnoxious growing up, and still are," he joked.

We made our way to the end of the garden, where we found a white gazebo. We sat on the bench inside, under the full moon.

"I've been doing a lot of thinking out here," Sammy told me.

"Me too," I said. "Listen, about Lisa—"

"This love Sanj and Needa have, it's pure. It's not based on owing anyone anything."

"Sammy, like I said, you don't have to make yourself want to be with her because you feel like you owe her for being there during a difficult time."

"Then why are you with your fiancé, Manny?"

The Patels sure knew how to interrogate someone.

"Is it because he was the first boyfriend who came along after your parents passed away?" Sammy must have seen my eyes widen—he winced at himself. "Oh, shit, I am sorry."

"No, you're right," I said. "Being out here with you made me realize that love is more than that. It's about family, friends, making each other laugh and smile, and being there for each other. You don't get into a relationship because you feel lonely or feel like you have nothing outside of work anymore. I love my company and what I do, but there is way more to love than that, and you've showed me that. I have a lot to think about when I get home."

Sammy looked at me, and under the moonlight, his brown eyes lit up.

"Manny . . ."

In one quick sweep, his lips were on mine, opening and welcoming mine. My arms fell to my side, and Sammy held both of my hands in his, working his warm fingers through my fingers and then pushing my hair behind my ears as he kissed each of my cheeks, before he slowly made his way back to the fire on my lips. A passionate kiss that felt like no other and yet at the same time way more familiar as the wet warmth made its way past my longing lips, to the nape of my neck, my trembling legs, and my aching heart. I wanted Sammy so badly. I wanted to be wrapped in his arms in my hotel bed in between the sheets, having that *Indian sex* that Aliyan talked about earlier.

But then he pulled back. "Manny, I'm sorry. I have no idea what came over me. I know you're engaged . . ."

"Sammy, no. It's fine. More than fine."

"Manny, it's not. This was a business deal, and I crossed the line. I'm sorry . . . I am going to go back inside, and I will see you tomorrow for the wedding."

He got up.

"Sammy, Lisa . . . she . . ." But before I could tell him, he was gone.

His kiss lingered on my lips and in my thoughts.

Chapter 30

Dear Breakup,

What's the difference between love and lust? Is there a different feeling for each? I think I love Nico because he makes me feel special and takes care of me, but I just want to rip off Eric's clothes and cuddle next to him. Can't I love and lust?

Talia

I watched the commotion of Aliyan's team as they worked their magic on me from head to toe, distracting me from the lingering kiss with Sammy. It was a weak moment. I was positive as soon as I saw him we would both laugh about it. And yet, I felt the kiss not just on my lips, it had taken over my body. I shook my head.

"Oy." The makeup artist applying a light layer of foundation muttered at me.

"Sorry." The artist continued to work on my face as I thought back to what Mr. Patel had said in the garden about my mother. I was reminded of her high cheekbones, her big smile, her beauty—physical, yes, but also that inner beauty that radiated through and touched every single person she came across. My mother wasn't an ace at selling houses because of the way she staged them, but because every house was filled with her warmth.

No tears, I told myself, batting my eyes, as if that would be enough to stop them.

"So, why are you not here with this fiancé of yours?" Aliyan asked as he reentered the room from a client call.

Four hours of face masks and makeup, tweezing and teasing, and a lot of hair spray. I had been wondering when Aliyan Auntie would get around to my love life.

"Adam. Oh . . . he's—"

"Adam? Sounds very, um . . . how do you say . . . non-Indian?"

"He is non-Indian," I said. "I mean, *not* Indian. Also, he's busy working all over the world and this wouldn't be his kind of thing, and it's also a business trip. So, he wasn't exactly invited. I came with Sammy, the client."

"You travel with your clients?"

"This is a special client, you could say."

"Do tell! What kind of *special* are we talking about? Above or below the waist?"

The room suddenly seemed awfully small.

"Aliyan! He's just a client who needed a favor and is sort of helping me out, too. And he's turned into a friend." A friend who had accidentally kissed me and made me long for more. "It's his brother's wedding."

"So, you're his date?"

"NO, not date. Not really."

"You're attending your client's brother's wedding, but you're not his date?"

I knew how ridiculous this all sounded.

"He's not your friend," Aliyan declared. "Indian guys don't bring a random Desi girl to a wedding full of family."

But do they kiss random Desi girls?

"We kind of have this arrangement, like you helping me get ready all week." I smiled at Aliyan.

"Arrangement." He repeated the word with doubt. "So back to your *arrangement* with your fiancé?"

"Yes. Adam. My fiancé." The title seemed less appropriate right now. "He's smart when it comes to work, and so we *work* well together. A good team, you know . . ." And there it was, the same word Adam had used to describe our relationship. A *team*. Except we were nothing more than a sort of business team now. Here I was, teaching Breakup clients to play for the same team in a relationship. The trouble with Adam and me was that neither of us was doing that anymore. There was no Breakup boot camp that could save us. I wanted something else. I wanted someone else.

"Beauty, bravery—"

"Holy shit!" I interrupted Aliyan.

Aliyan cocked an eyebrow at me and stopped teasing my hair.

I stared at him. The last few days had been flooded with the emotions that I had been numb to over the last two years—because someone had helped me numb them. And it took only a week with Sammy to undo all that.

"Love!" I squealed.

A week of falling in love with Sammy.

"Let me guess, my little Mintu is in love with someone other than this Adam?"

"I love Sammy. Aliyan, I am *in love* with Sammy." I got up quickly.

I heard whispers, "She loves Sammy," coming from Aliyan's team.

"Oh, my Mintu." He gestured to the women who were helping me get ready. "We all know you love Sammy."

I looked at them, and they smiled. They did all know, and so did I, but I had just been burying it like I had everything else in the last two years. This was real love, and not a *plan to love*.

Aliyan looked at his watch. "It's about time you admitted that to everyone, Parvati. And perhaps it's about time to send an email. I am sure you know someone who could offer a great discount with a Breakup email," he joked.

"You always make me smile even when I don't think it's possible."

"I think I may have *some* competition from Sammy, who makes you smile the most."

"Oh, Aliyan," I gushed back.

"Hang on to those Sammy feelings a little bit longer, though—we need to finish getting you ready. It's time to take a look at what's behind garment bag number one. And you are going to want to do that by yourself." He handed me the bag.

"What? Where are you going?"

"Trust me, honey. This is a moment you'll want to have alone."

"But, Aliyan, when will I see you next?"

"In your dreams, baby. And possibly a few nightmares," he joked. He kissed my cheek. "Don't worry. We'll be seeing each other. You're family now."

I hugged him tight and told him I loved him.

"Don't you dare make this old handsome gay man cry, Manny. There's a reason we aren't in Bollywood, girl. We are ugly criers."

I hugged Aliyan one last time before he walked out of my hotel room, but not out of my life. I waited for the last of his team to leave, and then I picked up the garment bag and slid open the zipper. As if the gown had been waiting to come out, it popped, making its escape. I stood in awe, not even sure where to look first. The two-piece gown sparkled in pink with silver specks, handcrafted with sequins, which lay on a net fabric in snowflake motifs. The blouse had sheer long sleeves and a sheer back, the bustier top had an underlayer of shimmering sequins and tassels that dangled from the end of the neck, and the skirt was layered so that it had just the right amount of poof. It was breathtaking, the kind of gown I imagined any Indian princess would like to wear on her special day.

I slipped it on. Still no mirrors. I had promised Aliyan that I wouldn't look in the mirror until I was completely dressed. He had left a pair of blue chandelier earrings in the bag. I placed one in each ear and then put dozens of matching bracelets on arms that were still stained with henna. A small cloth sat inside the bag. I peeled back a tiny pink bindi and secured it to the space between my eyebrows. I walked over to the shoes that Aliyan had placed by the door for me and slipped my newly pedicured feet into the sparkling gold heels. Everything felt so me, as if I had dressed up like this a dozen times before.

Mirror. I needed a mirror. I was ready to see my evolution. I pulled the sheet off the armoire in my room and stared.

My mother.

I looked like my mother had in those pictures from years ago in India. Happy, dancing, and in love. I was her. I was myself. I was a real Indian woman.

My makeup bright, as if the precious dew had been created just for this night. Red lipstick tinted my lips, while pinks and golds highlighted my cheeks and eyelids. I was myself, but my mother was there in all her grace and beauty. I touched the gold necklace around my neck and tucked it lovingly under the other jewelry, but not before it caught the light shining from the bedside lamp. A flutter appeared across my face, but this time it didn't fade away. This light was steady and finally beaming bright for my parents and Sammy Patel.

"Manny, oh my gosh, I thought you weren't going to come! I am so sorry about the other day. I shouldn't have called you . . ." Manisha leaned toward my ear. ". . . the b-word. I was just mad at Lisa, and I took it out on you. And I really thought we were friends. You and me. Two sisters—not sisters-in-law, because, like, you know, you are totally obviously not ever going to be mine." She stopped rambling. "By the way, you look—you look so HOT. Dayum, girl, you are totally outdoing me tonight." She hugged me. "I am so sorry."

"Manisha, it's all right. We are friends. More than friends. We are bahans, like you said." I hugged her back. "None of this is your fault. You had no idea what was going on. And I lied to you. I'm so sorry, really I am, but you have to believe me, I care about you and your family so much."

"I know you do. We all know you do. I was, like, totally mad about the Lisa thing, and she's the queen of all *b*'s, you know, not you. I took it out on you."

"I know, Manisha. Have you seen Sammy, by the way?"

"I haven't. Don't worry. He'll be here." She saw the look of concern in my eyes. "Is everything all right? It's Sanj and Needa's big reception party. This is the moment we've all been waiting for all week. Whatever it is can wait."

An arm settled on my shoulder.

"Beta."

"Mr. Patel—"

"Thank you for staying," he said.

"My goodness, my girls looking so amazing," Mrs. Patel said.

"You look amazing, too, Auntie-ji."

"Oh, I am old and with my husband. No need for that anymore. Amazing, shmazing. We only come for the food now." She laughed. "Manisha, come here. Let me fix that necklace."

"Mom, come on," Manisha said, but she still walked over to her mother.

"Dapha ho joa, you never know who will be here. Mr. Hot Stuff could be anywhere here tonight just waiting to pick you up and finally take you away from me! Mind you, at this point, you could pick him up." She gave Manisha a little slap on her behind.

"Ugh, Mom, you are so gross."

"Oh, I am gross? All I do is love all my children and now I am the gross one."

"Fine, Mommy dearest. You and Dad are equally gross." Manisha laughed.

Mr. Patel leaned over and whispered in my ear, "I see so much of your mother in you, beti. Including the way the corner of your mouth curls—like your mother's did when she was genuinely happy."

I was no longer frightened of Mr. Patel like I had been the day before, but found something comforting in his eyes that made me feel cared for. I held back the tears as he hugged me, too. "Your mother would be so proud of the woman you have become today, Manny," he whispered.

"Do you think so, Mr. Patel?"

"Beti, one thing I know for sure is that your mother was proud of being Indian, and she would be proud to have raised a charming and smart Indian daughter like you."

"Thank you, Mr. Pat—"

"Uncle, call me Uncle-ji."

"Oh my gosh, can we save whatever drama about your Bollywood mama for later?" Manisha joked.

I smiled at Mr. Patel, and he joined Manisha and his wife and hugged his daughter in a teasing way.

I looked around for Sammy.

"He's here; don't worry. You will find him and tell him why you have been so happy this week," Mr. Patel said.

We made our way to the main hall where the reception was being held.

"There he is. Hey, Sammy, come over here," Manisha yelled. He was just outside the doors, greeting guests.

"Coming. Sorry, I was trying to get everyone coordinated and—" Sammy stopped when he saw me.

The music faded away, along with the voices of the people who were crowded around. The only thing I could hear was my heart beating. Loudly. Manisha and her parents looked at each other. "Let's give them some space," Mr. Patel whispered.

"I don't like space . . ." Mrs. Patel said, but her husband took her arm, and they walked away.

"Wow, I don't even know what to say right now," Sammy said as he looked me up and down. "Manny, you are stunning. I mean absolutely stunning. Man, you are just lighting up the room here. Have I already mentioned that? You look . . . you . . ."

"Happy?"

"More than happy." He held my hand.

"You don't look so bad yourself."

He hugged me. It was exactly what I wanted. Sammy's arms around me.

"Sammy, I—"

"Manny, I owe you an apology for last night. I crossed the line, and I know this is a business deal between us."

"You didn't cross the line." *And if you did, I wanted you to.* "Last night, I was trying to tell you that Lisa—"

"Big brother, when does the show start? I have one very impatient bride-to-be waiting on our entrance," Sanjeev interrupted. "You look gorgeous, Manny. You two secretly get married? Thought Needa and I were the only ones pulling that stunt," he teased. "Needa wants to come in. Any idea of the timing on this thing? We're all an hour late. I mean, not that we're surprised," he joshed.

"Guys, let's get a family picture," Manisha said, appearing again at our side. "My social is so loco this past week. Like, I am not getting enough likes." She locked arms with both of her brothers, pulling them over to Deena, Nyla, Ali, Jameela, and others who were standing in front of a pink-and-red flower backdrop.

Sammy reached for my hand. "Don't leave me. Stay close by," he said to me.

There was no way I would ever leave Sammy.

"Manny, come in here. Join us!" Manisha said.

"Let me take the picture." I pulled out my phone from my purse and started snapping away, feeling like an honorary member of the Patel family.

"Oh, hang on, I'm getting a call." I looked at my phone. It was Marie from *Beyond More*. The timing was lousy, but I needed to take the call. I moved away from the group so I could hear her.

"Marie, I was going to email you—"

"Manny, sorry, I'm having a hard time hearing you—"

"The magazine cover—"

"Yes, Manny . . . still there?"

"Marie, why did the cover look the way it did?"

"Manny, sorry, I think we . . . bad connection or . . . but the cover, yes, you approved . . . can't hear . . . send you . . . sorry."

The call ended. My phone lit up.

You have one new email.

Manny, sorry, it was difficult to hear you. I was surprised by
your office manager's email; please see your recommendations
for the picture to be retouched below.

Marie

I scrolled down to the email.

From: Manny Dogra

Hi Marie,

A few changes below.

Can you lighten my skin? The dark tones make me look too
brown. I like to look more like a blank canvas so your audience
can paint me whichever color they want.

I'd appreciate it if we could get rid of that gold chain, too.

Manny

I couldn't believe what I was reading. Adam hadn't just approved the cover. He had requested the changes. Rage overcame
me. I backed farther away from the Patels and ran out of the hall,
into the garden, faster and faster until I couldn't run anymore.

I sank onto the bench in the back of the garden where Mr.
Patel had told me how much he adored my mother. I held Mom's
necklace, the very necklace Mr. Patel had given her, the one
Adam had so easily removed.

"What's wrong, Manny?"

I looked up. Sammy had followed me.

"I saw you run out and got worried, so I came after you."

"Sammy—" I stood up. "I . . ." I fell into his arms and he held me.

"It's okay. Whatever it is, we will figure this out *together*."

"I'm the one who crossed the line before you did." My eyes pleaded with Sammy to listen as I slowed down my words and they became softer as he and I moved in closer to each other.

"I was feeling . . . feeling like I was falling, falling . . ." My breath finally caught up to my words. "Sammy . . . I love you." I kissed him as I had never kissed anyone before. Rajiv had reminded me that it was taboo for Bollywood actors to kiss on-screen, but I couldn't hold myself back.

I wanted Sammy. I wanted him so badly.

Sammy returned my kiss, his soft lips caressing mine, the tip of his tongue playing with my mouth. He reached to push my hair back and pulled me even closer as I felt our bodies shaking and aching for each other. How was this kiss even more electric than the first? Because it was love. This was love. Love made you fall to your knees and plunge into the arms of someone you could trust. Love wasn't a business. It wasn't a plan or a folder in someone's inbox. This was true love.

"When you walked out of that dressing room in Little India in that purple number, I knew I was in trouble," Sammy said.

"Why didn't you tell me?"

"Why didn't you tell *me*! Manny, your humor, the way you care about everyone around you, about me. The way you talk about your parents. How could I not fall in love with every inch of you. And you do this wild thing with your lip—"

"I did want to tell you. I'm so happy when I'm with you. But

I didn't want you to think how I felt had *anything* to do with Lisa breaking up with *you*."

"What?" Sammy let me go and took a step back. "What do you mean, she broke up with *me*? It's the other way around, silly."

"It's not, Sammy." I looked into his eyes. "Lisa emailed the agency to get help to break it off with you."

"When?"

"A few days ago. Sammy, I've been trying to tell you ever since."

"*A few days ago*? Not hours ago? *Days* ago? Why didn't you tell me right away?"

"Please. Let me explain."

"What is there to explain? I told you about my accident, how Lisa nursed me back to health, and how I thought I owed her, and you couldn't tell me as soon as you found out? I introduced you to my entire family. I trusted you. And you've been lying to me this whole time? Was there ever an email sent to her from Breakup?"

Sammy was so upset he was shaking.

"Yes, of course. And I know, Sammy, I tried . . . you have to believe me."

"No, I don't have to believe you."

"Sammy, I—"

"Just because things aren't working out with you and Adam," he pointed to my engagement ring, "doesn't give you the right to keep the truth from me until you feel it's the right time to tell me."

I twisted the ring, wishing I wasn't wearing it. "I didn't know this was going to happen. I didn't know I was going to care so much about you . . . your family."

"You don't care. You don't care about anyone besides yourself. Even now, this moment, it's all about *you*. You were waiting for when *you* felt it was the right time to tell me *you* cared. You couldn't do it a few days ago at the lake? Why, was Adam still talking to you then?"

"Sammy, that is not fair. This is your brother's wedding, and I didn't want to make this about . . ."

"*You!* I rest my case. You know, this whole CEO act you got going on, it's not for me. I told you I do things for other people to make their days. You do what makes your day! You know what, while you might be on the cover of some national magazine and trying to find yourself this week, a lot of us don't give a shit about that, because we have already found what matters most. And I stupidly thought that was you, Manny."

"But I did find what matters most! It's being here, with you. With all of you. But especially you. I just couldn't tell you while you were so happy and in all that Patel love. Everyone loves you so much, Sammy."

He had started to walk away but turned around.

"Yeah, well some of us loved you, too."

Chapter 31

Dear Breakup,

How do you get over someone . . . quickly? And what if you really don't want to? Is there a way to make up a breakup when you know that it just needs a little bit of understanding?

I can't seem to find that package on the Breakup website. Not even a boot camp for the heart that desperately needs one more chance.

Why can't Breakup offer a service to get people back together one last time? I don't want to give up, and all your options make it seem like that's the only hope I have, to move on.

Katelyn

"Miiiiiiiss Dogra. Mannnnneeeee." It was Rajiv's voice I heard in the distance, as Rob pushed open the door to the building.

"Not today, Rajiv." I tried to smile back at him. He had my usual cup of coffee waiting for me.

"Don't worry. I bring it to you," he called, but I walked into the building with Rob, where we waited for the elevator.

"You sure you're up for getting back to work so soon?" Rob focused on business, knowing that I didn't want to talk about Sammy or the wedding.

"I'm sure. And thanks for flying to Marble to come get me."

"Manny, you sounded . . . you are devastated. There was no way I was going to let you get on that plane alone."

"I'm sure I would have been okay." That's what I said, but I wasn't sure. I was supposed to be coming back home with Sammy, in the seats he had bought us. Except not as agency and client but as lovers. After I had confessed my love to Sammy, and the news about Lisa, he had gone back to Sanjeev's wedding. I didn't blame him. I figured it was best for me to go home without seeing any Patel. It was time for me to go back to my other family, the ones who had been there all this time helping me not just with Breakup, but with the breakthrough that I needed to heal after my parents had passed. Rajiv, Anjali, Rob, and Jay were what I told all Breakup clients they needed in their lives after a heartbreak—friends who were there for you with a bottle of wine, a Taylor Swift album, and some much-needed laughs.

"Thank you."

"What is a gay ex-boyfriend slash best friend for?" he said and wrapped his arm around me.

The office was abuzz, as usual. Anjali was at the reception desk, tablets in hand.

"Manny, it's so good to have you back," she said.

"It's good to be back and to get to work. I'm heading into my office to get ready for our ten o'clock."

The office seemed quieter than usual. Or maybe I hadn't set aside the noise from the chaos of the Patel week. *Had it only been a week since I was last here?* I was back now, though. My life had been turned upside down, and I wasn't sure about anything except work. Sammy hadn't returned any of my calls, just as I hadn't returned the few calls that Adam had made to me. I settled into my office chair and swung around to look at the view of clouds. Not as comforting as usual.

After what I'd read in Marie's email, I had decided that Adam didn't deserve to hear from me again, and since he was still in Europe, it made it easy to have what few things he had in our home sent to the Jamiesons. I wasn't angry at what he had done, because he had done it to someone I didn't recognize anymore. A CEO who didn't seem to care about anything but being buried in her business. I didn't miss her. And given all that and the way I felt about Sammy, I didn't miss Adam. Not one bit.

But I did miss Sammy.

My thoughts were interrupted by Anjali's Monday-morning knock.

"Hi, Manny." She walked in quietly and asked nervously, "How are you?"

"Morning," I answered faintly. That was all I said.

"Manny, if I can say something? You went to find yourself, to discover another side of you. That's what you should take away from all this. I know it hurts, but you found a few more pieces of the Manny Dogra puzzle you were trying to put together. That's what you set out to do, right? Falling for Sammy was the icing on an Aja Raja barfi." She smiled.

I tried to smile back at Anjali, thinking about the note she had written and how proud she was of me as an Indian woman.

"You're right," I said. "I found me, and I also found my way back to honoring my parents. Along the way I just happened to fall in love with Sammy. And I have had enough naan for a lifetime," I joked.

I sat up in my chair and added, "Now, let's get back to what we do best—breaking up."

"Okay, if that is what the boss wants, that is what the boss shall get. I have a list of urgent emails we have to get through before our ten o'clock. We have a client who needs help telling his fiancée she's a bad cook, so bad that he's been secretly eating before he gets home every night to avoid her meals. It's urgent because she plans on catering their wedding. Another client forgot to divorce his first wife and has already proposed to his second, but has just found out the first one is pregnant. And we have another client who needs help getting the love of his life back."

"Did we already help him or her break up?"

"I mean technically no, but yes?"

"Anjali, I am really not in the mood for games this morning. I was already pretty asshole-y to Rajiv."

"Well, he just realized how much he loves this woman and made a mistake walking away from her."

"No more second chances, Anjali, under any circumstances. Next."

"Umm . . . that is what's next."

There was a knock at the door.

Anjali swung around as the door began to open. "You may want to reconsider this case."

Sammy stood in the doorway.

What was going on? I got up.

"I'll be outside," Anjali said as she slid past Sammy.

"Sammy?" We met in the middle of my office. His dark eyes had bags underneath them, same as mine. His wavy hair looked messy and he was wearing the green jacket he'd had on when I first met him.

"Manny, give *this* client a second chance," he said. "After I left the wedding celebrations, it hit me. I was leaving everyone behind, and the one person I wanted to come back to, I had let walk away from my life." He paused. "I love you, Manny. I love you more than I have loved anyone in my life. I love you more than all those women my aunties set me up with, especially the ones who ate my food." He tried to laugh. "I was just scared of how quickly I loved you but also how much I loved you."

I fell into his arms. I knew Sammy wasn't upset about how long I had held on to Lisa's secret. I knew he was scared that along the way, he had also found his inner Indian with me. His family, all those aunties and weddings he claimed not to miss— he had missed all of it. He had just buried it because of what he felt he owed someone. Just like I had with Adam. I wasn't the only one discovering things about myself this week—Sammy was, too.

"Like I said in Marble, Manny, this light of yours . . . it's so freakin' bright." Sammy kissed my lips and sent that familiar electrifying love voltage up my body just like he had in Marble.

"Well, maybe you should put on some shades." I teasingly

pushed him away, and then moved back into his arms. "Sammy, this light only shines so bright when you're with me. As soon as I came back to Baskin, it was dim again."

Sammy kissed me again, and I could feel the heat in our faces from the love, from the bright light.

"Mr. Patel, we still have a strict no-second-chances policy here at Breakup."

"You're right, Ms. Dogra. But I don't need a second chance to date you. I need a first shot at marrying you." He got down on one knee. "Manny, will you marry me?"

"Sammy . . ." I started to cry. "I will. Yes, I will."

"She said yes to the dress! Hollla!" I could hear Rob shout outside.

"She said yes! I am organizing all the wedding details as we speak!" Anjali exclaimed.

My office door flew open to Rajiv's "Om Shanti Om" playing on his portable boom box while he, Anjali, Rob, and the rest of the staff all peeked in.

"This calls for bottle service!" Rob said as he popped open a bottle of champagne.

"Finally, the gods have listened to my daily prayers," Rajiv added as he started to bhangra.

"You always said we Indians never show up on time. Maybe, for once, you, Sammy Patel, did show up at the right time." I kissed him again.

"Now, are *you* ready to meet *my* crazy family?" I asked my new fiancé.

Chapter 32

Dear Adam,

After reviewing my inbox, I was finally able to clear the trash.

Consider this email a notification that I am revising my current relationship plan, and it no longer includes you.

See, the thing is, the business of love isn't just on *your* hours of operation, at least not over here anymore.

Love is on my watch now, and I chose Indian Standard Time.

Your very Indian ex-fiancée,
Manny
(Courtesy of the team at Breakup)

ACKNOWLEDGEMENTS

A very special thanks . . .

To my agent, Jill Marr, who plucked me out of the universe of queries and found something special in my writing. To editor Brenda Copeland, who helped me find my Inner Indian while I wrote this story. To everyone at Simon & Schuster, especially Laurie Grassi, who took one phone call with me and knew she had to have *The Break-up Expert*. And a big thank you to Molly Crawford from Simon & Schuster UK, who could see Manny's story on an international platform. You have all welcomed me with such open arms, love, and kindness.

To my parents, who showed me the love of embracing creativity as a young South Asian girl in a world where it seemed impossible. To my sisters, Tina and Rupa, who are constantly the cheerleaders of all my work.

To Lee Parpart, who read the synopsis to this book and pushed me to send it out.

Lastly, I want to thank myself. In the words of Snoop Dogg, "I want to thank me for believing in me, I want to thank me for doing all this hard work." I did do all this hard work, and with a lot of love and support along the way.

ABOUT THE AUTHOR

SONYA SINGH is a former entertainment reporter turned communications professional who has followed her dream of telling stories in front of the camera and now behind the scenes. Her debut novel, *The Break-up Expert*, is an ode to her own personal dating experiences, during which she honed the art of writing the perfect breakup email/text. Sonya lives in Toronto, Ontario. You can follow her at **sonyasinghbooks.com** and on Instagram **@sonyasinghwrites**.